CAJUN IN A KILT

Love Regency Style

ROSEMOUNT MANOR
BOOK I

LOUISA CORNELL

Trademark Acknowledgements

Voodoo Beer
Ritz Carlton
Johnny's Po Boys
Cartier
Versace
Beckham's Bookshop
Brooks Brothers
Mr. Darcy from *Pride and Prejudice* by Jane Austen
Kermit the Frog
Lagavulin
Marriott
Sugar Bowl
Oscar
Jack Black
Batman
AK 47
Gucci
Crisco
iPhone
iPad

Waterford Crystal

Wedgewood China

DeLamerie Silver

Braveheart

Ashton Kutcher

Arnold Schwarzenegger

Weebles – Hasbro Toys

Disney World

Highlander

Daily Mirror

Keith Moon

William Shatner

Nike

Mary Poppins from *Mary Poppins* by Pamela Lyndon Travers

Steve Irwin

Rice Krispies

Rolls Royce

Café du Monde New Orleans

Professor of Enemy Languages
And Baton Rouge Cajun Extraordinaire
You taught me to speak German and Russian.
You showed me the real New Orleans
from the hole-in-the-wall eating joints, to the best bars for real
jazz,
to the home-grown Cajuns, Creoles, and Voodoo churches.
You showed me the spirit of the city and culture that refuses to
give up.
Thanks, Herr Professor
For True

Acknowledgments

I owe so many people for my writing career and the joy writing brings me.

The entire crew at Scarsdale Publishing for their amazing work. Especially,

Publisher Sharona Wilhelm for giving me this amazing opportunity and putting up with my slow ass!

Editor Penny Brandon for making me sound like a much better writer than I am.

Romance Writers of America for putting me on this path.

Southern Magic RWA for keeping me on this path.

Regency Fiction Writers for keeping me honest when it comes to all things Regency.

Andrea K. Stein and Kristine Hughes, my sisters of the heart, who are always ready with an encouraging word or a swift kick, whatever is called for at the time.

My mom for putting up with a romance writer living and working in her basement.

My five furry ankle biters for making sure not an hour goes by that I don't have to get out of my chair to let someone out to pee!

Chapter One

February 28
New Orleans, Louisiana

His nose twitched at the vinegary sting with a cayenne burn.... Hot sauce.

Shrimp. Fresh caught and fried.

French bread? And the tang of a good remoulade.

Chili fries.

And...Voodoo beer?

When it came to getting his bearings, Danny Arneaux usually trusted his nose. Then again, when a man came to in a strange bed, it was best to squint at least one eye open and check out the décor, just to be sure. As this was a technique he'd honed damned near to an art over the years, he dragged his head from beneath a thick comfy pillow and forced one eyelid semi-open.

Pleated ivory silk canopy. Mahogany bedposts. Expensive gold drapes and carpet. Fake antique chandelier. A pair of ivory, gold, and brown silk upholstered armchairs.

The Ritz Carlton.

"New Orleans," he mumbled.

His nose hadn't lied. He swiveled his head back enough to eyeball the source of the miniature dagger-shaped instruments digging into his naked left hip and butt cheek. Perfectly manicured nails painted crime scene red, and a big ass ruby ring glowed in perfect contrast to the rich ebony of the long, elegant fingers shaking his ass awake. Even the caramel toned skin he'd inherited from his French Cajun daddy and Creole mother looked bland in comparison.

"Got it in one," said a sultry voice with the exact tone of abrasive boredom to let a man know he was dealing with one smart bitch. "Care to try for your name?"

Danny shot a middle finger salute over his shoulder and rolled back under the expensive hotel pillow. "What time is it?"

"Nine-thirty. Care to try for my name?"

"Jesus Christ."

"Close enough." Jaqueline St. James, his agent and business manager, flexed her nails and gave him one last shake before she came around to the side of the bed where Danny did his damnedest to ignore her.

"Please tell me that lump on the other side of the bed is those two flea tenements of yours and not some nameless Bourbon Street bimbo."

Danny searched under the covers to pat the canine hindquarters backed up against him like a cat against a hot brick. First one tail wagged, then a second stirred the sheets next to him. Course, neither of the two one-hundred-and-twenty-pound drool factories made a move to leave the warm cocoon of pillows, blankets, and sheets they'd scratched around themselves. He was lucky to have any covers for himself, let alone a place on the bed.

Jacqueline muttered something in French, the only time her Caribbean ancestry appeared, and sat down in the armchair next to his side of the bed. The pop of a plastic to-go lid and the heavenly dense, dark aroma of chicory coffee had him reaching blindly toward her.

"Gimme."

The scent and heat moved away, just out of reach. "Roust your bony, ashy ass off that bed, and I might let you have a sip or two of this sludge you call coffee."

"That's plain old mean," Danny mumbled even as he struggled to wrap the sheet around his hips without exposing his agent to a full moon or worse. She didn't care, but he'd retained at least a few scraps of his Mama's upbringing.

"That's what you pay me for, baby," Jacqueline replied, the cup of coffee in one hand and her cell phone in the other.

"Not at nine-thirty in the morning, I don't. If meanness is what I pay you for, remind me to give you a raise." He sat up on the side of the bed, scrubbed his face with his hands, then reached for the coffee once more.

Her eyes never leaving her phone, she waved the cup in the air a bit and finally placed it in his greedy grip. "You need to suck down some of that nasty brew and hit the shower. You have a plane to catch this afternoon."

Danny concentrated on drawing as much of the heat and heavenly taste of Café du Monde's finest into his very bones. He'd spent most of the last twenty-four hours trolling the Quarter. Even in late February, Louisiana had the ability to cloak itself in the kind of heat that would steal a man's breath like a graveyard haint. Not that he'd noticed. He'd been cold for nearly six months. Cold in his soul, the old folks would say. Not even hot chicory coffee seemed to help. Maybe if he…. *Wait! What?*

"Give me that," he demanded as he rose from the bed to follow the cup Jacqueline had plucked from his fingers when he wasn't paying attention. "Why am I catching a plane? Where the hell am I going?" He stumbled and made a grab for the sheet that threatened to slide to the floor. "Give. Me. That. Coffee."

She rose from the chair, sniffed the cup, and carried it across the room as if it contained toxic waste. "This is not coffee." With a hip bump, she opened the bathroom door and placed the cup next to one of the sinks on the long double vanity. "It's motor oil with a dirt chaser. Get your ass in the shower. I'll try to find something decent for you to wear on the plane. Your winter wardrobe is already on its way to the airport."

Danny hitched up the sheet, wrapped it more securely around him, and tucked the end of it in at his waist. He traipsed to the bathroom and snatched the cup from the vanity to drain its contents in one scalding gulp, which peeled the hide off the roof of his mouth and made his eyes water, but he'd be damned if he'd utter a sound.

Jacqueline rolled her eyes and turned her attention back to her phone.

"What winter wardrobe?" he asked once his mouth stopped trying to turn his face inside out. "I don't have a winter wardrobe. What's wrong with the clothes I've got here?" He waved at the three opened suitcases on the long couch across the room. The ones that looked like a family of raccoons had been rummaging through them.

"The winter wardrobe I had Michael purchase and pack in your trunks this morning."

"Trunks? I don't own any trunks. Unless you count the ones on my cars."

"You do now."

"Why do I need trunks of new *winter* clothes? And why did you let Michael—"

"Because he has taste," she cut in. "Are you going to get in the shower, or do I have to strip that sheet off and shove you in there myself?"

She had him there. Michael, Jacqueline's personal assistant, had an uncanny eye for fashion. Not to mention a lawyer's skill at cutting through red tape, and a shrink's ability to calm Jaqueline down when she finally went nuclear. Whatever they were paying him, it wasn't nearly enough.

"You won't shove me into the shower. You might get your phone wet."

She didn't even pause as she flipped him off and continued to text at the same time.

"You could always have Michael shove me in the shower when he gets here."

"Michael is in the hotel business center getting the paperwork in order for your furry ass-warmers to travel on the plane with you. God knows who he is going to have to blow to get it all finalized in time." She turned her attention from her phone and pinned him with a look most Cajun mamas would envy. Not yet nuclear, but the fuse had been lit. "Shower. Now!" She turned and walked toward the suite's balcony.

Well, hell!

Since discretion was the better part of not getting a size eight stiletto up his ass, Danny deliberately dropped the sheet and strolled into the walk-in shower that was only slightly smaller than his first apartment in Hollywood. He turned the water on two notches below scalding and adjusted the six shower heads to target his aching muscles full blast. Standing in the middle of the pounding heat, he dropped his chin to his chest and braced his palms against the expensive marble tiles of the shower walls.

As the water's sting awakened his nerve endings, tiny needles of sensation scattered over him like fireworks over the bayou. The stinging turned to a caress as his skin grew accustomed to the water's temperature. He breathed in the steam, clearing his head to the point he could finally ask himself the questions he'd refused to ask Jaqueline.

Had she found a role for him? Or had she booked him on a reality show where has-been actors competed for charities like one of those survival, eat bugs and twigs shows…in frickin' Alaska? Was that why he needed a winter wardrobe? Great. Charity was fine, but the idea of body parts, *important* body parts, freezing until they dropped off wasn't his idea of charity.

It was his idea of desperation.

Reality shows were designed to play on the audience's sense of nostalgia. Worse, was the audience's sense of revenge against entertainers who'd committed the deadly sin of burning out, giving up, or finally showing the world they really didn't have a damned bit of talent to begin with. Wasn't that what actors did once their careers took a nose-dive? The last few small steps from has-been to never-was. He shuddered and grabbed his shampoo. Asinine as it was, the harder he worked the lather into his scalp the clearer the last several hours became.

How would Jaqueline feel if she knew he'd wandered the streets of New Orleans all evening, grabbed a sack full of take-out food from Johnny's Po Boys on St. Louis Street, and ended up back in his hotel room before midnight throwing himself a pity party with fried shrimp, hot sauce, and Voodoo beer until his eyes crossed and he'd crawled into bed with his dogs? He didn't have the glamorous lifestyle some thought he did. He wasn't the Hollywood bad boy. In fact, in five years, he'd be a failed actor nobody would remember.

Screw this!

The pity party was over. Jaqueline was up to something. She was never this cryptic. Well, not most of the time. He was catching a plane. To where? He needed a new wardrobe. For what? His dogs needed paperwork to travel.

Why? At the back of his mind, a sneaky little idea wriggled like a worm on a hook. He turned off the water and stepped out of the shower before he scraped the thick, fluffy bath towel over his body then wrapped it around his hips. While he shaved, brushed his teeth, and put on his ridiculously priced deodorant, that worm of an idea kept waving at him, luring him in as if he was a big old catfish looking to get caught.

Nope! Not going there.

"Only one way to find out, *couyon*." He opened the bathroom door.

"I don't care what you've decided," Jaqueline said into her phone. "That was not part of our deal. And that is not the person you said would be training him. You stick him with some amateur, and I'll have your ass, Wentworth." She stood at the balcony doors drumming her nails against the glass. "Of course, I won't tell him, but this is completely unnecessary. My client is a professional with a great track record and—"

He could imagine what the person on the other end of the call was saying. Actually, better *not* to imagine it.

"Fine. I'll have him on the plane this afternoon. You screw us on this, and I'll sue you so hard your grandchildren will owe me money." She stabbed the phone off, turned, and jumped at the sight of him.

Danny propped one shoulder against the door jamb and waited. In her red satin pumps and black linen skirt and jacket, she was an imposing woman who scared the hell out of most everyone who met her. She'd been his agent for ten years. He owed his very lucrative movie career as America's favorite action hero to her. The recent crash and burn of that same career he'd managed all by himself, starring in two of America's biggest drama flops back-to-back. Two drama flops he'd chosen to do against her advice.

"I can stand here all day, Jaqueline," he finally said. "Or I can go back to bed. You can join me if you like."

"Never with the customers, darling." Her nails clicked across the face of her cell phone again as she texted.

"Good policy. Same thing my Maw Maw used to say. Course, she ran a cathouse down on Basin Street."

"Thin line between pimping whores and pimping handsome young actors with a body grown women want to climb like a jungle gym." She stopped texting and gifted him with one of her rare, wicked smiles.

He couldn't help but laugh. "Okay, fine. But I'm not getting dressed until you tell me *why* I'm catching a plane this afternoon."

"Because you can't drive to Scotland." She stared at him expectantly, her fingers poised over her phone.

His brain hit pause for a few seconds. Finally, he spluttered, "Say...what?"

"You got the part."

Early in his career, Danny had done his own stunts. He'd had his clock cleaned more than once and the sensation—ears ringing, inability to breathe, and the world going away through a narrow tunnel of darkness—usually indicated he was about to land in a world of hurt. Standing in the doorway of the bathroom of his suite at the Ritz Carlton, Danny had a serious case of stunt man déjà vu. He shook his head. Violently.

"What did you—"

Jacqueline's phone rang and she raised a finger to silence him. "Did you get it all done?" Her tone, half drill sergeant and half Hollywood socialite, indicated she spoke with Michael. "The books too? Good. Bring it all up here. I need you to pack his luggage and ship it back to Cali." She ended the call and dropped her phone into the pocket of the *Cartier* embossed red leather shoulder bag draped over the back of the chair behind her.

"I found a decent pair of black jeans and one of the Versace dress shirts I'm sure Michael persuaded you to buy."

"He snuck it into my suitcase last week. Jacqueline—"

"Sneaked. The word is sneaked. And it was two weeks ago." She picked up the clothes and tossed them at him. "Get dressed." She started to reach for her phone.

He beat her to it, grabbed her purse, and flung it onto the bed. "What role, Jaqueline?"

They stood there staring at each other. He didn't know how long. His blood whooshed through his ears like the washing machine on his Maw Maw's back porch. His heart beat a few beats, stopped, then took off like a racehorse. *Dammit!* Her expression revealed nothing. How the hell did she do that?

"What part, Jackie?" She hated when he called her that. At this point, he didn't give a damn.

"A Matter of Honor. You got the lead."

He stumbled to the bed and sat down. Hard. Jacqueline dragged her purse out from under his ass and sat down next to him. Neither said a word. The young director of A Matter of Honor had allowed Danny to audition for the part, but deep-down Danny had been certain he didn't stand a chance. Oh, he wanted the part, dumb as the idea was. After all, what did an action star think he was doing trying to act like a romance hero? But aside from his lack of experience and the fact his British accent sucked, regency romance heroes were of the…lighter persuasion than him. But now—

There was a knock at the door to the suite and Michael barreled into the room, a leather messenger bag in one hand and shopping bags from Beckham's Bookshop and Brooks Brothers in the other. He took one look at Danny and Jacqueline then turned toward the suitcases on the couch.

"I see you told him." Michael dropped the bags at his feet and began to organize the contents of the suitcases. "Shouldn't he be getting dressed?"

"I'm sitting right here, asshole," Danny said.

"That's my point. Get up. Get dressed. You have a—"

"Plane to catch. Yes, I know. I got the part. I'm going to Scotland. Why am I going to Scotland?"

Jacqueline patted him on the knee. "Regency boot camp. At least three months of it before you start shooting. Wentworth's orders. It'll give you time to get used to the place. Scotland is home for the next year at least, *cher.* Longer if the filming schedule runs into issues. A place in the middle of nowhere called Rosemount Manor." She stood.

Danny grabbed her hand. The mention of the director's name, *THE* hottest director in Hollywood, finally woke him up.

"Wait." He shook his head so hard his teeth rattled. "How…. What the hell just happened?"

"Does he need socks and underwear?" Michael suddenly asked. "Or is he going commando?" He picked up the jeans and shirt Jacqueline had tossed at Danny and draped them over a nearby chair.

"This is insane. Why is he talking about me like I'm not here? How did I get the part? Why do I have to go to boot camp? What the hell is going on?" By then, he was on his feet and shouting.

The bed erupted in a chorus of bloodhound baying. The dogs fought their way out from under the covers, which made the whole thing look like a bad Halloween party trick.

"We know you're here. Who else would be sleeping with those mangy noisemakers?" Michael snapped.

"Screw you," Danny shouted above the baying of his dogs.

"Not even at gunpoint," Michael yelled back as he flung clean boxers, a t-shirt, and a pair of thick black socks at him.

The dogs finally broke cover and stood in the middle of the bed baying loud enough to shake the windows.

"Marie! Laveau! Shut! Up!" Danny and Michael yelled in unison.

Silenced, the pair flopped back onto the bed as if shot, tails wagging.

"If you make it through boot camp, I hope you leave those two monsters in Scotland," Michael said.

"Why don't you—"

"Shut it," Jacqueline ordered as she covered Danny's mouth with her free hand. She glared at Michael. "Both of you." She took a deep breath and released it with a huff. "You"—she pointed at Michael—"get his luggage packed. You"—she pointed at Danny— "get your shit together. Get dressed. You are the actor who just landed the role of a lifetime. Act like it."

Danny gathered up the clothes and organized them on the bed. His head continued to spin, but at least a little slower. He started to drop the towel, but suddenly remembered he wasn't alone. He really *was* losing it.

"Do you two mind?"

"Please." Michael snorted and went back to work packing everything Danny had scattered all over the suite in the last two weeks. "Every man, woman, and child in America and half the ones in Europe and Asia have seen your naked ass."

He had a point. Something struck Danny. "Is that why I got the part?"

"Because most of the world's population has seen you half naked?" Jacqueline snorted. "You got it because the guy Wentworth wanted for the part turned it down."

"Oh." Well, that was a nice shot to the ego.

Danny rolled that knowledge around in his head while he put on the clothes Jacqueline and Michael had chosen for him. Once dressed, he sat back down on the edge of the bed and petted Laveau's head. The trouble with getting what he wanted was trying to decide what to do with it once he did, especially if he'd only gotten it by default.

"Hey," Jacqueline said as she ended another phone call and came to stand in front of him. "Wentworth didn't have to give you the part. Apparently, whatever you said after you read for him made an impression. You weren't his first choice, but you were his second. I don't know why you want to do this film, and you don't have to tell me. Just don't screw it up."

"Come sign these so I can get them back to Wentworth's people," Michael said, indicating the array of paperwork he'd organized across the suite's dining table.

Danny hadn't noticed what Michael had done—he'd tried to concentrate on what Jacqueline had said. He'd heard every word, but for some reason it refused to make sense. He signed the contracts at each little red arrow. He didn't bother to read them. He trusted Jacqueline implicitly when it came to contracts. When it came to her maneuvering him into doing something? That was a horse of whole different color. A carousel horse. Painted by Picasso.

Why had he been so determined to play this part? Hell, if he knew. Now he had it, all for the price of some Scottish Regency boot camp, which was sure to be some whacked out waste of time with the producer's wife's yoga instructor who'd read a bunch of romance novels with underwear models in fancy britches and women in long dresses looking goo-goo-eyed at them on the covers. Easy, right?

He stacked the signed contracts to the side then dragged the leather messenger bag across the table. Inside, he found his passport, his wallet, copies of the contracts, a thick envelope of travel papers and health certificates from Marie and Laveau's vet, his laptop, and his cell phone.

Merde!

Michael, the little weasel, had creepy crawled into Danny's suite last night or early this morning and filched through his stuff to pack this damned bag they insisted he carry instead of putting everything in his pockets like a normal guy. He turned and jumped up from the table so quick he almost knocked the chair over. Fortunately, he caught the back of the chair and caught sight of Michael and Jacqueline across the room arguing before he opened his big mouth to cuss the assistant so bad a fly wouldn't light on him. They were arguing like a married couple at a neighborhood *fais-do-do*—quiet enough nobody could hear and with enough hand waving everybody knew.

"Is there a problem?" he asked, voice raised.

"No," they said way too fast and way too together.

"How about you two don't piss on me and tell me it's raining. *What* is the problem?"

Michael opened his mouth. Jacqueline shut him up with an elbow to the solar plexus.

She checked her perfectly styled ebony hair in the ornate mirror on the wall next to her. "You won't be flying to Scotland alone," she finally said. "Wentworth is sending his jet down from New York for you and the flea bags."

"And?"

"You'll be flying from here to Aberdeen with your Regency coach. They'll be working closely with you the whole three months. And they'll be staying on as a consultant during filming. Try to make a good impression."

Michael broke into a spontaneous coughing fit. Something was definitely screwy about this whole thing.

"What the hell is a Regency coach?" Suddenly this whole *role of a lifetime* thing was starting to stink like a cooler of shrimp left out in the sun the day after the barbecue.

"The person who is going to turn you into Mr. Darcy," Michael said with the kind of smile that meant Danny was *not* going to enjoy this nearly as much as his agent's assistant would.

"Who the hell is Mr. Darcy? That's not the part I wanted." That sensation of being punched in the head came back. What the hell was he doing?

Michael groaned. At least that gave Danny a small measure of satisfaction.

But the rest of it—the boot camp, the Regency coach, over a year in Scotland freezing his ass off, and the sudden realization this was his last chance, finally hit him. Some idiot director had decided to give him, Danny Arneaux, the most fought over role to come out of Hollywood in years. He was an action star, for God's sake. As much as he wanted it, his last two films had shown him he would never be a serious actor, let alone a serious actor in some fancy British dress up gig.

"Call Wentworth," he said as he dropped back into the chair he'd vacated. "I don't think—"

Michael grabbed Jacqueline's arm and stretched up to speak into her ear. "Tell. Him." His tone was nowhere near a whisper. Both Danny and his agent looked at the assistant as if he'd lost his mind. He flexed one shoulder. "I actually think he can do this. Sue me. But you need to tell him about the coach."

"What about the coach?" Danny, pitiful as it might be, was willing to do damned near anything to prove he was something more than whatever it was he'd become.

"I promised Wentworth."

"Screw Wentworth," Danny and Michael said together.

Jacqueline smiled that rare, wicked smile again. "Okay, fine. Get the rest of his stuff packed, Michael, and harness up those damned dogs. Sit down, Danny. There are some things you need to know about this Regency coach."

Chapter Two

Shoot. Me. Now.

Those three words played over and over again behind Samantha Higgins's lips. Only her monumental desire to keep her job kept them locked there, unspoken. For the last twenty minutes, she'd been listening to Dr. Cedric Wellesley-Smythe, to whom she'd played lowly assistant for five years, pontificate about his qualifications, degrees, and period films he'd saved from humiliating historical inaccuracy.

People often commented how they loved his—and her—British accent. But right now, he sounded like an old record that wobbled as it lost steam but refused to give up the ghost. She knew from experience this particular oration usually continued for another twenty minutes before the man ran out of steam enough to take a breath. She glanced at her watch. Nine o'clock in the morning was too early for one of her boss's self-serving speeches. Actually, any time was a bad time to suffer through the man's droning.

Seated across from her and Cedric, Erik Wentworth, one of Hollywood's most sought-after young directors, looked as if he wanted to jump out the thirty-second floor window of the New York high-rise where this meeting from hell was taking place. If this went on much longer, Samantha might join him. After the wrap of the latest period drama, she and Cedric had been in California for the last six months, checking the final edits. They'd flown to New York a few days ago for this meeting. At this point, all she wanted was to return to her lovely flat in London and perhaps visit her parents in Suffolk. She'd been traveling with Cedric too damned long, and she wanted to go home, even if only for a little while.

"Dr. Wellesley-Smythe." The director straightened at his desk so abruptly he startled Samantha and actually managed to silence Cedric. For the moment at least. "Does this little monologue have a point?"

Samantha nearly choked on her tongue. Apparently, so did Cedric.

England's foremost dialogue coach and historical continuity consultant spluttered a few times then issued his patented all-he-needed-was-a-monocle, *"Harrumph!* Very well, Mr. Wentworth, allow me to be perfectly clear." Cedric sniffed and brushed at his sleeves for effect. His face flushed a rosy pink. "There is no way I am going to risk my reputation trying to turn that sow's ear into a silk purse. Not to be indelicate, but the next Mr. Darcy is not a man of Color."

Samantha stiffened. Cedric could be a prig and even an asshole, but a racist?

Cedric lifted his brows. "You will have to recast the lead role before I will even *think* of lending my considerable—"

"Not happening." Wentworth said with a slight smile Samantha found funny and a little frightening.

"I beg your pardon?" The pink was well on its way to lavender.

"Danny Arneaux will be playing the lead in *A Matter of Honor*. Recasting the role is not up for discussion."

"Good God, man, did you not watch the same screen test I did? That hack is no more a nineteenth century British cavalry officer than Kermit the Frog." Cedric's face was now a lovely shade of puce.

Kermit the Frog?

Samantha didn't know which shocked her more, Cedric's assessment of the screen test or the fact he even knew who Kermit the Frog was. Of course, the actor's accent had been atrocious. And he'd obviously had no idea how to play an Austenesque hero with a Bronte sisters' twist, which was definitely what was called for in this role. She'd read the script. It was exquisite. However, there was something about this actor's portrayal in his audition that—

"Miss Higgins, come along. We're leaving." Cedric lurched from the leather office chair, picked up his briefcase, and headed for the double doors across the room.

"*Dr.* Higgins," she muttered, as she rose and grabbed the strap of her messenger bag from the back of her chair.

"No one in their right mind would take on this task," Cedric stated. "It is impossible. Completely and utterly—"

"I'll do it." When Cedric gawked at her, and Mr. Wentworth paused with his fingers on his cell phone, she realized she'd spoken aloud.

"Don't be ridiculous. You're not even remotely qualified to take on such a project," Cedric said, his mouth drawn into one of his four facial expressions. This one meant to evince disdain. If anything, it evinced constipation.

"I've worked every film and helped coach every actor you have for the past five years. I have the same degrees you have, despite the fact I don't feel it necessary to rattle them off every time I meet a potential employer. Mr. Wentworth, if you need, I can provide you with my credentials and my references, but I assure you, I can do this job."

She'd always wondered what running mad might feel like.

Apparently, it felt like reaching the top of the London Eye, swaying in the breeze, and seeing everything rather small and fuzzy. Her heart threatened to beat out of her chest. She used some of the techniques she taught actors to control her breathing. When tossing one's position into the rubbish bin, fainting dead away might be a bit much.

"I won't allow this," Cedric declared.

Samantha and Mr. Wentworth stared at him, then at each other.

"Are you serious about this, *Dr.* Higgins?"

"Dead serious. When do you want me to start?" What the devil was she doing?

"Miss Higgins, no one can turn this Arneaux person into the caliber of actor to pull off this role in three months. No one," Cedric said.

"Wanna bet?" Mr. Wentworth came around and propped his hip on the corner of his desk.

"Excuse me?" Cedric looked as if his head was about to explode. At least if Samantha's career was over, she would have the memory of the man's imminent decapitation to comfort her in her ensuing poverty.

"I believe he's proposing a wager," Samantha said as innocently as possible.

"I am. You are already signed to consult on the new adaptation of Mansfield Park after A Matter of Honor wraps." Mr. Wentworth fixed Cedric with a honed-steel glare. "If *Dr.* Higgins succeeds with Danny Arneaux, you will cede the Mansfield Park job to her. And if she doesn't—"

"If she doesn't, you will see that she never works in this business again." Cedric didn't bother to don an expression. He didn't have to. He was furious at what he saw as her betrayal.

It didn't matter what Wentworth said. Once she went through with this, the presumptuous little Yorkshireman who had everyone convinced he was from one of the finest families in London would do everything in his power to ruin her.

"Done," Samantha declared before Mr. Wentworth could speak. "When and where do I start, sir?"

The young director folded his arms and raised an inquiring eyebrow at Cedric.

"You will both regret this." Cedric turned, fumbled with his briefcase and the doorknobs, then burst out into reception without a backward glance.

"Need a drink, Dr. Higgins?" Wentworth asked once the somewhat shocked receptionist closed the doors to afford them some privacy.

"Absolutely. Whisky, neat, if you have it, please." Might as well toast severing ties with Cedric properly. Not to mention the dustbin fire that was now her career.

Wentworth went to the bar across the room and poured two glasses of Lagavulin. Samantha met him halfway, took the glass he offered, and immediately took him up on the offer of returning to the leather chair before his desk. She dropped her bag at her feet.

"Are you over the what-the-hell-did-I-do phase or do you need a minute?" He sat at his desk.

Samantha raised a finger and took a long sip of her drink. Once her eyes stopped watering she said, "Fine now. Mr. Wentworth, are you certain about—"

"Absolutely." He studied her face, his frightening little smile flitting across his otherwise bemused expression a few times. "In over your head, Doc?"

She laughed. "Without a doubt."

"Why'd you do it?" He sipped his drink with an intensely casual air. This was a test—one for which she had never studied in her life. Every decision she'd ever made had only been after careful consideration of the consequences. She had no experience with leaping before taking a good look.

"I haven't the foggiest idea," she replied.

"I think you do. I mean besides the obvious."

"The obvious?"

"You're as good at this as Ceddie-boy, if not better."

"Well, there is that."

This time Wentworth laughed, but only for a moment. His entire demeanor suddenly turned serious. "You saw it too, didn't you?"

"*It*, sir?" She understood the question. She merely wanted a pause to gather her thoughts because she wasn't certain she could describe exactly the *it* she'd seen.

"Stop with the 'sir.' My name is Erik." He leaned forward across his desk, his fingers steepled beneath his chin. "Arneaux's screen test. Forget the accent and the uncertainty. Something about him says he *is* Captain Rothgate. You saw it too. That's why you're willing to stake your reputation on this film. On him."

Samantha hadn't expected Wentworth to read her so well. How did she explain to a man like Erik Wentworth something she didn't quite understand herself?

"I believed him," she finally said softly. She cleared her throat and looked the director in the eye. "Despite the accent and the uncertainty, in that moment on screen, I believed he was the kind of man who would do the honorable thing, the right thing, even if doing so broke his heart. The pain, the hopelessness, not as if he was portraying a part, but...." She ran out of words.

"As if he'd lived it," Wentworth said.

"Yes." She offered the director an uncomfortable smile. "I hope, between the two of us, me coaching and you directing, we can make something of Mr. Arneaux."

Wentworth raised his glass, and she met it with hers. "From your lips to God's ears, Doc."

They finished their whisky in silence. It occurred to Samantha they were both taking a huge chance—with this film, with their reputations, in trusting each other and the abilities of an actor whose films she had to confess she'd never seen. Not her cup of tea. Probably best not to mention that to Mr. Wentworth.

"Can I assume you can leave immediately?" the director asked, stirring her out of her ruminations.

"Of course. My luggage is scarcely unpacked. Where am I going and when?"

"This afternoon. You're taking my jet to New Orleans to pick up Arneaux, then you are flying to Aberdeen together."

"Aberdeen?" Cedric hadn't mentioned a trip to Scotland. Then again, he wouldn't. He'd always assumed she'd go wherever he went, arrogant old fool.

"Rosemount Manor in the Highlands. Rented out the entire estate from some duke who needs the money. I've arranged for a Regency boot camp. Riding instruction. Sword and pistol instruction. You'll have everything you need to turn Danny Arneaux into a Regency officer and gentleman."

That feeling of swaying in the breeze at the top of the London Eye came back to her. She was really going to do this. She was the lead historical consultant on the most talked about period drama of the year—maybe the decade. Maybe she should have passed on the whisky.

"Then I'd better get to the Marriott and pack. With luck, Cedric will have already left in a huff." She stood and retrieved her bag once more.

"I'll have my driver take you. Then he'll take you to LaGuardia." Wentworth came around the desk. "One more thing, Dr. Higgins. Arneaux doesn't know this, and I would appreciate you not telling him, but there is a clause in his contract."

"A clause?"

"If you don't sign off on it, he doesn't play the role. The final decision is yours."

"Mine?" She hoped that wasn't as squeaky as it sounded. "And he doesn't know? How could he not know?"

"I put it in the contract after I discussed it with his agent. She said he never reads the contracts before he signs them."

"Very trusting of him, but a bit foolish." Samantha wasn't certain she liked the idea of keeping something this big from the man she would be training. It seemed…dishonorable. "Wait. When did you put my name on the contract?"

"I didn't. The contract reads *a person of the director's choosing.* I had my suspicions about Cedric when the three of us watched the screen test. Had my suspicions about you too. I go with my gut, Doc, but I'm not an idiot. Not when it comes to making money or movies. If, after three months, you think he can't do it, I want you to tell me. That way none of us ends up with egg on our faces. Deal?" He extended his hand.

She hadn't been thinking all day. No need to start now. "Deal." She shook his hand then left his office.

By the time the elevator delivered her to the lobby, a limo with a uniformed driver stood waiting at the curb. The ride to the Times Square Marriott gave her barely enough time to think about what she'd done.

Bloody hell!

◈

"You really haven't seen any of his movies?" the young, blonde flight attendant asked for at least the fourth time in the last forty minutes.

Samantha glanced at her watch and bit back a sigh. "Sorry. No. I'm not a fan of action films."

"You don't know what you've missed. He is *so hot*."

"Yes, I believe you said that," Samantha muttered.

The young woman practically purred. "Six feet of chai latte."

Samantha stared. She was shocked every bloody time people did this, especially women. Didn't they understand that by objectifying and fetishizing men, they were doing the same thing men had done to them since the dawn of time?

"You do realize he's a human being?" Samantha asked.

She sighed. "Yeah."

Samantha forced her attention to the window. Another instant, and she might say something that would make her first day on the job her last. Sitting on the tarmac in a luxury jet might be every girl's dream, but it lost its luster after over an hour, especially if that tarmac was in a place as hot and humid as New Orleans. Another hour of this and she'd be a puddle all over Mr. Wentworth's expensive carpet and big, comfy seats. She had to give it to him, his jet was the height of luxury. Even with the chattering flight attendant.

"Don't you think he's handsome? I do. And he's got a smokin' body. They say he has the best butt in Hollywood." This last was said in hushed tones behind the flight attendant's hand as if it were a great secret.

"Does he own a watch?"

"Huh?"

The girl's confusion might be funny if Samantha weren't at the end of her tether. The flight attendant looked cool and composed despite the heat, while Samantha sweltered like a pot of cabbage on St. Patrick's Day.

"You said he has a wonderful butt. Does he have a watch? He was supposed to be here over an hour ago. I was simply curious as to whether he or someone in his entourage is in possession of a way to keep up with the time."

The poor girl stared at her as if she'd suddenly sprouted a second head. "Um. I'll go check with the pilot. Maybe he's heard something."

"Brilliant idea," Samantha said with her sunniest fake smile. "Thank you so much."

"I do love your accent," the flight attendant said with a wave as she strolled to the front of the plane and disappeared behind a dark blue curtain.

"And I'd love a bottle of water and a student who knows the importance of punctuality."

Samantha stood and made her way to the back of the jet where a series of closets, luggage storage compartments, and powder rooms stood between the main cabin and a private sitting room and bedroom. Her irritation with the movie star had started about an hour ago when a team of baggage handlers had hauled no less than six monstrous trunks onto the plane. They'd filled up the empty luggage compartments in short order, then proceeded to stack trunks in front of her few suitcases. She'd have to become a mountaineer to reach her bags now.

She sighed, removed her suit jacket, then draped it across the ends of the two trunks shoved in front of her luggage. With luck, her jacket would be safe there until another team came to unload Mr. Arneaux's plethora of expensive leather trunks.

A rumble of voices at the front of the plane and some rather odd noises distracted her for a moment. She glanced up but being five foot six didn't help when trying to see over the backs of the tall spacious seats in the main compartment.

She *had* contemplated digging through her bags for a change of clothes. It was a long flight to Scotland. Not that it mattered now. The importance of making a good and appropriate impression on Mr. Arneaux had faded somewhere between his tardiness and the luggage blockade.

"Bollocks," she muttered.

She no longer worked for Cedric. She didn't need to look like a buttoned-up assistant. She was in charge now, dammit. She'd dress as she pleased—once she could get to her clothes.

She turned to return to her seat. Something landed square on her chest. "Ooooff!" she cried out, and landed flat of her back.

The weight held her pinned to the carpet. It took her a moment to catch her breath. She wouldn't have been surprised to see little birds circling her head as in a child's cartoon. Her eyes focused, and she wished they hadn't. A furry red hulk stood squarely on her chest drooling all over her blouse. Its breath was hot and smelled of…shrimp?

"Laveau!" a dark, rough voice called. "Laveau, get off her, you big goober."

Someone ran down the aisle toward her. Another creature bayed near the front of the plane. The flight attendant joined in, alternating between shrieking and saying over and over, "I can't believe it's you. I can't believe it's you."

Samantha squeezed her eyes shut and tried to shove her attacker off her, which resulted in some wet, slick, disgusting goo covering her hands, and a wide abrasive tongue removing her makeup.

"Are you all right, ma'am?"

She was a tough, self-sufficient woman, but she wasn't made of stone. If ever a voice said, *open your eyes and take a look*, this one did. Once she did, she had to blink a few times to take in the man bent over her, wrestling the red behemoth until it stood behind him.

The screen test Danny Arneaux had done didn't do the man justice. His eyes were a luminous green, not jade nor leaf, but some color in between. His blade of a nose had a bump halfway down, broken at least once in his life. His jaw was sharply squared, and his cheekbones could have been drawn by an architect. His hair was several shades of ebony from a dark chestnut to deepest black. His lips were the pale red ochre that drew her eyes to shells along the beach, the bottom one full and sexy as the devil, and the top one absolutely the sort that begged to be taken between her teeth and….

"Can you get up?" He reached down and took her hands in his, then pulled her slowly and carefully to her feet. "I am so sorry. Laveau is harmless, but he doesn't know his own strength. Laveau, apologize to the lady."

"No need for an apology." Samantha tried to straighten her clothes and retrieve her dignity from some corner of the luggage bin. "I'm certain your…." She glanced at the dog, now hanging his head in shame. In fact, everything on the dog appeared to be hanging. The creature was huge, red, and wrinkled. "Someone forgot to iron your mastiff."

He laughed, a wicked temptation of a laugh that sent little shivers down her spine. *Steady on, girl. This is most definitely not why you are here.*

"They're bloodhounds. And you're Dr. Higgins. My Regency coach." He extended a hand.

"Very good, Mr. Arneaux."

She went to shake his hand, but immediately stopped when she saw the coating of dog drool all over her palm. In a show of forethought, the flight attendant reached around the actor to hand Samantha a cloth napkin. Samantha wiped off the drool as best she could, then shook the entirely too tall gentleman's hand. He was a good foot taller than she, which meant she was in for three months of looking up and likely getting a stiff neck. *Wait!*

"*They?* They're bloodhounds?" she asked.

"Yes, ma'am." Mr. Arneaux pointed toward the front of

the plane where another huge red bag of wrinkles sat in the middle of the aisle scratching its ear. "That's Laveau's sister, Marie."

"Pleased to meet them, I'm sure." She plucked at the now wet blouse sticking to her boobs. "I wasn't told you'd be traveling with…pets."

"I found out early on, in Hollywood, if you want a friend, your safest bet is a dog."

"Oh, I think they're precious," the flight attendant gushed.

"Thank you." Mr. Arneaux smiled at the girl, who looked about ready to faint dead away. "You said your name was Tiffany, right?"

"Of course, it is," Samantha muttered.

Clothes stained and damp, her hair a shambles, she stood next to a clean, crisp, figure-hugging uniform-wearing Tiffany. Samantha sighed. So much for appearing the consummate professional on her first day as a period film consultant.

Mr. Arneaux glanced at Samantha. His lips twitched. "Tiffany, honey, could you let the pilot know we are ready to go? And maybe bring Dr. Higgins and me a drink?"

"Oh, absolutely, Mr. Arneaux. Right away." She actually clasped her hands under her bookshelf of a bust.

Samantha rolled her eyes.

"Call me Danny," he said, and waved the flight attendant giddily on her way. "Shall we?" He nodded to indicate Samantha go ahead of him toward the spacious seats at the front of the plane.

Once they reached their seats, she noticed two large dog kennels facing the plush high-backed airline bench capable of seating three, where someone had also dropped a messenger bag, a duffle bag, and a bookstore shopping bag in the space closest to the window.

Samantha sat down on the matching bench across the

aisle from his and attempted to use the napkin to wipe the drool off her blouse. And her skirt. And her shoes. She was vaguely aware of Tiffany closing the door at the front of the cabin and lowering the long handle to seal it. Mr. Arneaux spoke quietly to his canine companions. Once Samantha finally looked up, each was safely, though with sad faces, locked into one of the dog kennels. The jet began to move, backing then turning to taxi toward a runway.

"You probably ought to take that blouse off, Dr. Higgins."

She turned her head so quickly in his direction her neck cracked like a bully's knuckles. Contrary to expectations, he appeared sincere, rather than rife with typical male innuendo.

"I beg your pardon?"

"Here." He dragged the duffle bag closer, rummaged in it, and drew out an oversized purple and gold t-shirt. "Trust me, you don't want to fly all the way to Scotland wearing Laveau's slobber. That stuff is like glue, and your blouse and bra are soaked. In about three minutes you won't be able to peel them off for love nor money. Try this." He offered her the brightly colored, completely inappropriate item.

She looked up at him, remembering she was likely to spend the next three months doing so. "No, thank you. I'm fine."

The jet bounced along the taxiway in search of a runway.

"Oh, come on now, Doc. Nobody wants to fly eight hours trussed up like a—"

Suddenly, the jet jerked to a stop, and Samantha had a lap full of Hollywood action star. Actually, only part of him was in her lap. His face landed across her breasts. She didn't want to think where his hands were.

"Like a what?" she asked, her voice only slightly breathless as she attempted to push him off her.

He planted his hands, one on the armrest and one on her

knee, and levered himself slowly to kneel beside her seat. For a second or two, she could have sworn a bright crimson flush shone beneath the deep bronze of his face and neck. This close, she had to admit his face was a combination of rugged handsomeness and a sort of classic male beauty. His mouth was too damned sexy by half, but his eyes…behind all that green was the *something* she'd seen in his screen test. Though she hadn't a clue what that *something* was.

"I am so sorry." He dragged the shirt out from under his knee and draped it over her legs before he stood and dropped into his seat.

"No harm, no foul." She fiddled with the shirt and arranged her things along the rest of the bench of seats between her and the window.

The jet engines revved, and the pilot turned sharply before picking up speed. A disembodied voice filled the cabin with the message they were cleared for takeoff and to please strap themselves into their seats.

"Sounds as if we are on our way. Perhaps I will save the shirt for later."

He fumbled with his seatbelt and flashed her a grin. "Suit yourself. I promise not to look. Back home, a gal can shed her bra and change her shirt in less than a minute without showing an inch of skin. Guess they don't teach that in Regency Coach School."

"Certainly not."

Could her answer have been any more prudish? She wanted to kick herself. Fortunately, one of his dogs began to whimper, and he leaned forward to murmur through the wire door at the front of the nearest airline crate. He ignored Samantha completely while the jet picked up speed and the pilot got them into the air. She stared at the shirt with the bright gold LSU and fleur de lisle's on it. A quick glance revealed Mr. Arneaux had fastened his seatbelt and was pulling several books from the bookstore shopping bag.

Well, bollocks!

She'd spent the better part of her life following a singular plan in a logical progression to achieve her goals. She didn't participate in silly, useless behavior like drinking herself into oblivion, sex with any man who asked, or taking up stupid challenges to prove a point. That way lay madness. The shirt taunted her. Her latest bit of madness stretched his legs out across the fronts of the two kennels. Was she really going to do this?

As quickly as she could, she drew the t-shirt over her head and went to work unfastening her blouse, then her bra. In minutes she had them on the seat beside her and her arms through the sleeves of the t-shirt. It was too big by at least two sizes, but the cotton was thick and soft. Much as she hated to admit it, the ridiculous thing was far more comfortable than what she usually wore on a transatlantic flight.

"Nicely done, Doc." His voice was rich, dark, and laced with laughter.

She glared at him.

He raised his hands in surrender. "Didn't see a thing. Cross my heart."

"A likely story." She forced herself not to smile.

He'd goaded her into it, dammit. She refused to acknowledge his justified amusement. In his black designer shirt tucked into black jeans that fit like a second skin, Danny Arneaux had every right to laugh at the Brit in the pinstripe skirt and oversized t-shirt that reached her knees.

"My mama raised me to be a gentleman. Or at least I think she did." He held up an obviously new copy of *Pride and Prejudice*. "Guess I'll find out."

"You're reading Jane Austen?"

"My agent's idea. This Darcy is supposed to be the man when it comes to historical romance heroes."

"You've never read *Pride and Prejudice?*"

"'Fraid not." He gave her a sideways glance. A lazy curl at one corner of his mouth promised a smile. "I majored in football and partying at LSU. Not much room for reading in that curriculum." He opened the book and flipped through the first few pages.

"Actually, you majored in Broadcast Journalism and minored in French poetry." She smothered a smirk at his abrupt stillness, followed in short order by the tilt of his head her way, as she added, "And you graduated with a three-point nine average."

"How the hell did you—"

"You entered college at the age of sixteen on full athletic and academic scholarships. You graduated at the age of nineteen. After which you were drafted into the NFL, but you never signed a contract. You went into modeling then acting." Samantha fidgeted with the t-shirt. Useless. She still looked like someone's dumpy little sister. "Why was that?"

"Why was what?" In a kaleidoscopic shift, his eyes were more hazel than green now, flat and empty.

"Modeling instead of football? American football is far more exciting, from what little I understand of the game."

"Yes, ma'am—*if* you think getting your bell rung during the Sugar Bowl and wandering around New Orleans in a cross-eyed haze for two days is exciting. That sort of night life is more fun than an Oscar party at Jack Black's."

"Bell rung?"

"Getting tackled so hard by a member of the opposing team that you hear bells ringing that aren't there?"

She winced, but didn't say anything, only continued to focus on him and waited.

He slapped the book against his leg. His chest rose and

fell. "After the game, they found me wandering around Jackson Square and I ended up in Tulane Hospital. Concussion. My fifth or sixth." His shoulders rippled in a flourish of a taut muscles. "Maw Maw asked me not to play football anymore. Said it'd knock what little sense I had right out of my head. Then where'd I be?"

"A very wise lady."

"You have no idea. So, here I am, thirty years old, flying to Scotland for some kind of boot camp hoping to save my dumpster fire of a career before I get too old to have a career. Those action film stunts are rough as hell on the body." He flashed her a, *you-don't-need-those-knickers-toss-them-over-here* smile. "I don't suppose you'd let me in on what this boot camp is all about, would you?"

She forced herself in tedious increments to look away. "Read your book, Mr. Arneaux. I'll be interested to hear what you think of Mr. Darcy."

Samantha grabbed her messenger bag and wrestled her laptop free. While she focused on powering it up and gathering the brain cells burned to ashes by that smile, he stared at the open book in his hand and muttered. She caught a few words here and there and almost felt sorry for him.

"How did she... Learn prissy-assed dancing... Freeze my couilles off... Haggis. Fire Jackie... Again."

"Don't fire your agent," she said without looking away from her screen. "I always do a thorough background check on Cedri—on *my* subjects, um students—before I begin their training." Samantha blinked furiously and resisted the need to kick against her seat. "That's how I knew about your education." She still refused to look at him. She tapped the keys of her laptop. Typing what, she hadn't the foggiest.

"So, I'm your…subject, huh?"

"I misspoke."

"I don't think so, Doc. You're not a misspeaking kind of girl."

"I am not a *girl*, Mr. Arneaux. I'm a woman, and I do misspeak. On occasion."

"You are most definitely a woman, Doc. *Mea culpa.* And I kinda' like the idea of being your subject. Think of all the experiments we could do."

She rolled her eyes and turned to find him staring at her suggestively. A stray snort escaped her. "Does that sort of thing work on American girls?"

"On occasion."

"There will be no experimenting."

"Damn."

"And stop calling me *Doc.*"

"Stop calling me *Mr. Arneaux,* and I will."

"Very well, Dante. You can call me Samantha."

"Jesus."

"Samantha will do."

"Please don't call me Dante."

"It's your name. Dante Xavier Arneaux. Much more elegant than the plebeian *Danny.*" Oh, that didn't sound snotty at all.

"You just think I'm plebeian. Wait until you try to teach me how to dance. Samantha." He shifted away from her and opened his book for the umpteenth time.

"I didn't mean to imply…I mean, of course you aren't…." No matter how small her foot was, it was hard as hell to pull it from her mouth once she'd shoved it in there as far as she had. "After all, you're one of the highest paid actors in the world."

"I know who I am, Dr. Higgins. I'm a piece of Creole Cajun trash out of the poorest parish in Louisiana who won the genetic lottery and somehow managed to make a living off it. Don't forget it. Because I never do."

Of all the things she'd expected Dante Arneaux to be, nothing had prepared her for this. Now what?

Chapter Three

"Not long now, sir," the pilot replied over his shoulder. "Little over an hour maybe? Might want to wake the ladies."

"Thanks, Mike." Danny left the cockpit and closed the door behind him.

When he reached the two airline crates, he bent to check on Marie and Laveau, both snoring their heads off. They weren't the only ones. Stretched across the bank of three seats, Dr. Higgins gave the dogs a run for their money. She'd probably think that too *plebeian* a thing for her to do, but she'd been sawing logs off and on for the last eight hours or so. Then again, so had he.

By some sort of unspoken agreement, they'd taken turns sleeping or pretending to sleep so they didn't have to speak to each other after that first disaster of a conversation. The pretense had also convinced Tiffany to leave him alone, once he'd assured her he had no objection to her sleeping in the jet's bedroom. So long as she did it alone. Not a complication he needed—and he sure as hell wasn't going to go back there and wake her up now.

Dr. Higgins rolled over, and her blankets slipped to the

floor. Danny stooped to retrieve them and paused to study her. All women looked younger when asleep, especially those like his Regency coach. He knew the type. Ambitious. Stressed. Maxing out the *professional* look to make it in a man's world. When he first saw her, he'd assumed her hair was a sort of nondescript dirty blonde. Now that her librarian bun look had given up, and sections of her hair had cut loose to fall across her face, he realized she had hidden the whole golden-haired English beauty thing in an ugly hairstyle. And she was a beauty when she wasn't being *Dr. Higgins*. Her skin was a warm creamy white with a pink tinge just beneath the surface. The perfect shade of coral, her plump lips were tempting as mortal sin. The curve of her cheek begged to be kissed.

Kissed? Oh, hell, no!

He snatched back his finger, hardly aware he'd been about to touch her face, and leapt back feet so fast he almost lost his balance. Danny flung the blankets back over her and dropped into his seat, which sent the stack of books he'd left there sailing into Laveau's crate. At which point, Laveau erupted into a frantic round of barking fit to wake the dead —or a snoring English woman, who flailed her way out of the blankets and landed on the cabin floor with a squawk.

"Bloody freaking hell!"

He ought to help her, but he was laughing too damned hard to help anybody.

She cussed with every breath.

His whole body shook.

In that cute little British accent.

He clutched his sides.

"Shut it, you noisy bugger," she ordered the shaking, ear splitting crate of indignant bloodhound.

Laveau actually stopped barking. Danny didn't blame him. To hell with Regency coach. When she was pissed, this woman had a voice most linebackers would drop and give twenty just on general principle. One blanket had ended up wound around her arm like a python, and she couldn't shake it.

"Of all the—" She glared up at him, and if looks could kill he'd be a smoking hole.

"Stop laughing, you sniggering twit, and help me."

Danny managed one of her requests. He stood, scooped her up in his arms, then placed her gently back onto her seat. He couldn't stop laughing, though. Not completely. He retreated to the safety of his own side of the jet. She wriggled her arm out the plaid blanket and flung it against the window before she turned to him again. By that time, Danny wasn't laughing, just snorting from time to time.

"I did not ask you to manhandle me, Mr. Arneaux," she said as she tried to make the wrinkled combination of business skirt and extra-large t-shirt look like something it wasn't. Her mouth was drawn up like she'd been sucking lemons. "And *what* is so funny?"

"You, Dr. Higgins. Cussing up a storm with an accent like Batman's butler. What would Mr. Darcy think?"

The pilot's voice interrupted with the news they'd be landing in about fifteen minutes.

Danny leaned across the aisle and stared into Samantha's big blue eyes. "And I never manhandle women. Not even when they ask me to." He turned to glance at the back of the plane. "Hey, there, Tiffany. Did you have a nice nap?"

"Nice enough, Mr. Arneaux," Tiffany said as she walked between him and Samantha and stopped at the curtain between the main cabin and the service area before the cockpit. "Lonely though." She flashed him a suggestive smile and went behind the curtain.

"Poor thing," Samantha muttered.

Danny stared straight ahead, coughing to cover a laugh,

and was whacked upside the head by one of those little airline pillows. When he turned to complain, the prim little Brit was perusing a bound movie script like butter wouldn't melt in her mouth.

He snatched the pillow up from the floor as the jet began to descend. He cleared his throat. Twice. Finally, he leaned over and shook the pillow to get her attention.

She turned toward him and smiled sweetly. "No, thank you, Mr. Arneaux. I'm quite awake now and we're about to land." She went back to her reading.

He'd been dismissed, which suited him fine. Seeing the title on the front of the script she studied, dropped a couple of his cousin, Charlene's, famous biscuits in his belly. Charlene had been married five times, and not because of her cooking. Just like his stomach cramps weren't because the jet was losing altitude as they came in to land.

The script. The view outside the jet window—Scotland. No going back now. He'd flown across an ocean dragging two slobbering hounds and a stack of trunks full of clothes he'd never seen before to have his ass humiliated and whipped into shape by…a woman about ten miles out of his league who probably wouldn't give him the time of day if it wasn't her job. Not that he was interested. He had a career to save.

He might have a motive for getting involved with Dr. Samantha Higgins. Hell, Jacqueline had made it perfectly clear he needed to do anything and everything to make certain this woman signed off on his keeping the role he'd won by the skin of his teeth. And in Jacqueline's book, seduction was the first line of defense. It had only taken one transatlantic flight with Samantha Higgins for him to peg her as dangerous, a lot more attractive than she probably wanted people to realize, and smarter than the average man.

Danny didn't know if he even qualified as *average* by her

standards. He was damned sure he didn't qualify as Mr. Darcy, let alone the man she was probably falling in love with now, *Captain Rothgate*, the hero of the script she was reading. The hero he'd staked his entire future on playing.

"I hope you're buckled up, folks," the pilot said over the intercom. "We've got sleeting rain in Aberdeen and it's going to make this a bumpy landing. The current temperature is forty degrees Fahrenheit."

"*Merde!*" Danny pressed his head into the headrest and closed his eyes. He was going to kill Jackie if he survived three months and more in Scotland. And if there wasn't a warm coat and some long-handled drawers in those damned trunks, he was going to murder Michael too.

"Is there a problem, Mr. Arneaux?"

He raised his left eye lid and gave Dr. Higgins a one-eyed side glance. "Besides you still calling me Mr. Arneaux? No ma'am, no problem at all."

She smiled. That scared the hell out of him.

An hour later, Danny stood at the front entrance area of the Aberdeen airport surrounded by luggage carts loaded with his trunks, Dr. Higgins's bags, and his dogs' airline crates. He didn't want to know what Erik Wentworth or even Jackie had to do to have Marie and Laveau cleared with so little aggravation. Even his Regency coach had remarked on it.

"Do they always travel overseas with you?" She bent to look inside each crate in turn and was rewarded with some rowdy tail thumping.

The rumble of more luggage carts and the sharp clickety clack of stilettoes sounded somewhere behind them. He hoped no enthusiastic fans had gotten past the security people who'd escorted them to the far end of the entrance.

He was tired, dammit. A giant weight had settled across his shoulders from the moment he'd left the plane, and it had nothing to do with the fleece-lined black wool coat that reached below his knees. Being Danny Arneaux was beyond him at the moment. The clickety clack stomped closer. Dr. Higgins looked at him. She'd asked him a question. Oh yeah.

"I pretty much don't go anywhere without them, but I usually have more trouble than this. Wentworth must have pulled some strings. Where's our—"

"Or perhaps that bitch of an agent of yours made all that legalese just go away," an annoying female voice from his past declared. "Jacqueline St. James is very good at covering your ass, isn't she, Danny?"

Danny froze. Then took a deep breath and turned inch by inch. "Hello, Lily. What"—*Crack!* His cheek and jaw sizzled with her slap—"are you doing here?" He rubbed the cheek she'd slapped.

"Haven't you heard? We're starring in this movie together." Lily Randolph, former child star and present-day pain in the ass actress, turned to Dr. Higgins and extended a hand. "Dr. Higgins, I presume? I'm Lily Randolph." She shook the startled woman's hand for half a second. "Oh, look, there's our transportation. Shall we?"

She waved at the herd of skycaps who pushed her mountains of luggage behind her, then tottered off on her six-inch heels toward the stretch limo type bus parked outside the sliding doors. When he found out whose bright idea it was for him and Lily to arrive in Scotland at the same time, let alone be stuck in the same vehicle together all the way to this Rosemount Manor place, he might end up on the six o'clock news. If they had six o'clock news in Scotland.

"Are you all right?" Dr. Higgins asked, her tone sincere if awestruck.

"I'm fine. At least this time she didn't draw blood." He

picked up his messenger bag, then hers. "What role is she playing?"

"Blood? This time?" They walked to the entrance side by side. "How many times has she slapped you?"

"About six times over the last six years or so. I try not to run into her more than once a year. Thankfully, she only draws blood when she's wearing an engagement ring. Must be between fiancés again." He glanced at Samantha. It took his entire acting toolbox to look anything but embarrassed as hell. "Better put that coat on. That wind is whipping it out there. What role is she playing?"

"How many times has she been—" She finally shrugged into her heavy wool coat and wrapped a tartan scarf around her neck. "How many times has she been engaged?"

"I stopped counting at five."

"Five? Good Lord!" Samantha did a double take between him, Lily, who was arguing about where her luggage went in the limo, then back at him again.

"The good Lord's got little to do with Miss Lily Randolph. Maybe he's using her to teach me a little humility from time to time."

Samantha snorted, which for some crazy reason, he loved.

"Maybe's he's using her to teach you how to duck."

Danny tried not to laugh, so did Samantha but, by the time all the luggage was loaded, and he'd strapped Marie and Laveau's crates so they could see him, he and Samantha were still laughing. She had a great laugh, not feminine or silly, but full and real. It was probably the most real thing he knew about her at this point.

"Oh, Dr. Higgins," Lily called from the rear facing seats at the front of the limo opposite them. "Why don't you come sit with me?" She patted the spot beside her.

The Englishwoman grabbed her messenger bag and rose

to move across the length of the bus. "Any advice, Mr. Arneaux?" she asked softly.

"Don't turn your back on her and don't forget to duck." Danny winked.

"Lovely."

"One more piece of advice?"

"Yes?"

"Call me Danny or I'll tell them to put her in the room right next to yours for the next three months."

"You wouldn't." She glanced up at Lily and managed a weak, *I-shouldn't-have-had-that-airline-burrito* smile.

"Oh, yes I would, *Samantha*."

"She's playing Captain Rothgate's wife." Samantha fished the script out of her bag and tossed it on the seat next to him. "*Dante*."

Danny grabbed the script, muttering every Cajun cussword he knew as Samantha weaved her way across the open space between the front facing and back facing seats of the luxury bus, then plopped down next to Lily. Samantha and Danny faced each other across a thickly carpeted open area.

Each set of seats consisted of a long, overstuffed leather bench that looked like recliner sofas without the footrests. Across from the double doors, a couple of single seats stood on either side of a long bar that contained a nice selection of liquor decanters set into holes to keep them from falling over and a couple of ice buckets attached the same way. In addition, there were a couple of fridges set into the underside of the bar, along with a microwave and a television. Danny had seen a lot of these setups in the last ten years. This one was extra fancy. Not in a tacky way, but with some class. Hell, he had cousins who could live in this setup given half the chance.

Lily's voice rattled like an AK47, shrill and fast. Between the distance and the sound of the bus's engine, he couldn't really hear what she was saying. But he didn't need to know what she was saying to know she was worried. She only talked like that when something was wrong. What could possibly be wrong? She had the female lead in what was sure to be one of the coming year's top movies.

Someone had turned the heat up. Samantha unbuttoned her coat. She fidgeted with the LSU t-shirt and looked… awkward and uncomfortable. Something he'd not seen in her in the ten or twelve hours he'd known her. Lily was doing all the talking. Not unusual for Lily. She always talked like someone who'd been mainlining chicory coffee for three days straight. But the Regency coach wasn't saying a word. Definitely strange. He glanced out the window.

They were out of the city and traveling up a narrow two-laned road. Danny was disoriented. The traffic was coming at them from the wrong direction. He shook his head and looked away from the road—and was instantly mesmerized. Green. So green it hurt his eyes. Not the dusty gray green of the bayou. Not the fake constructed green of California. This was a real green, so alive he expected it to crawl across the road. The rain still pelted against the windows, but the hills rose higher and higher. A weird sort of mist swirled over the tops of the hills like whipped cream on a piece of pie. He clutched the script against his chest and watched the countryside roll by, more beautiful than any set, than any CGI he'd ever seen. He couldn't look away.

This was what Captain Rothgate came home to after the horrors of war. These hills were the ones he walked. Danny narrowed his eyes and drew the view into his body, into his soul. The hills rose and fell, and he imagined the sort of man they'd carve—a man who'd do the honorable thing at any cost, a man as solid and alive as the countryside flickering past the window like a waking dream. Playing Captain Rothgate was the role of a lifetime, but there was more to it than that for Danny. Much more. He wished he knew what the hell that *much more* was.

"You are no help at all, sir," Samantha whispered in his ear before she sat down next to him.

He'd started at the first touch of her breath against his neck. Now he dragged his attention from the window and blinked to bring her face into focus. "What?"

"I did everything but send up a flare," she said in a low voice as she reached back and scratched Laveau's muzzle through the door of the crate.

"You didn't enjoy your conversation with America's little sweetheart?"

Danny watched Lily, who knelt on the seat and spoke through the open glass panel to the burly driver behind the seat. Her lime green skirt looked like she grew up in it, and it came just below the curve of her ass. At eighteen she'd been tempting in a girl-next door sort of way. At twenty-four she was sex in stilettos.

"Typical," Samantha said. She plucked the script from his hand and moved down the leather seat away from him.

"What'd I say?" He suspected it wasn't something he'd said, but he'd learned a long time ago never to assume he knew what a woman was thinking.

"It wasn't what you said, it was what *I* said, which you obviously didn't hear because you were listening to the call of the wild." She nodded at Lily.

"I was listening to the theme from *Jaws*. That's what I hear when I see Lily. What did you say?"

"*Jaws?* You're horrible."

"You're the one sending up flares." He gave her his undivided attention. "What *did* you say?"

"I said, it is not a conversation when only one person is speaking." She tugged at the neck of the t-shirt and sneaked a furtive look toward the front where Lily continued to flirt with the driver. "I cannot believe Wentworth picked her to play Captain Rothgate's wife." Samantha flipped aimlessly through the pages of the script. Danny noticed little notes and highlighted passages as she did.

"That makes two of us. Are you her Regency coach too?"

"No, my services are engaged for you alone. Apparently, Miss Randolph has done period drama before and won an Oscar for it, as I recall."

"Yeah, when she was twelve." Danny winced. He was allowing his fear to make him petty.

He returned to watching the enigmatic Scottish countryside. He didn't need any more reminders of how wrong he was for this part. No matter how bad he wanted it. He kept staring out the window, and the silence settled between them like an old *tante* chaperone.

"What do you see?" she finally asked. "What has you so captivated?"

He thought about it for a minute. Rain. Grass. Hills. Sheep. That was the easy answer. He saw much more than that. People didn't expect him to make deep or thoughtful observations. Not the good old boy from Louisiana. Would she expect that? She might be the only person on earth who might understand what he truly saw in the land spread out in front of him like a moving painting.

"I see what he saw. Home, after a long time at war, after doing something terrible for all the right reasons. Home always forgives you, even if you don't deserve it. Home doesn't judge. That's what Captain Rothgate saw. And I think I get it, sort of. At least a little bit."

Her little inhale of breath made one side of his mouth kick up. At least she wasn't laughing.

"You read the book. *A Matter of Honor*. You read it."

"Surprised?" He turned from his view out the window and looked at her.

"No." She drew the word out in a softer version of her precise British tones. "I don't think I am."

"Sure you are. But I appreciate the lie."

"I saw your screen test."

Well, that was the last thing he expected her to say. What the hell was he supposed to say to that besides, "How bad was it?"

"I cannot believe you dragged those two bags of drool all the way to Scotland," Lily announced from the front seat. "Do you sleep with those creatures?"

"Much safer than sleeping with an eighteen-year-old actress looking to boost her career," he murmured.

"Bastard," Lily snapped in unison with Samantha's gasp.

Lily narrowed her eyes to slits . "At least I didn't—"

"Don't," Danny warned in a soft voice. "Okay, Lily? Just don't. I'm jet lagged, I'm cold, and I don't have the strength to play nice."

Samantha followed this exchange like a spectator at a Wimbledon tennis match, her eyes now on Lily as Lily muttered loudly enough to be heard, "At least they didn't have to hire a Regency coach for me." She rifled through her lime green Gucci bag, pulled her phone out then pretended to scroll the screen.

Danny wiped the condensation from the limo window. "Is there a loch near this place we're going?"

"I believe so. I've never been there." Samantha opened the script once more. "Why do you ask?"

"Is there a monster in it?"

The limo climbed the hills taking them deeper into the Scottish countryside. A low hum settled in his nerves, the kind that used to run through him before a dangerous stunt.

It took her a minute. "I don't think even Nessie could take on Miss Randolph."

Her voice sent a weird sort of warmth into his chest.

Weirder still, he didn't need to see her face to know she was smiling. Not a big fake Hollywood smile, but the kind a woman smiled when she'd discovered a secret she didn't intend to share.

His phone dinged faintly inside his messenger bag. He fished it out to check the message.

Is your finger broken?

Jackie. Damn! He was supposed to text her once they landed. He'd been a little distracted. He shot her a text.

Danny: *Did you know Lily Randolph was cast opposite me?*

Jackie: *I plead the fifth.*

Danny: *You're fired.*

Jackie: *Again?*

Danny: *A heads up would have been nice.*

Jackie: *Was it bad?*

Danny: *No worse than a body cavity search in the Savannah City Jail.*

Jackie: *I so don't want to know how you know that. How is the Regency coach?*

Danny: *No comment.*

Jackie *That bad?*

Danny: *My signal's getting low. I'll check in when we get to boot camp.*

He shut off his phone then dropped it back into his bag. He sensed Samantha's focus on him, but when he turned to her, she'd gone back to making notes in the script. Danny stretched out his legs, crossed his ankles, and settled into the comfortable seat, still drawn to the rain-streaked images running past the windows of the limo like a tourist's videos. His eyelids dipped and rose. He fought the mixed rhythm of the rain and the sound of the tires against the road.

His sleep on the plane had come and gone at best. Jackie's last instructions to him, meeting Samantha Higgins, Regency boot camp, had all run together into a bizarre brew of questions streaming through his head on a continual loop like a demented musical earworm. He needed to sleep, but not now. Not trapped in a limo with two women, each with their own agenda where he was concerned. Kind of like napping in a johnboat with gators on one side and water moccasins on the other. A man would have to be able to walk on water to get out alive.

Despite his best efforts his eyes grew heavy.

THIS ROAD WAS BUMPY AS HELL. DANNY SHIFTED IN HIS SEAT, but the sound and sensation of a flat tire flopping shook him until he had no choice but to open an eye and figure out where he was. It only took a second. To his left his new Regency coach looked up at him, her eyes full of questions— and just a smidge of amusement. In front of him, across the limo, Lily Randolph lay sprawled across the plush bench under an ugly lime green puffy coat and five or six plaid blankets. Her mouth hung open and her hair was a mess. He let the idea of taking her picture with his phone slide across his mind. Nope. Not something a guy did to a woman he'd have to kiss on screen several times. Good way to lose a lip.

He scrubbed his face with his hands and twisted his upper body across the back of the seat to check on Marie and Laveau. They were sound asleep. He settled back into his seat, but the rattling of the limo didn't stop.

"Cobblestones," Samantha said.

"'Scuse me?"

"The drive is made of cobblestones. I assume that's what woke you?" She closed the script and slid it into her messenger bag. She'd buttoned up her long winter coat over the t-shirt.

"How long was I asleep?"

He buttoned up his own coat. The air in the limo had

cooled considerably, even with the heater blasting. Outside the window a long line of towering trees went by and a quick glance at the window closest to Samantha showed the exact same sight—trees lined up like fence posts and green lawns prettier than any football field.

"Long enough. We've arrived."

"Arrived?" Danny slid to the side edge of his seat and pressed his face against the window. "Where? All I see is grass and trees."

"Rosemount Manor. Your home for at least the next year or so, after three months of boot camp with me, of course. We've been on the estate for the last half hour."

"What manor? All I see is—Holy *merde!*"

The line of trees ended and opened into a circular driveway. In the middle was the biggest fountain he'd ever seen, which made the ones in Vegas look like garden gnomes. Four horses looked like they were about to run up the driveway, but a big, ripped guy in a chariot held them back. What was behind the fountain, however, made even all that look small. The reddish gray stone house was massive and older than anything he'd ever seen in New Orleans or anywhere else. He angled his head and tried to see how many stories high it rose skyward.

"That's no manor, that's a castle. Nobody said I'd be living in a castle." Danny sat back.

Samantha stared at him. Damn. He must sound like a complete idiot.

"I believe the remains of the family castle are on the estate, but it contains His Grace's private offices. Rosemount Manor is only a little over five hundred years old."

His Grace?

"Is that all?" Danny reached for the door handle as the limo drew to a halt. A young guy in a fancy jacket beat him to it and opened the door as at least a dozen more men swarmed around the limo like paparazzi. Danny grabbed his bag and stepped out onto the cobblestone driveway in front of the fancy covered entrance to the *manor.*

"Good afternoon, sir," the one holding the door said. "Welcome to Rosemount Manor."

The guy wore a skirt—a plaid skirt with knee socks and black dress shoes. They all wore the same getup. Danny shook his head and turned to help Samantha out the limo.

"Shouldn't we wake Miss Randolph?" Samantha asked as she wrapped her scarf around her neck.

"Let one of the guys in the skirts do it. She won't bite them. Probably."

Samantha grabbed Danny's arm and stood on her tiptoes to whisper in his ear. "Those are footmen. And they're wearing kilts. Not skirts. And if you call them skirts again, they *will* bite you."

"Got it. I knew that."

Her expression said, *Bullshit.*

Busted!

Danny started toward the back of the limo where the army of guys in fancy dress were moving the piles of luggage onto rolling carts. Once a cart was full, one of the guys rolled it toward the front door. It took two of the guys in kilts to lower the airline crates from the back of the limo. The minute they'd loaded the first one onto one of those carts, Marie spotted Danny and began to bay. A familiar shriek had everyone staring at the open side door.

"Run for it," Danny told Samantha. "I'll get my dogs and follow."

"Are you sure you'll be all right?"

"I'll throw a few of the guys in kilts at her."

Danny opened the first crate and leashed up Marie. He handed a second leash to one of the footmen who opened Laveau's crate but failed to catch the dog barreling through the open gate and out onto the perfectly cut lawn. The footman took off after the dog. Marie tried to follow her brother. Danny pulled her back.

He handed the leash to Samantha, but she took a step back. "Not me."

"I've got to go after him," Danny said in exasperation.

"No, you don't."

"Did neither of you think to wake me before now?" Danny and Samantha turned as Lily teetered out of the limo. "I wouldn't expect Danny to, but you, Dr. Higgins, aren't you part of the help?"

Danny winced.

A tall, leggy redhead in a sort of peasant top and denim skirt topped with a bright purple hooded sweat jacket strode around the fountain, her hand extended to the screeching actress who was about to get punched by the Regency coach, unless Danny had misread that fire in Samantha's blue eyes.

"Miss Randolph," the redhead said with the happiness only someone who had never met Lily could express. "Welcome to Rosemount Manor. Let's get you out of the cold. Dr. Higgins? Mr. Arneaux? Shall we?" Smart woman. She tried to tug Lily toward the open double doors on the other side of the fountain.

A series of shouts drew everyone's attention to the front lawn where Laveau was heading back toward the limo baying his head off. Marie took off toward him, snatching her leash out of Danny's hand and adding her voice to the noise. Marie reached Laveau and they both raced toward the driveway crowded with carts of luggage, footmen, and innocent bystanders.

"Oh dear." Samantha nodded toward the far side of the fountain.

A tall, lean, dark-haired guy in a sweater and kilt strode toward them. He didn't look happy. Worse, Lily pulled away from the redhead and started toward the not-so-happy guy, a big smile on her face.

"They're going to scattered them like bowling pins." Danny lunged toward the group, but too late. Laveau and Marie burst through the crowd of footmen and they did, indeed, go flying out onto the moist green grass like bowling pins.

"Damn," Danny cursed.

The scene unfolded like a really bad movie. Marie and Laveau reared up onto their back legs before Danny could reach them and their paws landed on the man's chest.

"Bloody hell," Samantha cried.

"Noooo!" Lily shouted.

Splash! The man fell backwards into the fountain.

"What the—" Danny skidded to a halt at the fountain in unison with another splash as Lily tumbled into the water after the man.

A couple of footmen grabbed the animals' leashes and dragged them away from the fountain, both dogs perfectly dry. Danny reached for the leashes, but long fingers grasped his arm and he turned to see Samantha beside him. She shook her head and they watched as the rest of the footmen rushed to help the tall guy out of the fountain while the redhead managed to get Lily, soaked from head to toe, back onto dry land—er…cobblestones. The footmen backed away from the guy in the wet kilt, their heads bowed.

"What the devil is going on here?" the drenched man demanded.

Chapter Four

Samantha couldn't stop staring at her reflection in
the exquisitely framed full-length mirror. In five years of
working as an advisor to period filmmakers, she'd never had
the occasion to get kitted out in Regency dress. In fact,
despite her membership in every sort of Jane Austen society
and the like, she hadn't done so since her days at Oxford. Yet
here she stood in a period furnished bedchamber in one of
the most elegant and wealthy manor homes in Scotland
while Bridie, a maid Eleanor had assigned to Samantha,
styled her hair in a period updo complete with pearl-tipped
Regency style hairpins. Her gown of rich, blue silk fell from
an Empire waist. The netted overskirt glittered with tiny
white jewels, and she wore matching silk slippers with blue
ribbons she'd laced up her stockinged legs. An Austenite's
dream come true.

This could be fun—so long as she didn't think about the
duke in the fountain, the screeching actress dripping across
priceless Persian rugs, and the butler who'd glared at
Samantha as if *she* were personally responsible for the two
furry behemoth banshees living in the equally opulent

bedchamber across the hall because the "*actor fellow*" refused to send them to the kennels.

Dante had refused to send them to the kennel after, of course, apologizing to "*Mr. Grace*" for Laveau shoving the man, their host, a duke, into the fountain.

Samantha groaned and shook her head. Three months of this? More, once filming started—*if* she signed off on Dante and was still around herself. What the hell had she gotten herself into?

"Are you all right, miss?" Bridie had the most wonderful Scots lilt to her voice. A soothing tone that settled Samantha's nerves.

"I'm fine, Bridie. Thank you. And thank you for this." She indicated her current costume and hair. "Jane Austen herself could not have done better."

"Thank you, miss. We're all a bit excited to play fancy dress for the next few months. It's deadly dull working here most of the time."

"I don't think dull is going to be a problem with the Americans here," Samantha muttered as she picked up her paisley pashmina and her fan from the foot of the four-poster bed then headed for the door.

"Did Mr. Arneaux's dogs really knock Himself into the fountain?" Bridie asked as she trailed behind her, brushing at the back of Samantha's evening gown.

"I'm afraid so."

"Not like Himself couldn't use a good dunking," Bridie said.

Samantha glanced over her shoulder, and Bridie clapped a hand over her mouth.

Samantha grinned. "All men could use a good dunking from time to time, Bridie."

"Ain't it the truth," Bridie said before she hurried off on another chore.

Out in the corridor, it took Samantha a minute to get her bearings. The walls, hung with medieval tapestries and heavy gilt-framed paintings, stretched as far as the eye could see in both directions. She'd been so horrified, tired, and exasperated when the footmen had escorted her, Dante, and a soaking wet Lily and their luggage up to this floor, she hadn't paid a great deal of attention as to the way back to the first-floor drawing room where all the guests were supposed to meet before dinner.

"Fat black horse, then old woman in an ugly gray dress," a deep and familiar male voice said behind her. "Thataway."

"How do you…oh." Samantha's throat went dry.

She'd wondered why women threw themselves at Danny Arneaux. Cedric had said the next Mr. Darcy couldn't be a man of Color, but he couldn't have been more wrong. Who knew silk knee britches, a shoulder hugging evening jacket, and a white shirt and cravat were the things that would turn her on? No wonder all those Regency girls got weak-kneed at the sight of Mr. Darcy. She swallowed hard.

"You look very nice," she said, her voice perfectly calm and professional. Okay, fine. Calm, then.

"I'm glad you think so, Doc. I've never been so uncomfortable in my life, and I once had to spend a whole week in a wet suit. You"—he made a production of raising her hand to his lips and kissing the tips of her fingers just like Mr. Darcy would—"on the other hand, look stunning. Blue is your color."

"Flattery will not get either of us out of the duke's bad books." She pointed in one direction. He turned in the other, placed her hand in the crook of his arm, and continuing forward. "Especially if we're late. Are you sure this is the right way?"

"Yep." He indicated with his free hand. "Fat black horse." She noted the fat black horse painting on the wall to their left as he kept talking, "Dougal tried to explain this duke business to me, but I still don't get it."

"Dougal?"

"The guy who got me into this getup. My…*valet*." His English accent on the last word was spot on.

"He did an excellent job."

The two of them turned down another corridor, their footsteps near ghosts of sound, muffled by Turkey rugs over some sort of padding between them and the worn stone floors. If not for the discreetly placed electric light fixtures, they might have been wandering the halls of Rosemount Manor two hundred years in the past, especially as those light fixt cures were dark and only oil lamps and sconces with candles lit the halls.

"Old woman in ugly gray dress." He stopped at the huge portrait hung on the polished mahogany paneled wall. "Am I seriously going to have to wear crap like this twenty-four seven for the next three months?"

So much for two hundred years in the past.

"A gentleman does not say *crap*." She had no choice but to fall back into the role for which she'd been hired. Otherwise, she'd be laughing her head off at the unhappy-five-year-old tinge to his voice.

"I'll bet a gentleman doesn't go without drawers 'cause they ruin the look of the *breeches* either."

"Oh?"

Don'tlook.Don'tlook.Don'tlook. It was either the sexiest thing she'd ever heard or—

"He had to use my shirttails to wrap up my…equipment, so I don't scare the ladies, and I'm still freezing my—"

She held up a hand as they started down the wide, grand staircase to the first floor. "I don't need to know the details." Mostly she didn't need to visualize the details. He might be cold, but she had flashes of heat shooting through her body like fireworks.

"Not to mention," he continued, "I thought Dougal was going to have to use a shoehorn and a can of Crisco to get me into this outfit. I haven't been manhandled like that since the last time I visited my great-*tante* Stella's monthly bingo game with her girlfriends."

Samantha bit her lip. Her body shook. The dratted man looked at her, his eyes wide and his face completely open. Innocent? Not in his entire life.

They came to the double doors to the drawing room. The footmen on each side opened the doors in tandem, and she and Dante Arneaux strolled into the drawing room, just as a disobedient snort of laughter burst from her lips—which would not have been quite so terrible if the room had not suddenly gone silent as a tomb.

It wouldn't take a large hole. She wasn't terribly tall or broad. Just a small hole opening up in the floor right that very instant was all she asked. Preferably somewhere not covered with a priceless red, gold, and black Aubusson rug. The room was full of people in Regency dress, people she knew from her work with Cedric in the period film business. People who were no doubt stunned to see her here without him, taking his place.

"Dr. Higgins," the tall redhead from earlier said as she strode toward them. "I hope your rooms are comfortable. Mr. Arneaux? You both look wonderful."

"So do you…Ms. Witherspoon, isn't it?" Dante turned his infamous *bad boy* smile on her, and of course, the willowy event manager blinked for a moment like a deer in head-lamps. "That dress is a stunner."

"Why thank you, kind sir." Ms. Witherspoon bobbed a creditable curtsy. "And you look very handsome. The best part of this whole thing is the clothes, isn't it? Dr. Higgins, you look like you stepped out of a period film or a history book."

It would be so easy to hate the woman. Ms. Eleanor Witherspoon's dark emerald off the shoulder gown of watered silk was the perfect complement to her golden-brown complexion and brilliant auburn hair. She didn't *look* the part of an elegant Regency lady; she was elegance personified. And an American, no less. So not fair. Samantha's skin prickled, the tiniest of fissures dancing along the low neckline of her dress and up the back of her neck exposed by her period updo.

"You ladies are both exquisite," Mr. Arneaux said, his eyes fixed on Samantha like a man who hadn't eaten in a week, and she was a fish and chips wrapper. "Are those gowns as comfortable as they look? I'd hate to be the only one trussed up like a bale of hay."

"The gowns, yes," Samantha said. "The corsets, not so much."

"Ouch." He winced, and Ms. Witherspoon laughed. "Thank God Regency men don't have to wear those," he said.

"Actually," Samantha said as she plucked a flute of champagne from the tray a footman offered them. "Do you see the distinguished gentleman standing by the fireplace talking to His Grace?"

Mr. Arneaux and Ms. Witherspoon each took sips of their own champagne and cut surreptitious glances across the room.

"Mr. Sylvan Goode is a renowned Regency dance instructor, and he is most definitely wearing a corset."

"I wondered what that creaking noise was," Ms. Witherspoon said, her eyes bright with unvoiced laughter.

"Are you serious? Holy...." The actor coughed then focused his attention on the duke like a laser. "Why am I tied up like a Christmas ham, and he gets to wear a skirt?"

"Who?" Samantha asked though she and Ms. Witherspoon shared a conspiratorial glance of perfect understanding.

"*He* is the master of the house, and I daresay he isn't part of your Regency experience, is he, Ms. Witherspoon?" Samantha replied.

"He *is* the Regency experience." Ms. Witherspoon's tone indicated far more than met the eye. "Trust me. But I wouldn't call it a skirt again. These Highlanders find it very offensive."

"Hard to worry about offending a guy dressed like that."

"Until one remembers our ancestors used to eat our dead." A hand broad as a dinner plate landed on Mr. Arneaux's shoulder. The only thing broader was the newcomer's brogue. "Welcome to Scotland, Mr. Arneaux. I'm a big fan of your films." The speaker released Mr. Arneaux's shoulder and crossed the Aubusson to the fireplace.

The man wasn't quite as tall as the actor but more than made up for it in breadth. About sixty or so, with unruly dark gray hair and an equally feral beard, he was a mountain dressed in formal Scot's attire. For all that, he offered the duke a bow of such sincere respect it brought a sudden catch to her throat.

"What the hell was that?" Mr. Arneaux asked softly. He downed the rest of his champagne and took the glass Samantha handed him.

"His Grace's steward," Ms. Witherspoon said. "Mr. Angus McGinty. Don't let him fool you. He's a teddy bear."

"Would it be really tacky if I snuck my phone out and took a shot of him? That's the kind of *teddy bear* my Maw Maw would like to find propped up on her bed."

"Mr. Arneaux!" A blush heated Samantha to her toes. She'd spent so much time ogling the way he looked in his fitted evening clothes, her role as his teacher had flown right out the window. "A Regency gentleman does not—"

Ms. Witherspoon threw back her head and laughed. Everyone in the room stared at the three of them, and still the American beauty laughed. The way Samantha often longed to laugh, without giving a damn what anyone might think. Mr. Arneaux's lips twitched.

Once Ms. Witherspoon's laughter subsided, the other guests went back to their clumps of conversation. Her eyes met those of the duke, and her entire expression changed, as if someone had put out a light in the vivacious woman. Samantha felt bad for her. The man obviously disapproved of the bossy Yank in charge of what he probably saw as an invasion of his life and home.

"Your Maw Maw sounds like my kind of people, Mr. Arneaux," Ms. Witherspoon said, pointedly turning her back on the men warming themselves at the giant hearth.

"Okay, you two ladies are going to have to stop with the *Mr. Arneaux* stuff. If you don't start calling me Danny, I am going to get really ticked off. Not *eat-my-dead* ticked off, but, ticked off."

"I'm going to let Dr. Higgins explain the Regency rules about that sort of thing. I'm about to tick off everybody in the room." Ms. Witherspoon picked up a large green velvet drawstring bag from a pretty antique inlaid side table. "Your Regency experience starts now, *Mr. Arneaux*."

He sidled up next to Samantha as Ms. Witherspoon moved elegantly to the center of the room and briskly clapped her hands three times. The scent of his cologne, sandalwood with something clean and light, combined with the heat of his body, did strange things to Samantha's senses. It had been entirely too long since she'd found a man attractive. She chalked it up to him being criminally handsome and a professional charmer.

"Ladies and gentlemen, can I have your attention, please?" Ms. Witherspoon smiled broadly, showing perfect white, even teeth.

"I'm not going to like this, am I?" Mr. Arneaux asked out of the side of his mouth as he leaned down toward Samantha.

"Probably not."

"I am Eleanor Witherspoon, Rosemount Manor's event planner, known from this moment on as *Miss* Witherspoon. I want to welcome you and thank everyone here for allowing us the run of this beautiful home and estate, most especially His Grace, the Duke of Turra." Miss Witherspoon put her palms together and tilted them in the duke's direction. To which he returned the slightest inclination of his head. "For the next three months we will be turning back the clock and living the lives of Regency era men and women in every way possible."

A few of the guests appeared genuinely excited. Most looked bored to tears. Samantha was torn between fascinated anticipation and abject terror. Her entire future was to be decided in the next three months. She swallowed.

Bloody fricking hell!

Miss Witherspoon spoke again. "When you return to your rooms, you will each find a copy of your schedules and a book on the rules and manners of this Regency experience."

Rules?

That got everyone's attention.

"And the first rule is…" she opened the velvet bag and began to move around the room, "no cell phones."

"What?" a woman said.

"This is ridiculous," a man growled.

"I need my phone," two people said in unison.

"I didn't agree to this," another woman said.

Samantha had to admire her tenacity. Miss Witherspoon faced down each and every complaint with a steely gaze and an insistent shake of her velvet bag. One by one, the guests dropped their phones inside, their expressions running the gamut from utter disbelief to indignant fury to pathos of loss worthy of the best actors *Coronation Street* ever produced. Sadly, it was easy for Samantha to let go of her own connection to the outside world. She'd already spoken with her parents. Her work the last five years left them with no expectations of hearing from her on a regular basis. She had few friends, most of whom were reclusive history types like herself, and she had not had a boyfriend in ages.

"Is this really necessary?" Mr. Arneaux asked, even as he dangled the latest model iPhone over his fellow American's pretty green reticule. "My agent is the clingy type. She expects to speak with me at least three times a day."

"She signed the waiver for you," Miss Witherspoon said sweetly. "Such a sweet lady."

"*My* agent?" He dropped the phone into the bag. "I want a recount. Jackie's not even sweet when she's asleep. Did you know about this, Doc?" he asked Samantha as Miss Witherspoon moved on to the next group of guests.

"Will you stop calling me *Doc*?"

"That depends. Will you stop calling me *Mr. Arneaux*?"

"You need to read the book Miss Witherspoon has left in your room."

"You're no fun."

"This experience is not meant to be fun. At least not for you. This is work. For both of us."

Perfect. Her equilibrium tilted back toward normal. Nice. Professional. Normal.

"I don't care who you are. I have no intention of giving up my phone," came Lily's voice.

Mr. Arneaux's...*Dante's* full mouth twitched. His back faced the storm brewing across the drawing room, but he sighed.

"This is ridiculous," Lily said. "I don't need a Regency experience. I can play this part in my sleep."

Samantha couldn't vouch for Lily Randolph's acting skills at this point, but her ability to project her voice and capture a room was top notch.

"I see the *not fun* part of the program is about to start." Dante handed his glass to Samantha.

"Where are you going?" Samantha whispered after him as he turned and headed toward the grouping of red and gold striped damask chairs and settee where the actress and the program manager stood toe to toe whilst a couple of men Samantha recognized from previous period films watched like spectators at a cock fight. She refused to shout at him in a formal parlor larger than her first flat in London filled with scholars, film people, actors, and a bloody duke.

Once she shook off the spell he cast while striding in period evening clothes fitted to him like a second skin, Samantha tried to suss out the brief, jerky conversation between Lily Randolph and Dante Arneaux. Most of the jerking was on the actress's part as she spat out words in time with poking her finger into the middle of Dante's perfectly tied neck cloth. Samantha should have spent more time watching silent movies with Grandda as her lipreading skills were sorely lacking.

Dante plucked the phone from Miss Randolph's hand and dropped it into Eleanor Witherspoon's drawstring bag, which Eleanor yanked closed. Lily's mouth fell open and she turned her glare onto him. He whirled and walked away as Miss Witherspoon turned. Samantha shifted in an effort to hide the laughter she worked to suppress but stilled when Eleanor immediately ran into the duke. Samanth couldn't believe her eyes when the tall redhead didn't reply to him. She merely patted his chest and walked away.

"Wonder what's up there?"

Samantha jumped. Dante's deep voice in her ear was the last thing she expected. How the hell did a man as tall as him move so quietly?

"Maybe we don't need to know," he said. "The only drama we need is what's in Wentworth's script, right?"

She shot him a recriminating look. "I don't know. Is your little convo with America's sweetheart going to stir up any drama? I cannot believe you took her phone."

The woman in question still stared daggers at Dante's back.

"Neither can she. There won't be any drama on my part unless she kills me in my sleep. Promise you'll get my dogs back to my agent if she does."

"Done."

He grinned, and she couldn't help but smile back. Until Lily Randolph started toward them. The double doors opened, and a gong sounded somewhere down the corridor. Rosemount Manor's butler stepped into the room. Samantha released a quiet sigh of relief when Lily halted and looked at the man.

"Your Grace. My lords, ladies, and gentlemen. Dinner is served."

"Shall we?" Dante offered his arm and hustled Samantha out into the corridor behind the butler.

"Protocol dictates the duke and the highest-ranking lady lead the way to dinner," Samantha informed him even as she hurried to keep up with his long strides.

"What does protocol say about a pissed off actress whupping my ass before we ever make it to the table?"

She managed to dig in her heels and stop him just short of entering the sumptuous formal dining room. The other guests ambled down the hall toward them, chattering away until Mr. McGinty paused in the middle of the corridor, the duke and Miss Randolph coming up the Turkey rugs in his wake.

"Do you think she'll *whup* your…posterior with the duke on her arm?" Samantha whispered.

"Only if she can do it without letting go of him. Poor guy has no idea. Lily isn't a catch-and-release kind of woman."

"She *released* you."

Samantha started at the mask that abruptly snapped closed over his expression. What the bloody hell just happened? Embarrassment heated her cheeks, and she started to pull her hand from where she grasped his forearm, but he laid a hand on hers in what, warning, as they followed the other guests into the dining room?

The devil seized her, and before she could stop herself, she said, "You needn't worry, *I* have no intention of throwing you back."

His head jerked in her direction and her breath caught. The mask had evaporated, and a strange light burned in his eyes. Her mouth went dry.

She had no idea how to respond, so said, "You are incor-rigible."

"You don't know the half of it, Doc," he whispered.

"God help me," she muttered.

Dante threw back his head and laughed, a dark sexy rumble of a laugh as he held her chair before the footman could do so. Of course, everyone stared at him, eyes wide, mouths pursed. Because he laughed as if he meant it? Because he'd usurped the footman's position? Because they wondered what Erik Wentworth was thinking, casting *this* actor in the period film of the year?

Without a thought to manners or protocol, Samantha dropped into the carved mahogany chair with the ivory and gold silk striped upholstered seat and back. She had her napkin shaken free and flung in her lap before the duke cleared his throat and took his chair at the head of the table. The footmen served the first course, split pea soup.

Polite conversation buzzed about the table. Samantha took in the room. The furnishings were all dark mahogany, the endless dining table, the chairs, the sideboards. The color scheme was an ecru color and a sort of antique gold. Massive chandeliers lit the room. Fireplaces, framed by carved black marble mantelpieces, stood at either end of the room. An Aubusson rug in a gold, black, and white pattern decorated the floor.

The table setting of Waterford Crystal, DeLamerie silverware, and fine bone Wedgewood china in the duke's family colors of crimson, gold, and black could have graced the set of any period film. Samantha had served as Cedric's assistant on dozens of film shoots. This, however, was the first time she had been allowed to truly experience the period she'd devoted her life to studying. Silly. She suddenly felt a little overwhelmed by it all. The entire experience, especially with Dante Arneaux added in was frankly—

"Cold."

Samantha started. "I beg your pardon?"

"Your soup is getting cold," Dante said softly. "It's not bad, but I don't think it improves with age. Might want to eat it while it's hot."

She refused to look at him, but she did take up her spoon and begin to eat.

"Is the furniture that interesting or are you ignoring everyone on purpose?" he asked.

"Don't be ridiculous."

The nerve of the man.

"Not that I blame you. I never knew there were so many ways to talk about the weather."

"Eat your soup."

"I already did. Didn't slurp or spill a drop."

Now she did look at him. He winked and leaned back in his chair so one footman could remove his bowl, and another could place the second course onto the obnoxiously white tablecloth. Samantha shook her head.

The dance instructor, who sat to her right, asked after a mutual acquaintance in the business. She responded to his inquiries, all the while trying to keep an ear out for Dante's voice as Miss Bella Stepford, the film's costume designer and one of England's most well-known period clothing experts, engaged him in conversation. Samantha needn't have worried. He had the gray-haired lady in fits of giggles by the time the third course was served.

"I see Dr. Higgins has already begun your tutelage, Mr. Arneaux." From across the table, Teddy Rousseau, fencing and Regency weapons instructor, made certain everyone in the room heard him. "Your table manners are quite impressive."

Teddy was a renowned swordsman, but his most deadly weapon was his mouth. He was a notorious social climber. Mr. Rousseau wore his long hair in a period film style, tied back with a thin, black gross-grain ribbon. He was British for God's sake. An arrogant bastard to boot. He had hard grey eyes, was tall and lean, and was too damn good looking for his own good. And every beautiful woman he encountered knew it.

"Actually, Teddy, Mr. Arneaux and I haven't discussed anything pertaining to the Regency as of yet. His table manners are his own." Samantha had an immediate and unnatural urge to toss her glass of wine across the broad table at Teddy.

"My apologies, old man. I assumed…."

"No need to apologize. I'm pretty sure those Regency folks observed people at the dinner table all the time. It's a great way to find out who the assholes are."

"So right," Teddy said.

Samantha bit back a sigh and leaned over, resting her hand on Dante's forearm. "One does not refer to *assholes* at a Regency dinner table. Especially a duke's dinner table."

"Then maybe a duke should invite fewer assholes to dinner."

A riot of coughing, glasses clattering, and voices raised in concern all erupted from the head of the table. The duke's face turned bright red as he hacked and attempted to drink from his water glass at the same time. Mr. McGinty jumped out of his chair and began whacking the duke on the back. Good thing His Grace was a stout fellow, or he'd have been face-down in his plate from the force of the blows. Through this entire debacle, Dante continued to eat as if nothing at all was wrong.

The duke waved his steward away, took several sips of his water and set the entire dinner party back in motion with a mere glance. Samantha had never had fantasies of being a duchess or the like, but having that sort of authority? Nice. Even better, in a perfectly timed moment, she witnessed a wordless exchange between Dante and His Grace that spoke volumes about them.

Men!

"What did we do now?" Dante asked.

Damn! She'd said that out loud.

"Nothing at all." She fidgeted in her chair as the footmen removed the next to last course and delivered the dessert. "Eat your cranachan."

"Are you going to keep up this kiddie treatment for the entire three months And what exactly is cranachan?"

"Kiddie treatment?" She had all sorts of treatments in mind for this man. *Kiddie* had nothing to do with any of them.

"Eat this. Eat that. You sound like my Maw Maw."

"I beg your pardon."

Samantha had been told she reminded men of their boss or their sister or their best friend. Grandmother was a new low for her. She spooned up a healthy portion of cranachan from the beautiful crystal dessert dish and shoveled it into her gob. The sweet and cold hit her senses like an ocean wave. Her eyes crossed as she worked the confection in her mouth.

All the while, the damned Yank chuckled under his breath —until he took the first bite of his own dessert. He closed his eyes and hummed in a sort of ecstatic trance.

"Are you quite all right, Mr. Arneaux?" the duke asked from the head of the table.

"Give me a minute. I'm having a religious experience," Dante replied, eyes still closed.

"Mrs. Gordon's cranachan has that affect." The Duke of Turra was apparently incapable of smiling, but his eyes crinkled the teensiest bit at the corners as if he might have known how to smile at some point.

"I think I'm in love. This stuff is amazing."

"The way to your heart, Mr. Arneaux?" Halfway down the table, a woman wearing Regency-looking spectacles and with tortoiseshell combs pinning up her dark hair asked her question in such a truly interested tone Samantha wondered if the poor thing was at the wrong dinner party. She sounded so...nice. In fact, her face looked familiar in a *I've-seen-you-somewhere-before,-haven't-I* sort of way.

"I'm from New Orleans, Miss Chase," Danny said. "Good food is better than the GPS when it comes to getting to a Cajun's heart. The only thing better is a good story."

Chase. Where did Samantha know that name from? The woman blushed and tugged at the neckline of the plain burgundy gown she wore.

"You're a gifted writer, ma'am. *A Matter of Honor* is an

amazing book. Captain Rothgate is one of the most complicated heroes I've ever read," Dante said.

The buzz of conversation went silent. Everyone stared at the innocuous-looking woman who couldn't be more than thirty years old. Samantha, however, was struck by Dante Arneaux in a completely new way. She'd obviously spent way too much time with cynics and historians who used their knowledge like a cudgel over those for whom history was just words in a thick, dusty book. It took her a minute or two to assess the directness of his tone and the weight of the regard with which he spoke to the authoress.

"You're the author who has brought us all together?" Teddy blotted his mouth with a silk embossed napkin and pushed his half-eaten dessert away. "You don't look like a romance writer."

Miss Chase pushed her spectacles up onto the bridge of her nose. "What exactly does a *romance writer* look like?"

"Oh, you know. At least forty, heavy set, frizzy gray hair, and sexually frustrated?" He laughed. Worse, several of the other dinner guests laughed with him.

Miss Chase's cheeks pinked and she went back to picking at her dessert.

"I meant no offense, my dear," Teddy said. "I'm sure your little book must be of some interest. Wentworth bought the rights, and the man knows how to make a good film out of almost anything. You have to admit though, Captain Rothgate is no Mr. Darcy."

"Teddy, really." Samantha had suffered the man's arrogance before because of her position as Cedric's assistant. She didn't have to put up with it now she was the lead coach on this film. "Have you even read Miss Chase's book?"

"Aren't most historical romance novels simply rewrites of *Pride and Prejudice?*"

Dante opened his mouth to speak, but at Miss Chase's

blatant *please-don't* expression, he made a lip-zipping motion and tossed away an imaginary key. Who was this man? Samantha feared she was finding out, and the knowledge was a dangerous thing.

Fortunately, the table erupted into a variety of opinions of Jane Austen's work, each one wordier and more esoteric than the last. Dante rolled his eyes and mouthed the word *"Morons"* to the authoress. She and Samantha shook their heads.

"What is your opinion, Mr. Arneaux?" Lily Randolph's voice carried over the voices of the others.

"'Fraid I don't have one." Dante dropped his spoon into the now empty cranachan dish and pushed slightly away from the table.

"Have you not read *Pride and Prejudice?*" Miss Stepford asked. "Don't you find Mr. Darcy a fascinating character as well?"

"Oh, I've read it. I just can't express my opinion without using one of the words Dr. Higgins here says I cannot use at a duke's dinner table."

"Not at all, Mr. Arneaux," the duke said. "Feel free to express your opinion. I am certain we would all like to hear your thoughts on Mr. Darcy. Be as blunt as you like. I find American directness refreshing."

"Yes, do enlighten us, *Mr. Arneaux.*" Lily draped her hand over the duke's only to have him slide his from beneath hers to take up his wine glass.

Samantha's stomach sank. In her short acquaintance with Dante, that glint in his eye was becoming an all too familiar signal.

Don't say it. Don't say it. Please. Don't say it.

"Mr. Darcy's an asshole. That's my opinion."

Chapter Five

DANNY SNATCHED THE INSTRUMENT OF TORTURE FROM around his neck and turned back to the two ladies coming up behind him on the stairs leading to the second floor. They were laughing, which explained the idiotic grin he couldn't wipe off his face. Thanks to him, the evening had ended early. Good thing because the damned jet lag was kicking his ass. They reached the hallway where his and Dr. Higgins's rooms were. A footman was just coming out of Danny's.

"Just took the dogs out, sir. They should be good for the night," he said as he bowed to the ladies.

"Thanks, Robbie. You're the man."

The footman gave him a thumbs up and hurried down the hall. Danny turned back to his companions.

"Well, Dr. Higgins, Miss Chase, I think the evening was a great success. How about you?"

"Which part?" his Regency coach asked. "The part where you caused a duke to nearly choke to death?"

"Twice," the authoress said. "When you said Mr. Darcy was an *arse*, I thought the poor man was a goner." She snickered then clamped a hand over her mouth.

"The only thing gone was the tablecloth. I've never seen anyone spew wine that far. It was awesome."

"Awesome is not the word I would use."

"Oh, come now, Dr. Higgins. That is exactly the word I would use," Miss Chase remarked.

"Which is why you are the writer, Miss Chase." Dr. Higgins's smile, her real smile, the one that lifted her cheeks and made her eyes squint just a little, made a spot in the middle of Danny's chest hurt.

"Please call me Anna. And you too, Mr. Arneaux. Any man who defends my work has to call me by my first name."

"You've got a deal, Anna, if you call me Danny. Is that proper enough for you, Doc?" Danny could kick himself. Her smile faded, but at least this time it didn't go away completely.

"Anything to stop you from calling me *Doc*," she muttered.

"Well, my room is down the next corridor," Anna said with a little wave. "I'll see you two at breakfast?"

"Will there be cranachan?" Danny asked as he opened his door.

"Good Lord," Anna and Samantha said together.

They said their *good nights,* and Anna started down the hall.

"Hey, Anna."

She turned and gave Danny a head tilt and another wave.

"I meant what I said about your book. Rothgate is…well, I consider it a privilege to play the part ."

"Thank you."

Her voice barely carried, but he heard her. She shrugged and disappeared around the corner. When Danny turned back, Samantha stared at him like he had two heads.

"What?" He patted himself down in search of food stains or missing buttons. Understanding crept up on him like sunrise in the thickest parts of the swamps. "I didn't mean to embarrass you at dinner, you know. When I'm tired, my filter kind of goes to Jamaica. Once I get a good night's sleep, I'll be—"

"This would all be so much easier if you weren't you." Samantha spun on her heel and fumbled her way into her room across the hall.

Danny stared at the six-paneled oak door she'd slammed behind her. "I'm sorry?"

He rubbed the back of his neck and let himself into his own room. Someone had lit oil lamps and placed them on nightstands on each side of the giant four poster bed. They had also put a screen in front of the fireplace that covered half the wall on one side of the room, but it didn't block the light or heat. Lying on top of the thick quilted duvet, Marie and Laveau both gave a soft *woof* of greeting and promptly settled back down to sleep. Danny was supposed to pull the bellpull thingy to get Dougal to come and help him undress.

To hell with that.

He was perfectly capable of wrestling his way out of these crazy clothes. He was already going phoneless and dealing with no electric lights or heat in Braveheart's damned deep freeze. Not to mention they'd locked the adjoining bathroom, which meant no showers, and if he needed to pee, he had to do so in some kind of pot. A bourdaloue, Dougal called it. Danny didn't want to think what happened when he needed to…. He shuddered. Nope, not thinking about it.

It took a couple of tries, but Danny managed to strip down to just the long-tailed shirt. He spotted something white lying across the long wooden chest at the foot of the bed. Once he picked it up, he started to laugh.

"*Now* I get to wear a frickin' dress? Oh, *hell* no."

He flung the nightshirt over the dogs and went to dig through the chest of drawers on legs where Dougal had put away most of Danny's clothes. Danny was already plotting his revenge against Michael. The bastard knew this whole three months was going to be one long Halloween. That new winter wardrobe he'd provided Danny was a winter wardrobe of Regency clothes from the flimsy-assed *stockings* to the actually pretty stylish and warm *many-caped greatcoat* —which was a long name for a heavy wool coat that covered Danny from neck to ankles. Maybe he'd sleep in that.

"Aha!" He pulled a pair of flannel sleep pants from the bottom drawer.

The number of limbs Michael was going to keep intact went up as Danny dug deeper, finding several pairs of sleep pants, some t-shirts, some heavy sweats, and even some flannel boxers. Yes, Michael would live to aggravate Danny another day. And Dougal needed a bonus for not confiscating them when he took Danny's laptop, kindle, iPad and chargers. Not to mention his electric razor. Apparently, Eleanor Witherspoon took no prisoners when it came to this Regency experience thing.

The look on Lily's face when Witherspoon demanded her phone. That. Was. Priceless. Of course, knowing Lily, she had at least one back up phone hidden in her bra or God knows where.

He stepped into the sleep pants and nearly moaned at the warmth they brought to his chilled skin. As he turned out the oil lamps, the wind rattled the windowpanes behind the heavy velvet drapes. The fire in the fireplace burned pretty well, but it'd be out by morning. Danny pulled off his shirt and climbed into bed, wiggling his way into the spot between his two dogs. He picked up the nightgown, ready to toss it onto the chair where he'd thrown his shirt and the rest of his clothes. The sissified thing was too big for a woman, and the material was pretty heavy—wool or some kind of flannel.

The neck was open, and the sleeves were long with a ruffle at the end of each.

"Screw it," he muttered.

He drew the garment over his head and shimmied his way into it. The damned thing was warm, and between it, the flannel sleep pants, the blankets and duvet, and a hundred plus pounds of dog pressed against him on each side, he might make it through his first night in Scotland without freezing to death.

He recalled Samantha's words, *"This would all be so much easier if you weren't you."*

"You don't know the half of it, sister," he muttered as he maneuvered the half-dozen or so pillows into a workable configuration.

He liked Samantha Higgins, dammit. She was smart and determined with a sense of humor that kind of snuck up on him. And she saw people. She watched him, talked to him, listened to him. Him. Not his ass or his body or even his face. *Him.* Which, considering what Jackie had told him he had to do, was not necessarily a good thing. But he wasn't completely against seducing Samantha. His motive for doing so was another thing, a confusing and a little bit shameful thing.

"The Regency coach has the final word. If you want to play this role, you need to do whatever you have to do to convince her to give Wentworth the okay." Jackie had said. *"If that means you sleep with her, you damned well better sleep with her. Early and often. Got it?"*

His agent was *not* the sentimental type. He paid her for her career advice, and not taking her advice had nearly tanked his career. God knows he'd done worse to get where he was. Hadn't he?

He scrubbed a hand over his face. Sleep. He needed sleep. Dougal had informed Danny he had a horseback riding lesson at seven tomorrow morning. With luck he'd break his damned neck and wouldn't have to worry about Lily Randolph killing him. Or about how he really had the hots for his British Regency coach but didn't want to seduce her just to get a part in a movie.

"What the hell am I doing?"

Laveau rolled onto his back with a groan. A size twelve paw caught Danny in the chin. That pretty much summed up the last twenty-four hours. Danny turned and settled onto his side with one arm thrown over Marie.

"No snoring and no farting. I don't want to have to explain drool stains and nasty funk to Dougal."

Thank God he'd had some experience with horses. If he managed to get through tomorrow's riding lesson without embarrassing Dr. Higgins, she might recommend he play the part without him having to seduce her. Sleep settled over his body in waves just as some sort of weird breeze carried an earthy smell and ruffled his hair. A woman's soft laughter whispered somewhere across the room. What the hell was so funny?

❦

Turned out, seven o'clock in the morning in Scotland came a helluva lot earlier than it did in LA or even in Louisiana. By the time Dougal rousted Danny out of bed and arranged the hunt coat, shirt, and skintight leather britches for his riding lesson, there was no time for breakfast.

"Breeches," the valet said as he handed Danny the thin stocking things and black riding boots.

"Huh?" Danny struggled to shove his feet into the boots and drag the soft black uppers to his knees. No wonder these Regency guys had someone to help them get dressed. It was a wrestling match just to get into his clothes.

"They're not *britches*, they're breeches." Dougal handed Danny a pair of black leather gloves, which he shoved into his coat pockets.

"They're cutting off the circulation to my balls is what they are." Danny adjusted himself and headed for the door. "I thought these guys were supposed to be all about good manners and gentlemanly behavior."

Dougal followed him down the corridor and brushed at the back of the dark green wool hunt coat. "Yes, sir. Why do you ask?"

"I don't see how it is good manners to walk around in no underwear wearing something so tight a woman can tell what religion you are." Danny continued down the stairs and across the marble foyer to the thick double doors that looked like something out of a Dracula movie. Behind him, the valet's choked coughs sounded suspiciously like laughter. "Okay, Dougal, where does the duke keep his horses?"

Danny dragged one of the doors open and went down the steps that led to the fountain where his dogs had dunked the duke. Dougal was hot on his heels.

"The stables are that way, sir." He pointed to the left where the cobblestone driveway curved toward the back of the house. "Urquhart is expecting you."

"Who—what?" Danny stopped and turned back to the valet.

"Urquhart," Dougal said, pronouncing each syllable with care. "He's His Grace's horse master, and Miss Witherspoon has recruited him to teach you all to ride properly."

"Miss Witherspoon, huh?"

"Yes, sir."

"The same Miss Witherspoon who took my phone and has us all living with no electricity, no showers, and wearing getups that are instruments of torture? That Miss Witherspoon?"

"Yes, sir." Dougal stared, his expression as bland as unseasoned rice.

"Great," Danny muttered as he turned and strode toward the stables. "This guy's probably the Marquis de Sade of riding instructors. The horses probably have the whips and spurs."

The morning air, though as cold as an ice bath, smelled clean and green, something Danny didn't get to experience much since he spent so much time in Los Angeles. He paused to stand and follow the manicured lawn and neatly trimmed hedges that seemed to go on forever until they disappeared into a silvery mist rising out of the greenery as if by magic. There were hills in the distance. How high did they have to be to be called mountains? It didn't matter. They were beautiful, painted in shades of gray, green, and brown as if some master had climbed a ladder and drawn them across the sky.

"Ready for your lesson, Mr. Arneaux?" A short, sixtyish man dressed for riding walked toward him from the direction of the stables, his hand outstretched. Danny was impressed at the strength and efficiency of the man's handshake. The old guy was wiry, built like most of the senior stuntmen Danny worked with on film sets all over the world. His comfort level with the situation kicked up a notch or two. In his world, strength and experience meant competence. Competent people usually didn't get you killed. Usually.

"Ready as I'll ever be, Mr. Urquhart, is it?"

He followed the man through a gate and into a sort of courtyard surrounded on three sides by rows of stalls, each one with a half door open out to the middle. Several men of various ages and builds were busy with buckets, rakes, shovels, and wheelbarrows. There had to be at least three or four dozen horses to take care of and their coats, manes and tails looked better than the hair of a lot of Hollywood stars Danny knew.

"Just Urquhart. Mr. Urquhart was me father. Here you go, Mr. Arneaux. Let's get you up on Grenadier. I understand you've had some experience riding horses?"

It took Danny a minute to decipher the man's question. His Scottish accent was thicker than Dougal's. Then again, the roar in Danny's ears didn't help. Standing several feet away, its breath visible in the chill, was the tallest, blackest horse he'd ever seen. Its feet were the size of pie plates and the fur, hair, whatever they called it was feathered over its hooves. He swallowed and wiped his hands on his coat.

"You want me to ride that?"

"You're not afraid of wee Grenadier, are you?" The old man flashed him a crooked grin.

The men who'd been busy around the stables suddenly didn't have a thing in the world to do. This had to be a joke. Where was Ashton Kutcher?

Since there were a good dozen or so Scottish dudes standing around waiting for the American to chicken out, Danny did what every dumbass American would do in this sort of situation. He walked over and took the reins from the red-headed teenager standing at *wee* Grenadier's head. Trouble was, Danny had no idea how the hell to get up on the damned Arnold Schwarzenegger of horses.

"Hey, Urquhart?"

"Yes, Mr. Arneaux?"

"Where the hell is the saddle?"

"It's right there, Mr. Arneaux. On his back."

"That's not a saddle. That's a damned leather doily. Where's the horn?"

There was a round of badly covered laughter from the men now crowded around Danny and the monster horse.

The horse that was giving him a good dose of side-eye to add insult to injury.

"Och! You'll find no saddles with horns here. You'll be learning to ride Sassenach." Urquhart spat onto the cobblestones.

"Sassenach?"

He needed to be taking notes. English accents. Scottish accents. Weird ass words. And a saddle that looked like a WWE championship belt.

"English style. But Sassenach is what we call anyone not lucky enough to be born a Scot. Means foreigner, and not in a good way, mind you." Urquhart grinned then pointed to a huge worn square stone next to the corner of one of the rows of stalls. "We have a mounting block if you need it."

"It's for the ladies," one twenty-something man in a tweed jacket, tweed cap, and blue plaid kilt said.

For the ladies?

Hell no," he muttered, and could have sworn stifled laughter emanated from somewhere behind him.

Danny looped the reins around his left hand and after two tries, got his left foot into the flimsy metal stirrup—which tightened the grip of the leather pants on his nuts pretty damned efficiently. He winced and hopped a few times on his right leg. When he finally launched himself at the saddle, Urquhart cupped Danny's knee and basically tossed him up on the horse's back. Danny slid his right foot into the right stirrup and shifted around to keep his ass on the pancake of a saddle, which would have been a hell of a lot easier if the horse wasn't dancing in place like a chorus girl.

"How does that feel, Mr. Arneaux?" Urquhart checked the saddle and adjusted first one stirrup before he ducked under the horse's neck to walk around and check the other.

"Like you and your buddies are having way more fun

with this than I am." He took the reins with both hands and tried to remember how to hold them correctly.

At least they were all honest enough to laugh.

"Are you nervous now, Mr. Arneaux?" Urquhart smiled, but his tone was dead serious.

Danny cut his eyes down toward the cobblestones. Damn, that was a long way to fall. "As a virgin at a prison rodeo."

Complete silence. He glanced at Urquhart. It took a minute, then the old man shouted with laughter. He said something undecipherable to the others, and suddenly the whole stable yard cracked up. The horse wasn't amused. He sidled into the middle of the stable yard. Danny tightened up on the reins. The horse tossed his head then craned his neck to give Danny a full on *I-will-eat-you-alive* glare.

While he struggled to gain a little control of the horse, someone led out a broad-backed, shaggy horse not nearly as tall as Grenadier and a whole lot friendlier looking. With a leg up from one of the stable workers, Urquhart was in the saddle and ready to go.

"Shall we, Mr. Arneaux?" He nodded toward the far end of the courtyard where another gate opened into what looked like miles of green fields divided by hedges, rock walls, and a narrow dirt lane that carved through the middle. Urquhart steered his horse through the gate.

"Do I have a choice?"

Danny focused every fiber of his being on not falling off the horse. The group of guys working in the stables had to be standing there watching, taking bets on when the American action hero got thrown like a frisbee. He got to the gate and looked over his shoulder.

"Put me down for twenty," he shouted back at them.

"Staying on or falling off, gov?" the young redhead called to him.

"Falling off. I'm no sucker."

He kicked the horse into a trot to the sound of applause and laughter behind him. Every bone in his body rattled as he caught up to his riding instructor. They rode along in silence for a while. Not that Danny minded. The countryside was something no computer could ever put on the screen. The mists were clearing, but entire sections of fields still had a sort of fuzzy blanket of gray and white covering them. The air was so clean it hurt to breathe.

That wasn't the only thing hurting. The so-called saddle wasn't much protection for the family jewels, especially once Grenadier picked up speed, which he did once he followed Urquhart's horse from the lane into one of the fields.

"You're doing better than I thought you would," the horse master said. "You've surprised me, Mr. Arneaux."

"That makes two of us. It's been a long time since I rode a horse."

"I saw the western you were in. It was good. I like westerns."

"It was one of my first films. I was a lot younger then." In more ways than Urquhart could imagine.

"Och. And you're so old now?" The old man sat on his horse like it was a recliner in somebody's living room. No fear. No tension. How many years did a man have to ride to feel like that?

"Some days, yes. Some days I feel very old."

"Aye." He pulled his horse to a halt at the top of a hill. "But not today?"

Danny managed to get Grenadier to stop. Or maybe Grenadier decided he wanted to stop. A sure thing that Urquhart's horse was a girl. Danny never underestimated the power of a female no matter the species. He suddenly noticed the view from the top of the hill. Off in the distance stood a castle, or at least part of one. The wind picked up, and the sky blended from slate gray to bright blue. The quiet beneath the wind struck him—deep and profound and full of meaning.

"No. Not today." He glanced at his companion. "The man I am playing in my next film, he's an English cavalry officer from Scotland."

"Aye. That's why the American woman hired me to teach you how to ride. I come from a long line of cavalrymen. Me grandda rode with the Scots Greys in the Great War."

"Did he talk about it?" Danny asked as they walked their horses down the hill and back toward the lane.

"Never."

"Neither did my cousin. He was the only brother I ever had growing up. He was a Marine. Afghanistan. Iraq. He came home and didn't talk about it. Not even the night he blew his brains out." Where the hell had that come from?

"You can come back from war, but you can't always come home. The duke's brother, Lord Lachlan, served in Afghanistan. He's been back here a while. I'm nae sure if he's really home yet."

They rode slowly. Urquhart offered brief suggestions. Sit back. Keep your heels down. Don't grip with your knees. Balance. Move with the horse. All in that Scottish brogue that was as much a part of the country as the rocks and hills and eerie mists. All the time, Danny grew more comfortable on the horse, and whether for better or worse, he began to think he might actually be able to play this part.

"This character you're playing, he comes back from war?" Urquhart asked as they turned onto the lane back to the stables.

"He survives Waterloo. Comes back to Scotland to… figure out who he is." Danny gripped the reins tight, almost before he realized it.

"The Highlands will do that for ye. If ye let them."

Danny decided two things. Urquhart wasn't talking about

a movie character, and the old man was a whole lot smarter than the average riding instructor.

"Same time tomorrow then?" Danny asked as they came within sight of the stables.

"Aye. We'll go for a good run tomorrow."

"Let's not get ahead of ourselves."

Urquhart snorted.

Something red with a fluffy tail ran across the road at Grenadier's feet.

A bunch of birds burst out of the hedge at the side of the road.

Grenadier half reared.

"Oh, shit!"

Danny saw it coming—and couldn't do a damned thing about it. His ass was sliding one way, his knees the other. He pulled on the reins and leaned back. He grabbed one handful of mane and then another. Grenadier picked up speed. It would have been fun if Danny wasn't scared shitless, if the gate into the stable yard wasn't closed, and if he couldn't feel the horse gather the muscles of his hind legs to—

The next thing Danny knew, he lay on his back surrounded by a circle of about seven or eight wind-chapped men, one slobbering horse, and one very concerned blue-eyed beauty. Great. Samantha had witnessed his abandon-ship dismount. He groaned.

"You're meant to take the jump *with* the horse, gov," one of the stable hands said.

"Tell it to Grenadier," Danny muttered through clenched teeth.

He couldn't decide which hurt worse. His entire body or his pride. Why was his Regency coach here now? The wind cut through him, carrying that earthy scent with a touch of lavender and…. What the hell? Was someone laughing at him?

"Can you get up or do we need to call an ambulance?" Samantha didn't sound like she wanted to laugh. A good sign.

Her forehead was wrinkled, and she was biting her bottom lip. Another good sign. Right? She held one of his hands between hers. Even better, especially as that was now the only place on his body that wasn't throbbing like a subwoofer. Another groan escaped as he closed his eyes.

"Is there a third option?" he finally asked.

"Well, you can't lie here all day," Urquhart said. "Come on, lads. Let's get him on his feet." Several of the men made to help him up, but they backed away when Samantha put up a commanding hand.

"Are you certain he should be moved?" she asked. "He took a terrible fall."

"Should have seen it from my side. I've got another lesson tomorrow. Can't I just lie here until then?"

The horse touched his muzzle to Danny's cheek, and dripped slobber down his neck. Danny opened one eye.

"Too late to apologize now, you big sissy. Running away from a bunch of birds."

Grenadier stamped a foot and snorted, spraying horse snot all over Danny's face.

Danny grimaced. "Get me up before he drowns me. That stuff is cold. And nasty."

He didn't let go of Samantha's hand, but he did let a couple of the stable hands hook him under the arms and slowly lift him to his feet. A spot on the back of his head pulsed with every heartbeat. His bones ached like he'd gone a few rounds with Alabama's defensive line. He shook his head and his surroundings swam. So not a good idea.

Urquhart snapped his fingers in front of Danny's face, and said in his thick Scottish brogue, "How many fingers?"

"What?" His Scottish translator wasn't working.

"How many fingers is he holding up?" Samantha asked.

Her soft but stern voice reached through the haze over his brain.

"Three, but I wish they'd quit spinning." Danny swayed slightly, and she immediately put her arm around his waist. The side of her breast pressed against his ribs. "You almost make it worth the fall, Doc," he said in a half whisper.

"What?" she frowned, and he tried to smile, but only God knew if his mouth actually moved. Her gaze narrowed. "Good Lord."

"Sounds like he's all right," one man snickered.

Urquhart ran his hands over him. Danny tried to limit his response to grunts and flinches. Until the man touched the sore spot on the back of Danny's head.

"Ow, dammit, that hurts. My hide's not as thick as Grenadier's, you know."

"That remains to be seen. You'll live," Urquhart declared. "Nothing's broken and that goose egg'll be gone by morning. Go have a lie down and a tot or two of His Grace's best whisky, and you'll be right as rain."

"After a few tots of Himself's whisky, he won't care if anything's broken or not," one of the men who'd helped Danny up said.

The others snickered.

Danny suspected they believed the Yank couldn't hold his liquor. He'd like to treat them to a couple of bottles of Voodoo beer and see them take Grenadier for a little spin after that. Preferably over a gate or two.

"Mr. Urquhart, might you have one of the men take us back to the house in the cart?" Samantha tightened her grip around Danny's middle. It hurt, but he couldn't care less. She was warm and stronger than he thought she'd be.

Cart? What cart?

Someone led Grenadier toward a stall across the way. The horse looked back at him with what had to be a horsey grin.

Asshole! A rumble came toward them from the far side of the stable yard. He must have hit his head harder than he thought. A small, rickety wooden wagon thing pulled by a horse built like a sumo wrestler stopped next to him and Samantha.

"I'm good," he said. "I'd rather walk."

"After the fall you took?" She maneuvered him around to sit in the back of the wagon. "I don't think so. Just consider this part of your Regency experience." She hopped up next to him so they sat side by side, their feet and legs dangling off the back of the old contraption.

"I think I should win that bet," Danny said in as loud a voice as he could muster. "It's not my fault that horse couldn't keep me in the saddle."

Uproarious laughter followed.

"Walk on, sir," Samantha said to the older man sitting on the seat at the front of the wagon. The horse started forward.

The wagon jostled and his head throbbed. "I've had about all the Regency experience I want for one day," he said to Samantha. Not exactly a lie because in the same moment, a very enticing part of his Regency experience sat with her thigh pressed against his and her hand on his shoulder.

"But your Regency experience has just begun," she replied. "You have at least three more months to go."

"You're a mean woman, Samantha Higgins. It isn't enough I lost my dignity and most of my pride back there? I'm sure they'll be laughing all day about the American actor getting dumped on his…."

"Arse?" she whispered with the smallest hint of a grin.

"That'd be the one."

"I don't know about that. The laughing, I mean. Mr. Urquhart said most Sassenachs would have cried like a little girl after the spill you took. I think you made quite an impression."

"Better than the impression I made in those cobblestones when I went over that gate *before* the horse did?"

The front doors of the house stood open as the cart pulled up in front of the steps. His aches and pains set up a chorus of *what-the-hell-were-you-thinking* so loud Danny didn't know if he was going to make it up the stairs to his room. He slid out of the cart and let Samantha draw his arm across her shoulders.

"Works better if you let the horse go first." From the seat of the wagon, the gray-haired man in the bulky sweater and faded kilt touched two fingers to his cap and drove around the fountain, headed back toward the stables.

"Thanks for the tip," Danny called back.

"Mr. Abercrombie, could you send for a doctor?" Samantha asked as the butler came out to help Danny up the steps.

"Belay that, Mr. Abercrombie. I don't need a doctor. I need a warm bed, a hot toddy and a vat of Bengay."

"Bengay? I am not familiar with that particular brand of liquor, Mr. Arneaux."

Danny started to laugh but cut it off with a wince. The three of them—he, Samantha, and the butler—eased their way up the wide staircase. They paused on the first-floor landing, and Danny debated asking them to bring a cot down and let him sleep there.

"Urquhart sent one of the lads from the stable up as soon as you fell…sorry, had your accident. Dougal is seeing to the drawing of a hot bath, and Mrs. Gordon is going to send up a tray for luncheon."

"Thank God for fast lads and efficient butlers. You can say fell, Abercrombie. Because I sure as hell did." Danny winced and tried to lift his foot to the first step of the staircase.

"Yes, sir. Oh, and Mrs. Wallace will be up to see to your injuries."

The idea of a hot bath, even if it was in a metal tub that looked a copper horse trough, finally set Danny's feet in motion.

"Who is Mrs. Wallace, the local veterinarian?" Danny asked as he climbed the stairs to the second floor.

"Not quite, sir." Abercrombie sniffed, stepped out from under Danny's arm, and opened the door to Danny's room.

"She's the housekeeper," Samantha whispered. "Abercrombie just thinks he runs the house. Mrs. Wallace is the one really in charge."

"Great." Danny released a long sigh as Samantha helped him into one of the overstuffed high-back chairs to one side of the fireplace. "Is she going to treat me with Regency medicine?"

Dougal had done his job well and had filled the big copper bathtub nearly to the rim with steaming hot water. Between that and the fire roaring in the fireplace, Danny sensed the chill and some of the aches and pains leaving his body.

"If you dirty that chair, she'll likely treat you with a horse-whip," Samantha replied.

"Oh, hell." Danny wanted to get up but didn't have the strength. "Where are my dogs?"

"One of the lads took them for a run," Abercrombie said, his face a clear indication of his opinion of Marie, Laveau, and probably Danny too. "I'll see to your tray then see to the location of your…dogs."

Danny waved as the butler left the room. "He doesn't like me."

"Does that hurt your feelings?"

He lurched out of the chair, muttered a few choice words,

and slowly wiggled his way out of the stained hunt coat. "Nope. I don't think Abercrombie likes anybody."

He dropped the coat on the floor and tackled the neckcloth thing next. Had to be a damned serial killer or a sailor to tie something like this. The shirt only had three buttons at the neck. Pulling it over his head was like landing on those cobblestones again. His back screamed for mercy until he finally got the damned thing off and flung it back into the chair. He glanced at Samantha.

"What?"

Chapter Six

LOOK AT THE BRUISES. SHE REALLY NEEDED TO LOOK AT THE scrapes and bruises. Doing so would stop her gobsmacked response to the sight of Dante Arneaux half naked. She hated to think what her response would be to Dante *completely* naked. He had a lean physique, but that didn't hide the fact every inch of him was ripped. From powerful shoulders to sculpted pecs to a ripple of abs that disappeared into his leather riding breeches, he had a body that begged to be touched. Or maybe she was the one begging. Her mouth had gone completely dry. The rest of her, however, was hot and damp and shivering with sensation.

"Is it that bad?"

"Wha…."

"The bruises. Are they bad?" He turned slowly.

Bloody hell. His back was even more beautiful. Perfect symmetry. Perfect strength and power. A perfect jungle gym for a woman's fingertips. She pushed her toes so hard into the rug over the stone floor she nearly fell over. A hard, sharp breath through her nose helped a bit.

There *was* a large black and blue spot wrapped around

from his back to the side of his ribcage. She took a step closer. A different bruise marred one shoulder blade. Another step. There were nasty looking cuts and scrapes on his elbows and the backs of his forearms. His knuckles were bloodied too. Yes, knuckles. Check those. Much safer than touching…anything else. She caught his hand at the same time he reached for the waist of his breeches, bringing her hand with him.

Whoops!

"Um, your hands look bad. Didn't you have riding gloves?" Neither of them moved.

"Yeah. Dougal gave me some. I just didn't wear them. Next time." His attention seemed to be drawn to where the backs of her fingers pressed into his stomach. His hot and rock-hard stomach.

"Good idea." She took in the fire, the hot bath, the huge bed. Anything but his face. "Definitely wear them next time. You'll probably feel better once you get in the tub."

"Uh-huh. I'm looking forward to it." He brushed a thumb across the back of her hand. "But I probably need to take these leather pants off first."

"Right." Still, they didn't move.

The fire hissed and cracked. Her breath was quiet, but audible. His was harsh and heavy. He was in pain. Right. Bathtub. Now. She withdrew her hand and took a step back.

"I'll turn around, unless you need help." Could she be any more obvious? She was a professional, dammit. She turned toward the bed so quickly she almost fell over.

"Aww come on, Doc. How about that offer of help?"

"Dougal will be back any moment." She heard grunts, groans, a few swear words, then splashing.

"Spoilsport." A long, satisfied moan and more quiet splashing gave way to silence. "You can turn around now,

Samantha. Just don't look down. God, this water is perfect. Is this really how they bathed back then?"

Questions. Good. She could do questions. She picked up the folded towels on the blanket chest and placed them on the chair next to the fireplace. "Pretty much. Although many of them bathed in a shift or in the case of men, in their shirts."

"Were they really that modest?"

She glanced toward the tub. He was submerged up to his neck with his arms draped along the rim of the tub and his head resting against the raised back. His knees rose out of the water out of necessity, to accommodate his height. His eyes were closed.

"It was partly modesty and partly a way to stay warm."

"They should have had Dougal and his boys to fill their tub."

"Putting the tub in front of the fireplace is no accident either. It helps to keep the water warm. Though hot water was a luxury, it takes a lot to heat it using the wood burning stoves, and it was more important to use the stoves for cooking." She picked up a thick velvet dressing gown and draped it over her arms as she sat on the side of his bed. "You frightened me. When you fell off the horse, I was afraid you'd broken your neck or worse." She shouldn't have said it, even though it was the absolute truth.

He didn't open his eyes. "I saw you."

"What?"

"Before I fell, I saw you. I wondered what you were doing there. You looked like something out of one of those Highlander movies. That dress and the thing around your shoulders."

"The shawl?" Samantha stood and turned to the cheval mirror next to the wardrobe. The dressing gown fell from her hands. She wore a simple wool Regency walking dress, a sort of slate blue, with a heavy silver and gray paisley shawl wrapped around her against the cold. Perfectly ordinary, even if it was a costume.

"With your hair down like that you were like a romance novel cover walking toward me. Until I lost my grip on the horse. Why were you there?"

"He must have kicked you in the head on the way down." She cleared her throat to try and rid it of the inconvenient catch in her voice. Samantha turned back toward the tub. He was sitting up, his shoulders and upper body glistening with rivulets of water still running down the dips and clefts of taut muscles and tendons. His eyes the green of English moss fixed on her in a way that raised goose bumps along the back of her neck and sent them thrumming down her body.

"You're a beautiful woman, Samantha Higgins, and smart as hell. That combination makes a man feel like he's been kicked in the head. You didn't answer my question."

"What question?"

"Why were you at the stables?" He shifted his legs in the tub.

Soft, harsh breathing punctuated the minutes ticking by on the mantel clock. Samantha's hands, which she'd tangled in her shawl and clasped beneath her breasts, rose and fell. Dante's expression, unsmiling and fierce, refused to allow her to look away. She took a step closer. Then another.

The door burst open so sharply they both jumped as if shot. Water sloshed over the sides of the tub. A tall, spare white-headed dynamo stormed into the room, a wooden box in one hand and a bundle of cloth strips in the other. She wore the uniform of a Regency era housekeeper, although the clothing looked so natural on her, Samantha wouldn't be surprised to find the woman dressed like that all the time. A long-skirted black dress buttoned up to the ruffled collar at her neck, a simple cameo pinned at her throat, a small pocket watch pinned to her breast pocket, long sleeves, and sensible laced-up black shoes made up her ensemble. She looked to be in her early sixties, though she had the purposeful vitality of a much younger woman.

Samantha exchanged a bemused glance with Dante.

"With muscles like those, I'd have expected you to do better by our Grenadier," the woman said as she stared into the tub and gave him a thorough inspection. She marched to the bedside table then began to take various items out of her wooden box.

Dante waved at Samantha, his hand flapping so swiftly the breeze stirred the fringe on her shawl. He nodded at the stack of towels on the chair just out of reach. She grabbed one and tossed it to him. He draped it across the tub, hiding his important bits from their uniformed visitor. He gestured again, pointing at the woman in the black dress, then raised his hands.

"I am Mrs. Wallace, the housekeeper. Let's get you out of that tub and see what the damages are."

The look of terror on Dante's face!

Samantha covered her mouth with her hands as Mrs. Wallace strode to the tub and grabbed his elbow. For an older woman she seemed to have a good deal of strength—and she had the element of surprise on her side. She hauled Dante halfway to his feet. He scrambled to cover himself with the towel. All the while he winced and half-gasped in pain. In answer to his pleading eyes, Samantha snatched up the dressing gown and scooted around Mrs. Wallace to hold it in front of him.

"Could I get a minute to dry off, Mrs. Wallace?" He struggled to use the towel and get an arm in the dressing gown at the same time. With one leg in and one out of the tub, he nearly toppled over. "I don't think the duke would take too kindly to me mooning his housekeeper *and* my Regency coach all in one day."

"Och, as if you've got something I haven't seen before." She released his arm and went back to her box of medicines. "Get over here and sit down." She patted the bed.

Samantha clasped her hands behind her back and raised her eyebrows. Dante dried himself off, stepped out of the tub, and tripped over the half-off, half-on dressing gown.

"Merde," he muttered, sprawled face down on the rug. "Merde, merde merde."

Samantha dropped to her knees beside him and tried not to look at the long, expanse of beautifully muscled and even more beautifully naked flesh.

Mrs. Wallace stood over him, arms crossed. "I take it back."

She bent down and gripped his elbow once more. Samantha threw the dressing gown across his back, drew his arm across her shoulders and put her arm around his waist. With a tacit nod to the housekeeper, they helped the injured actor to his feet.

"Ow. Ow, ow, ow, ow." He limped to the bed and, once they let go, managed to belt the dressing gown and cover himself.

Mrs. Wallace took his chin in her hand and turned his head from one side to the other. "Lucky your face missed getting bruised. From what I hear, you've made a nice living with that face. The magazines say you're thirty, but you don't look a day over twenty-five." She ran her hand over his hair but stopped when he pulled away. "Urquhart said you took a knock on the head." She poured some noxious smelling stuff onto one of the cloths she'd brought in then pressed it to the back of his head. He hissed in pain. The housekeeper took Samantha's hand and pressed it to the cloth. "Hold that."

With him seated on the bed, his face was at the perfect

level to turn up and look into Samantha's—which he did as Mrs. Wallace dragged the dressing gown down to his waist and started poking and prodding each bruise and scrape on his torso. Strangely enough, despite the pain he had to be feeling from the housekeeper's brisk inspection, Dante didn't utter another sound. He stared at Samantha, some earnest and intense thread drawn between them.

"Hand me that blue jar," Mrs. Wallace ordered.

Samantha used her free hand to pick up the unlabeled item and hand it to the housekeeper. Mrs. Wallace opened it then spread a heavy coating of the contents on the extensive bruise over Dante's ribcage and back. Samantha could feel the heat from the concoction from where she stood. His eyes watered, but he refused to complain. Not even when Mrs. Wallace picked up a length of cloth, wrapped it around his middle up to his armpits, and fastened it with some safety pins.

"Any dizziness?" Mrs. Wallace asked as she packed her medicines and cloths back into the box. "Nausea?"

"Not until you basted me and wrapped me up like a turkey, no."

Mrs. Wallace let loose a wicked laugh. "Any injuries to your legs?" She reached for the knotted belt of his dressing gown. "Or anywhere else?"

"No!" He shrugged his arms and shoulders back into the garment and folded the two sides over his lower body.

Samantha removed the cloth and her hand from the back of his head. She faced the bedside table to place the cloth into a china bowl to hide the laughter choking her nearly to death. It was bad of her really. The big, bad action star terrified of a Scotswoman old enough to be his mother.

"Very well," Mrs. Wallace said as she picked up the box and the remaining clean cloths. "Get him into bed, lass. That will do him more good than anything. Send for me if need be." She marched toward the door.

"Wait, Mrs. Wallace," Dante said. "Tell me something."

She stopped and looked back at him one eyebrow half-cocked.

"You said you take it back. What did you mean?"

"Ah. You do have something I've never seen." The old woman flashed him an evil grin and left the room.

Samantha lost it. She snorted, fell back against the bedside table, and fairly roared with laughter. Tears squeezed from the corners of her eyes. She couldn't stop, not even when Dante levered himself awkwardly into bed. He propped up the pillows, punched them into position, and eased back against them.

"So glad I can provide you with such hilarious entertainment," he said once she finally settled into sporadic snorts and chuckles. "Then again, I'm sure you enjoyed my spectacular parting with Grenadier. So, why were you at the stables?"

She tried her best to adopt a serious expression. "I was worried about you. I wanted to suggest to Mr. Urquhart that he introduce you to English riding slowly, so you didn't...."

"Fall on my ass? Good thing you didn't get there earlier. You'd have deprived yourself of even more entertainment."

"I think you provided Mrs. Wallace with far more entertainment than you have me."

"That can be taken care of if you like." He picked up the bedcovers and stuck one leg out.

"No, no." Samantha waved her hands, then tucked his leg back into the bed. She pulled the duvet, blanket, and sheet up under his arms. "I've already seen that entertainment, thank you."

"You looked? Why, Dr. Higgins, you wicked woman."

"It was difficult not to with you sprawled all over the floor with your…fundament stuck in the air."

"My what?"

"Fundament. It's a Regency word. It means bum."

"Arse."

"That's the one."

"Good word."

"Indeed."

He settled back onto the pillows but maintained that warm green eye contact that made her think all sorts of things that had nothing to do with teaching him to play the film role he'd won. She stood and folded and unfolded her hands at her waist. Better than doing with them what she wanted. She'd never thought she'd be jealous of an elderly Scotswoman with the subtlety of a beer lorry. Samantha needed to leave this room immediately.

"Dougal should be along with your food in a bit. Try to get some rest."

She had said the words, and she'd even visualized her walking purposefully to the door. Her feet, however, had other ideas. They refused to bloody move. This was not the way she intended to start her career as a period film consultant. One foot in front of the other, silly twit. Walk. She gave him a curt nod and backed toward the door, hoping he didn't hear the drag of her shoes across the rug.

"What about the rest of today's lessons?" His attempt at an innocent blink failed miserably.

"I beg your pardon?"

He indicated a stack of books on the secretary in front of one of the windows. "The schedule and handbook you gave me are over there. I need to check my schedule."

She went to the desk. "I think it best we reschedule the rest of today. You're in no condition for lessons."

"Come on, Doc. It'll take more than a little fall from a

horse to keep me down." He pushed himself up against the pillows and grimaced. "Well, a fall from a horse and an assault by a Viking in a black dress."

Samantha handed him the thick binder Miss Witherspoon had asked Cedric to prepare for all the participants before Samantha had taken over. Actually, as she'd done most of the actual work on the handbook, it was just as well she was the one in charge. She kept the leather journal where Dante had copied his schedule.

"Mrs. Wallace struck me as quite efficient," she said as she perused his schedule. "And Vikings usually kill you."

"Give her time. She was efficient all right. She efficiently poked every bruise on my body, burned my hide off with her potions, and saw more of me than my Maw Maw has seen in twenty years."

"Your grandmother hasn't seen your movies?"

"I told her we use a body double for those scenes." A creeping rosy flush splashed across his bare shoulders, up his neck, and across his cheeks.

"And do you? Use a body double?"

He gave her a *what-do-you-think* look.

"Shame on you. Lying to your poor, old granny."

"You wouldn't say that if you'd had her chase you around the dining room with a hickory switch." He shuddered. "I'd rather fall off Grenadier another five or six times."

"Well, that won't be happening today," she replied as she dropped the open journal across his lap. "Neither will your dance lesson."

"Thank God."

"Or your fencing lesson."

"Damn. I was looking forward to stabbing that Rousseau dude. He's an arrogant horse's…fundament."

"Teddy is one of the finest sword masters in the world. Of course, he's a horse's arse."

"Language, Dr. Higgins." He patted the spot beside him on the bed. "You've worked with him before, on other films?"

"A few." She sat at the very edge of the mattress.

"Then he should know how to treat you with respect. I don't like him."

"No one does, but he knows what he's doing." It had to be her imagination. Dante Arneaux radiated heat. The kind of heat a woman wanted to wrap herself around on a cold, rainy day.

"So do you. He needs to respect that." His jaw tensed, and he tightened his hands ever so slightly on the covers.

Samantha didn't know what to say. She took a breath.

"Since I can't do anything strenuous because of my delicate condition"—he waggled his eyebrows—"let's do my Regency rules and behaviors lesson." He began to leaf through the pages of the binder.

"We're already breaking several of the rules. As an unmarried lady I shouldn't be in your bedroom, especially alone and with you half dressed."

"Not even to take care of an injured man?" He fake-coughed and made a sad puppy-dog face.

"Not even then. My reputation would be ruined, and you might be forced to marry me."

Stupid. Stupid. Stupid. Of all the ridiculous—

"A fate worse than death," he replied as he reached up to push her hair behind her ear. "For you."

A knock at the door saved her from saying something even more idiotic.

"Come in," she and Dante said together.

To his credit, Dougal pushed a tea cart loaded with plates of food, a pot of tea, and all the necessary accoutrements into the room without a single indication he saw anything untoward about her sitting on the actor's bed. Which was fine.

Samantha had enough misgivings about the while situation for them both.

"Heard you've had a morning of it, Mr. Arneaux," Dougal said as he maneuvered the cart close to the bed beside Dante, then placed a legged tray across his lap.

"That's one way to put it," Dante said. "The worst part was having Dr. Higgins witness my unplanned dismount."

Dougal grinned. "Me old da used to say an injured pride hurts worse than a broken leg when a pretty lass is involved."

"Wise man." Dante gave Samantha a wink as Dougal placed silverware and a silk napkin on the tray set a similar place on the teacart for Samantha.

"You two are a pair and no mistake." She put two thick slices of bread, some cheese, some ham, and a small crock of butter on a plate, then placed it on Dante's tray.

"If there is nothing else, sir, I'll take your clothes down to the laundry and see what the dogs have done with poor Robbie." Dougal moved around the room gathering discarded clothes and wet towels. "I'm sure Dr. Higgins will take good care of you," he said as he hurried toward the door.

Samantha raised a hand. "Dougal, wait." The door creaked closed behind him.

"Another wise man," Dante murmured as he put together a sandwich. "I assume butter is the Regency equivalent of mayonnaise?" His expression was half disappointment and half hope. He really was so American.

"I'm afraid so."

"Oh well. Can I have some of those pickles? Aren't you going to eat?"

She dropped a forkful of pickles onto his plate then began to organize the cups of tea—which kept her from looking at his chest as the covers had now slipped to his waist. Mrs. Wallace's wrap hid some of him, but not nearly enough to suit Samantha's piece of mind.

"Let me see to our tea, and I'll join you."

He made an odd little pleading noise.

Samantha rolled her eyes. "Oh, for pity's sake. I'll join you in eating lunch." She turned from pouring tea long enough to fix him with a stern glare.

"What? I didn't say anything."

"You really should work on your poker face, Mr. Arneaux."

"Danny. And what's wrong with my poker face?" He took the cup of tea she handed him and managed a sip. She arched a brow. "Have you any idea how many times in this film you have to drink tea?"

"About a million. Why?"

"If you want people to believe you're an English gentleman you may want to try drinking tea without making that face."

"What face?"

She screwed her mouth into a tight frown and crossed her eyes.

He cracked up, then grabbed his bruised side. "Can't be that bad," he said with a groan.

"I watched you last night when we were in the drawing room after dinner."

"Yeah, well, I enjoyed the cigars and brandy with the guys more than I did the tea, even if the company over tea was prettier and nicer." He tried the tea again but didn't do much better.

"Here, give me that." Samantha took his cup and handed him the one she'd prepared for herself, complete with milk and sugar. He tried it. No grimace this time and he nodded.

"Better. This is how my Maw Maw fixed coffee to get me to drink it." He picked up a few pickles with his fingers and popped them into his mouth.

"You don't like coffee either?"

"My mom didn't want me to have it. She thought I was hyper enough without caffeine. I was kind of a handful. Maw Maw didn't get me started on it until after Mom died." He shrugged. "Guess it never really took." He bit into his sandwich and stared at his plate while he chewed.

Samantha drank her tea then ate a bit of cheese. "How old were you when she died?"

"I was ten. Breast cancer. By the time they caught it, it was too late. She was thirty-six years old."

"I'm so sorry. That must have been difficult for you." Samantha felt terrible, but she wanted to know more. For some reason, she wanted to know everything about him.

"Wasn't so bad. I had Maw Maw. It could have been a lot worse."

"What about your father?"

Dante smiled more to himself than her, she thought, and said, "He was a Cajun oil rigger. Mom met him when she was in grad school at Tulane. She didn't intend to get pregnant. He tried to do right by her as much as he could. He didn't marry her, but he stayed around long enough for her to get her doctorate. I think I was about three. Got my body from him, but Maw Maw says I got my good looks from Grandaddy Arneaux."

"I would never argue with your grandmother."

He nodded, his expression serious, and looked her directly in the eyes. "There's a reason I insisted that fencing asshole treat you with respect, Samantha. I didn't have my mom with me very long, but I had her long enough to know they don't hand out doctorate degrees just for showing up. And they damned sure don't hand them out to women, especially Black women. She earned hers. Just as I'm betting you earned your way. Even my agent Jackie didn't—doesn't— have it easy. We men get a free pass on just about everything. Women don't."

Samatha recalled Cedric's refusal to work with Dante and wondered how many others had felt the same and Dante never knew. Then again, the grim line of his mouth made her think maybe he did.

"My mother became a tenured professor of British history at Tulane before she died," he went on. "Not bad for a woman descended from freed slaves and French trappers. I hardly ever saw Mom because she worked all the time, teaching and writing. When I made it to Hollywood, I took her last name to honor her."

"She sounds like a formidable woman." It hurt to breathe, her eyes stung but she wanted him to keep talking.

Instead, they ate the rest of their lunch in silence, her still sitting on the edge of mattress next to him. She knew she should move, but she wouldn't have done so for anything. Eventually, he asked for more tea. Once she filled his cup and added milk and sugar, she mustered the courage to ask the question that had burned in her since she'd learned they were going to coach him.

"Did you really grow up in a…brothel?"

"I see you like to read the tabloids," he said without looking up.

"I'm sorry," she quickly replied. "It's none of my business."

He shook his head. "I'm the one who's sorry. I've never tried to hide where I came from. You learn early on there's no such thing as privacy in Hollywood."

He took a sip of his tea and she had the impression he was fortifying himself with a breath. He set the cup back on the saucer as gently as Mr. Darcy himself would have and went on. "My mom was Creole trash—after all, her mother ran a brothel. The place was one of those big, old Victorians in the French Quarter. The business was on one side and Maw Maw's house was on the other, which is where Mom grew up and where she and I lived after I was born. I wasn't allowed on the business side—neither was Mom, for that matter *ever*. Maw Maw finally retired a few years ago." He shrugged. "Mom and I both ended up doing pretty well for ourselves"— he flashed that amazing smile—"for Creole trash, wouldn't you say?"

"For anyone," she whispered.

Gratitude flitted across his face and he grew serious again. "I just hope my mom's proud of me because I'm damned sure proud of her."

"As you should be." What else could she say?

He took a bite of his sandwich. "One good thing about living on one side of a brothel, it sure as hell taught me a lot about how to deal with Hollywood."

"Good Lord."

"The Lord doesn't have a whole lot to do with Hollywood, Samantha. Don't ever forget it because I don't."

"Cynic?" she asked as she offered him the last of the pickles.

"Realist. The result of ten years of experience. God knows it taught me the hard way, but it taught me. Regency rules aren't the only ones that force people to be together even if they don't want to be."

"Is that what you think?"

"Weren't arranged marriages a big thing? I remember reading something in here." He leaned to the side of the lap tray and thumbed through the pages of the manual she'd given him.

"They were, but it's not that different to the arranged marriages nowadays. Like Hollywood, for instance."

"I wouldn't say they were marriages. More like hookups and shack ups. Anything to sell movies and keep people in *People* magazine. There's not a lot of difference between marrying for money and hooking up for publicity." He continued to flip through the pages of the thick binder.

"Is that what happened between you and Miss Randolph?" Samantha regretted the words the instant they passed her lips. She'd told herself she needed to know in order to effectively prepare Dante for his role—and if she told herself that often enough, she might actually believe it.

"She was only fourteen years old when I first met her, for God's sake," he said.

The vehemence in his voice startled her, but she couldn't stop, her business or not. "And?"

"Things sort of changed when she turned eighteen, but hell, by then I was twenty-four. Too damned old for her."

"That's only six years difference in your ages."

"Sometimes it's not the years, Doc. It's the mileage."

"Was it your idea or hers?"

"I'm not sexist, Samantha. I'm not the type of man who doesn't like a woman to take charge. Is that what you think of me?" He covered her hand with his and brushed his thumb across her knuckles, slowly, one at a time.

"I...I'm sure I don't know." She flushed all over with the kind of heat that turned bones to molten mush.

He caught her gaze and held it, which drew her muscles taut and slowed the blood in her veins.

"Samantha, I don't mind a woman climbing the ladder in this business. It's only right and fair. But I do mind sex with me being nothing more than a rung on that ladder, especially when it's with an eighteen-year-old girl being pimped by her agent who also happens to be her mother. Sex should be much cleaner and...simpler than that. Not to mention, between two consenting adults who actually understand the score."

Something in the way he emphasized "understand the score" clenched her heart. He hadn't wanted to use Lily, a young woman he considered to be a kid, a kid who was being used by her mother. How many men would have taken that high road?

Danny Arneaux wasn't staring at her like he thought she was a kid. The darkening of his eyes sent her heart pounding so hard she was sure he could hear the rhythm. Who was this guy? He was her student, that's who. But the admonition did nothing to make protest when he slipped a hand around the back of her neck and drew her close.

His lips touched hers and her insides turned to the same molten lava women had experienced since Adam took the apple from Eve, then kissed her. The cup and saucer on his tray rattled when he hugged her against his chest and Samantha understood how well-deserved was Danny Arneaux's bad boy reputation. He made her want to drop her panties right then and there and ride him into—

He pulled back, and she reeled. Through the haze, she registered the languid half-smile that curved his dangerous mouth.

"And since I am learning to be a Regency gentleman, you will excuse me if I tell you that if you want to know what happened between Lily and me, you will have to ask Lily Randolph herself."

The door to his room flew open. "Ask me about what?"

Samantha never dreamed she'd be glad of Lily Randolph's snarky presence, but for once she was. Her bursting into Danny Arneaux's room the other day had saved Samantha from making a huge mistake. Kissing that man once was dangerous as hell. Any more than that and her will to resist him would be non-existent and so would her reputation in her chosen profession.

She sat down in one of the window seats along Rose-mount Manor's ancient gallery and flipped through her consultant journal. A check of the dainty Regency watch pinned to her pretty Regency day gown and she saw her student was late. Again. Perhaps he wouldn't show at all. She was torn between being relieved she wouldn't have to see him, and worried she wouldn't be able to turn him into Captain Rothgate by the time filming of A Matter of Honor began.

"Oh, do get over yourself, Samantha," she muttered. "He's just a man and it was just a kiss and there is no need to speak of it ever again."

"Talking to yourself, Doc? Even in Louisiana that isn't a good sign."

The man in question appeared at the end of the gallery and strolled toward her. Dressed in the kilt, boots, and loose white shirt of a Highlander during the Regency he looked far more at home in the current setting than she felt.

"You're late, Mr. Arneaux." She picked up her script from the stack of books next to her on the window seat and began to page through it, all but ignoring him. "Regency gentlemen are only late when attending Almack's."

"Sorry about that." He grabbed an antique chair from against the wall and placed it before her. With a heavy sigh, he dropped into the chair in a casual sprawl. "I had to change out of my breeches after my riding lesson. Dougal kept trying to get my neckcloth right and I finally told him to forget it."

She glanced up at him. "You don't ride in a kilt?"

"No ma'am, I do not. I tried it once and had to go sit in the loch for the rest of the day before my...parts stopped screaming at me. Won't make that mistake again."

Samantha cleared her throat. "A gentleman does not discuss his...parts in the presence of a lady. Shall we begin with some diction practice? Do sit up, Mr. Arneaux. We practiced this just yesterday."

He drew himself into a respectable and period appropriate position on his chair. "Better?"

"Much. Now, shall we—"

"I would apologize for kissing you, but I'm not sorry, Samantha."

She blinked, and started to blurt an answer, but caught herself. And waited.

His eyes were more green than hazel today. And his lips were drawn in a tight line as if he wanted to say more. But he didn't.

Thank god for small mercies.

She took a deep breath. "We're not here to discuss our mistakes or to make more. We're here to prepare you for the role of a lifetime. Let's concentrate on that, shall we?"

She flinched inwardly at the flicker of disappointment that crossed his face. A soft cool breeze swept down the gallery and turned up a section of one of the long Turkish carpet runners. The waft of air carried the faint scent of heather and earth.

Arneaux stood, gave her an exaggerated bow and walked over to straighten the rug. When he finally turned back to her, his face was nearly blank in severity.

"I see." He clasped his hands behind his back. "Very well," he said in his burgeoning aristocratic British accent. "What shall we practice today? Doc."

The coldness of his tone startled her, but she'd wanted him to be…professional, didn't she? She stood and offered him her script. "This section of dialogue needs work. You're a's are still a bit too long. We'll start here."

He studied the page she held open. "Right. I don't need the script. I know the lines." He waved the bound pages away. "I need to walk. Helps me to think."

He paced down the gallery, turned, and walked back toward her. In a few steps he was no longer Danny Arneaux. His posture, stride, and face were those of a Regency gentleman, a soldier returned from war.

"You behave as if the decision is mine and mine alone, Eudora. Perhaps you would rather it be so, as then the blame would fall on me. Not you. Not William, but me. As much as I love you and would do anything to save you pain, you must tell me what you wish me to do. No man should have to choose between his honor and duty as a husband and his honor and duty as the heir to his ancestral title. In the end, I must either honor the dictates of my heart or honor the dictates born and bred in me for the last five hundred years. What would you have me choose?"

"I…uhm." Samantha stared. Stunned.

He waited.

"That was very good," she finally said. "Almost perfect, in fact."

"Almost, huh?" He sat down on the edge of his chair, his hands clasped between his knees. "So hit me, Dr. Higgins. What did I get wrong?"

"Well, let me see." She looked down at her journal page, a page where she hadn't written a thing. "You're a's in 'rather' are too flat and in 'dictates' are still two syllables. Well, closer to one and a half syllables actually."

His lips twitched in a little smile. "Most vowels have two syllables where I come from. Okay, show me again. I've got to get this right."

She repeated the word slowly several times. The way he studied her mouth and cocked his head to listen sent a warm shudder through her. He repeated the word back to her over and over again. He got up abruptly and walked up and down the gallery swinging his arms and repeating the word rather in rhythm with his steps. His concentration astonished her.

He seemed utterly focused on pronouncing the word correctly every single time. This was the man she'd seen in the screen test.

"Did Regency gentlemen really live their lives that way, with honor being so important?" he asked from the center of the room.

"Most did. A man's personal honor was part of his soul, or at least it was for those who were raised to live no other way."

"Men like Captain Rothgate." He nodded. "I get that. He does the right thing according to his code of honor no matter how much it tears him up inside to do it. He gives up his wife, his home, his whole existence for the sake of his honor."

"Yes, I believe so." She thumbed through the script. "Is that why you wanted to play him?"

"English aristocrats aren't the only men who were raised to be honorable, Doc. Even Cajun bayou trash know about honor." She opened her mouth to speak, but he raised a hand to stop her. "Sorry. I didn't mean that. I'm just frustrated. I want to get this right. And I want things to be right between us. Whatever that means."

Their gazes locked. Time stood still. He was several feet away, but she could smell his cologne and feel the heat of his body as if he stood only inches away.

"How goes the coaching, Dr. Higgins?" a familiar and annoying voice called from the entrance to the gallery. "Is he an Englishman yet?"

She and Danny jumped slightly as they turned to acknowledge Teddy Rousseau's poorly timed entrance.

"Do you mean do I sound like a snotty Brit sword fighter with a stick up his ass? Not yet, Teddy. Maybe you can help. Say the word 'dictates'." Danny winked at Samantha who shook her head but smiled in spite of herself.

"Dictates?" Teddy frowned. "Why the bloody hell would I say that?"

"Why wouldn't you? The way you teach weapons handling, 'dictate' should be your middle name. Come on. Say it again. 'Dictates.'" This time Danny said the word with an exaggerated southern drawl.

"Oh, for pity's sake." Teddy threw up his hands "'Dictates.' There. Are you satisfied? Dictates."

"Dictates," Danny repeated, matching Teddy's tone and inflection perfectly. "Dictates."

Teddy stared at him in complete shock. Finally, he said "By George, I think he's got it."

Samantha threw the script at Danny and her copy of the Regency boot camp manual at Teddy. "Idiots, the both of you. Run along, Teddy. Mr. Arneaux and I have work to do."

Chapter Seven

"Dr. Higgins asked that I remind you of your dancing lesson this afternoon," Dougal

said as he and Danny left the drawing room.

"I remembered. Why do you think I'm wearing these lame-ass shoes? Did she say anything else?"

"No, sir." The valet stopped at the bottom of the stairs that led to the first floor. "Was she meant to say anything else?"

"You are so not funny, Dougal."

"At least Grenadier hasn't dumped you. Again." The young Scot coughed and covered his grin with his hand. "Not like Dr. Higgins. Wagers have been made about what you did to her."

Danny started up the stairs. "Bite me."

"Is that a Regency term, sir?"

The servants might be betting on it, but Danny didn't know what he'd done wrong when it came to Samantha. Whatever it was, he'd done a bang-up job of it. She was still his Regency coach. Too damned much his Regency coach.

He'd had seventy-year-old hard-ass algebra professors with more warmth. In the week since he'd kissed her, they'd spent hours together.

Etiquette lessons.

Elocution lessons.

Dancing lessons.

Walking lessons.

History lessons.

And not a single word about the kiss they'd shared since the day after when he'd declared he wasn't sorry. Not a single word about his personal life or her personal life or anything more personal than "How are you this morning?" and "Here is your schedule for tomorrow." He was fine with her stand-offish attitude, except when he wasn't, which irritated the hell out of him.

Head bowed, he ambled down the hall toward the ballroom, ignoring the portraits in the thick, gold frames and the tapestries on the walls. After what Jackie told him about Samantha's power in him securing this role, he hadn't been happy about the idea of seducing his Regency coach. He still wasn't. Oh, he wanted to seduce her, but not because of the advantage it might give him regarding the role of Rothgate. He liked her, and he'd kissed her just to see if something was possible.

Unfortunately, Dougal was right. Danny had been dumped as a possible...something to Samantha, and it was driving him crazy.

"Bollocks," he muttered in a pretty damned good English accent.

"Look who's been practicing his British." The sly tone of this observation left no doubt about the speaker.

Lily stood two steps inside the ballroom dressed in a wine-colored silk gown with a four-inch sash at the waist tied so tight he didn't know how she was breathing, and a gravity defying neckline that must have been illegal during the Regency period because it was at least a felony today.

"Back off, sweetheart. I'm not in the mood." He squeezed past her and nearly made his escape.

She grabbed his arm and sidled up to whisper in his ear. "Is the little British teacher giving you a hard time? I wondered why she asked me to be your dance partner."

Danny peeled her fingers off his arm and walked over to the wall of windows looking out over the formal gardens at the back of the house. He perched a hip on one of the windowsills and folded his arms across his chest. When Lily had burst into his room last week, he and Samantha were too damned flustered to come up with a good answer to her question. Or at least he had been.

"Ask me about what?"

His head had been spinning, but apparently, Samantha wasn't nearly as enthralled with their kiss. She'd popped off the side of his bed and asked Lily to partner Danny in his dance lessons. Then she'd left the room like it was on fire and left him to listen to Lily make fun of his first encounter with Grenadier for the next fifteen minutes. If Dougal hadn't brought the dogs in wet from their morning walk, Danny would have crawled out a window to get away from Lily's bullshit, injured or not.

Mr. Sylvan Goode entered the ballroom. "Good morning, Mr. Arneaux. Shall we begin?"

Danny couldn't help but smile. Every time he saw the dance master and really nice guy, the phrase *"Weebles wobble, but they don't fall down."* came to mind. The man was about five feet five and as round as a billiard ball. Danny was pretty sure Mr. Goode wore a corset to bed. Amazingly, the man was so light on his feet it was scary. And he had the patience of a French quarter carriage horse.

"Hey, Mr. G." Danny offered the cheerful Brit a fist bump,

something Danny had taught the other man at Danny's first dance lesson. Goode always complied with a very precise bump followed by a flair of his fingers and a smug grin. Danny glanced around. "Shouldn't we wait for Dr. Higgins?"

"She's consulting with Miss Witherspoon this morning, and then she's arranging your kilt fitting. Shall we begin?"

"Why the hell not?"

The pianist and fiddler started tuning up, and he and Lily assumed their dancing positions.

"Kilt fitting?" Lily raised an eyebrow.

"Don't ask."

They walked through the steps of the *Roger de Coverley*, or at least that was what Mr. G called it. Mapping out the dance steps was fine with Danny because he didn't have to spend a lot of time in close contact with Lily. It was all he could do not to bust his ass in the slick-soled shoes he had to wear when he wasn't wearing boots. Gentlemen didn't wear boots to dance. However, every time he and Lily were brought together by the steps, she managed to push at least one of his buttons.

"Miss Higgins seems to be avoiding you, Mr. Sexiest Man Alive." Lily smiled sweetly as Danny missed a step and had to run to catch up.

"She's my Regency coach, not my girlfriend. She has a lot of things to oversee for this movie." He contemplated how many ways he could trip the actress without it looking deliberate.

They came together in the middle of the ballroom, then circled each other while touching hands.

"My sources tell me she's in over her head. Apparently, this is her first time as lead consultant. None of the others know how she got the job. She's just a glorified errand girl with a fancy degree."

They joined hands and danced down the center of the ballroom.

"Better check your sources, Lil. Erik Wentworth hired her. He only hires the best."

"One wonders why he hired you then." She hit him again with that little sweetheart smile, the one so sweet it made his teeth hurt.

"Same reason he hired you, honey. Our names are known, but with where our careers are, we both work cheap." He twirled her around and allowed the steps of the dance to separate them. When they came back together, he said, "Do me a favor."

"What would that be?"

"Shut the hell up for the rest of the lesson or I'll tell Eleanor about your second cell phone."

It was her turn to stumble. She opened her mouth, probably to deny she had another phone. He shook his head.

"You wouldn't dare," she said between gritted teeth.

"The hell I wouldn't." He bowed as the music came to an end.

"Let's try a waltz, shall we?" Mr. G suggested. "Now remember, you don't dance as closely for a Regency waltz as you do for the waltz today."

"Thank God for small favors," Danny said as he walked to the spot the dance master indicated.

While Mr. G showed him how to stand, Lily shot Danny a bird and flounced to the window until she was called.

For the rest of the hour, he tried his very best to keep his mind on the dance steps, which was hard as hell with the screwed-up shit going on in his head. Not about it being Samantha's first film or anything. Everybody had to start somewhere, and she was competent as hell. In that context, her avoidance of getting close to him actually made sense.

Maybe she was avoiding him because she needed people to think she was the ultimate professional. Or maybe she just wasn't interested. That idea made his ribs hurt worse than the fall from the horse.

The quadrille finally ended, and Mr. G said, "I think that is enough for today."

Danny gave Lily a stiff attempt at a bow. She didn't bother with a curtsy.

"You're progressing nicely, Mr. Arneaux. We shall make a Regency officer and a gentleman of you yet." Mr. G hooked his thumbs in his suspenders and rocked on his heels. "Of course, you, Miss Randolph, were already an excellent dancer."

"Thank you, Mr. Goode. It is always nice to have one's accomplishments appreciated."

Danny turned and, with a backhanded wave and a promise to see them tomorrow, he strode out of the ballroom and headed down the hall toward the stairs. The pitter patter of dainty determined feet caught up with him at the top of the stairs that led down to the foyer. Lily grabbed his arm. Again.

"Your career may be over, Danny Arneaux," she said, digging those talons she called fingernails into his nice wool morning coat, which was not to be confused with his nice wool evening coat. "But mine is just beginning again. And I won't let you or some prissy little Regency Coach fuck that up. Oh look. Speak of the devil. Miss Higgins!" Lily released Danny's arm and waved at the two women who had just strolled into the foyer. "I heard the most interesting thing about you last night." She made a beeline down the stairs for Samantha and Eleanor Witherspoon.

Danny groaned. "Shit."

Knowing Lily as he did, she was going to tell everyone that this was Samantha's first time as head consultant, and

Lily would do so in such a way as to make them all doubt Samantha's ability to do the job. Danny took the stairs two at a time and intercepted her just as she reached the two ladies. He caught Lily's hand, spun her in a circle, and reached into the pocket she'd had sewn into the end of the sash tied around her *hey-look-at-my-tiny-waist* dress. Poor girl was so shocked she couldn't speak. Thank God. He pulled out a pretty pink iPhone and handed it to the manager of their little boot camp.

"Here you go, Miss Witherspoon. Guess she forgot about this one. Good thing I saw this lovely gown vibrating when we were dancing. Come on, Dr. Higgins, let's go for a walk." He hooked his arm through Samantha's and started for the front doors.

"It's pouring rain."

"Fine. Not outside. We'll go for a walk Regency style in the gallery upstairs." Danny did an about-face and dragged Samantha back toward the stairs.

She contorted her body in an attempt to see what Lily and Eleanor were doing. Danny could have saved her the trouble. Eleanor was giving Lily hell.

"I shall be eternally grateful she didn't hide her phone in her bra," Samantha said.

"I would never reach into a woman's bra unless she asked me. Besides, she's not wearing a bra. Or a corset. I did her a favor. Knowing her taste in men, one of them is probably tracking her phone and will show up here with chloroform and duct tape. This way." He led her to the opposite side of the landing than the one he'd come down and along the hall until they came to a narrow set of stone steps off to the right.

"Chloro— Where are we going? Will you please stop?" Samantha planted her feet and refused to move. "What on earth is wrong with you?"

"We don't have that kind of time." He took her hand. "I

told you, we are going to take a walk Regency style. The gallery runs the whole length of the house, and it has some great views from the windows. The dogs and I go up there every morning and before bed to get some exercise, just like people did in this house hundreds of years ago, according to His Grace."

He started up the narrow stone steps and, to his amazement, Samantha followed. The winding staircase eventually opened into a long, wide room that stretched as far as the eye could see and then some.

"This is lovely," Samantha said softly. "I didn't even know this was up here."

"This is the oldest part of the house. They just kept adding on and adding on over the years. This is called the gallery and it is almost six hundred years old."

He was babbling like some kind of demented tour guide, but he'd found a book on the history of the house in the library, and he'd studied it. Because he wanted to impress her? Probably. Because he wanted her to like him again? As pitiful as that sounded, yes.

Samantha stood halfway down the gallery with the strangest look on her face, a combination of disbelief and... fascination? "How did you—"

"The footman, Robbie. I asked him where I could spend time with my dogs without worrying about them knocking somebody over. Even the duke has told me some things about the house and the family. Pretty cool stuff, actually." He stretched his arms wide and turned from side to side. "There's not much up here Marie and Laveau can break, so it works."

There were tall windows like those in a church spaced a fair bit apart down the outside wall. Wooden window seats with faded blue velvet cushions were set in every other window. Each window had heavy velvet drapes tied back to let in the light. Danny sat in one of the window seats and watched Samantha take it all in. This was her thing—the history, the idea of being in a place where people lived their lives all those years ago. Her face it up and she looked more unguarded than he'd ever seen.

"These suits of armor are authentic." She inspected the two metal monstrosities on each side of the doorway they'd come through at the top of the stairs. "And these are all Turkish rugs." She bent down and flipped the end of one of the big, worn rugs covering the wooden floors. "They are at least two hundred years old." She went to the far wall and tilted her head back to study the humongous paintings. When she turned and opened her mouth to speak, she suddenly stopped. "What?"

"You." He couldn't help but smile.

"I what?" She raised her hand to her hair, braided and pinned to her head.

Samantha belonged here, in a place like this, in another time. Her rust-colored dress brought out the soft rose of her cheeks, the sapphire blue of her eyes, and the gold of her hair. But it was her mind running ninety to nothing as she drew in the history of the house and the wonder that was her real beauty.

"You love this stuff. The house and"—he waved a hand around—"all of this."

"Well, of course I do." The light in her eyes dimmed. Her face settled into that professional film consultant pucker he'd grown to hate. "It's my job."

"Is that why you keep avoiding me?"

Well, that was subtle. *Not.* He forced himself to stay on the window seat, one foot up on the cushions with his forearm resting on his knee.

"I beg your pardon?" She'd started toward him but stopped a few steps from where he sat.

"Was kissing me so bad?" Holy hell. The connection between his brain and his mouth had completely shorted out and was about to burn him down.

"I am not having this conversation with you." She turned toward the stairs.

"You're not having any conversation with me at all. That's the point. Did I offend you?"

She turned back. "Offend me? How?"

"When I kissed you."

"Will you please stop saying that?"

"There is no one up here but you and me and the duke's dead relatives." Danny indicated a set of portraits across from where he sat.

"I cannot believe you have been talking with His Grace." She crossed her arms. "Eleanor says he wants nothing to do with any of this film business or us."

"You're avoiding the subject, but I'll bite. Just because you don't want to talk to me doesn't mean nobody does. Besides, I haven't kissed His Grace. Yet. If I do, maybe he won't talk to me either."

"You're insane."

"I'm an actor. Of course, I'm insane. And you're still avoiding the subject."

"Which is?"

Danny sighed. "I obviously misread the situation. I'm sorry I kissed you. Please accept my apology." He got up to leave and started toward the door.

"Mr. Arneaux, please wait."

Danny stopped mid-step. Then strode to one of the window seats and stepped up onto it. "If you call me Mr. Arneaux one more time, I'm going to jump out this window."

"Oh, for pity's sake." She rushed over, grabbed his hand,

and dragged him down. "Those windows probably haven't been opened in centuries." Samantha didn't release him. So, when she started to stroll down the gallery, he walked with her, his fingers wrapped around hers. "You didn't offend me. And I'm not sorry you kissed me. Dante."

He waited. They walked to the very end of the gallery then circled past the fireplace that filled the entire back wall to start back up the long room. It seemed she wasn't going to say more, which meant he needed to say something. Wouldn't be a problem if he knew what the hell to say. It'd been so damned long since a woman had left him tongue-tied it scared the hell out of him.

"So, you're not sorry, but…"

She stopped and let go of his hand. "I was hired to help you. Not to"—she waved her hands around—"hook up with you."

"I really hate that expression."

"Hook up? Then what would you call whatever this is between us?"

Danny threw his hands into the air. "I don't know what to call it. I don't know about the British version, but in the States one kiss doesn't make much of a—"

Samantha grabbed the back of his head and dragged him down to plant a kiss on him +that had his brain short-circuiting and his buckskin knee-breeches cutting off circulation to the entire set of his family jewels. Once she made a soft little sound and her tongue slipped past his lips, a jolt shot through him, and he woke up quick.

Danny wrapped an arm around her back and gently pulled her to him. He laid the back of his other hand against her neck, so his fingers rested against the silky texture of her hair. He wanted to unravel her braids and pins and see if her hair was that enticing all the way through, but he was too interested in prolonging their kiss to try. He struggled to get closer.

Melded from thighs to hips to chests, he marveled at the way their bodies fit together. Every inch of her cushioned and welcomed him. The cradle of her hips aroused him to the point of delicious, erotic pain. Samantha was made for long, slow lovemaking, and he had never wanted a woman more. She stroked and caressed his tongue with hers. Damn she tasted good. *She* was good. His head was about to explode when she finally drew apart to grab a short breath.

He took the opportunity to kiss the spot behind her ear he'd been fantasizing about this last week. He ran the tip of his tongue around the shell of her ear. She shivered, which gave him a flash of heat powerful enough to burn through a stuntman's fire suit. She worked her hands over his short-cropped hair as he angled his head to kiss down her throat as far as her dress would let him.

Oh, hell yes!

"Dante."

"Mm-hmm." He kissed her eyelids and slid both hands down her back to rest on her hips.

"Dante...."

He nipped her chin, and she gasped. She ran her hands inside his coat and underneath his waistcoat. He groaned. She settled against him for moment with a little sigh that sent a weird sort of pain into his chest. Just as quickly, she pushed against him.

"Dante!"

He raised his hands and stepped back. What the hell?

"I didn't mean for you to... I mean...." She stepped closer and pushed his arms down so she could rest her hands on them. "I don't regret kissing you because I liked it. I liked it a great deal. But I have a job to do here. My professional reputation is very important to me. I can't afford to be another name in the *Legend of Danny Arneaux* tabloid chronicles. I'm afraid no one will take me seriously." She'd said all that in one breath, and when she ran out of air, she stopped speaking. Her eyes didn't.

"Anyone who doesn't take you seriously is fucked in the head."

She burst out laughing.

"I'm serious, Samantha. You're good at what you do. I don't stand a snowball's chance in hell of playing Rothgate without your help, and I am not ashamed to say it."

Her laughter cut off as fast as it'd begun. She rested her head against his chest and muttered something he didn't catch. When she finally looked up at him, he thought she might tell him this was her first Regency coach assignment. Not that it mattered to him. Well, except he wanted Samantha to trust him. *Insane?* Definitely.

"It's my job to get you ready to play Rothgate. It's also my job to get everyone here ready to do what Mr. Wentworth is going to demand of them. I can't let anything, or anyone, get in the way of that." She bit her bottom lip and shook her head.

"And whatever this is between us? What do we do about that?"

"I don't know," she whispered. "But I think I'd like to find out. If there's a way to do it without—"

He touched his fingertips to her lips. "We'll figure it out. Somehow, we'll figure it out."

Never in his life had Danny had to work to have a relationship with a woman. It always came so easily to him. With everything he knew and everything that was going on, this was going to be one hell of an adjustment. He knew she had the final say as to whether he got the part, which he wasn't supposed to know. However, if he confessed everything now, he'd blow this fragile thing between them all to hell. He leaned in to kiss her again.

"Dr. Higgins? Mr. Arneaux? Are you there?" Dougal's voice drifted up the stairs.

Danny had to give Samantha credit. She didn't jump back, but her deer-in-the-headlights expression set him in motion. He stole a quick kiss to the corner of her mouth, clasped his hands behind his back, and strolled to one of the windows. Dougal entered the gallery, huffing and puffing from the climb.

"His Grace said you might be up here. Mrs. Wallace is here to fit your kilt, sir."

"Mrs. Wallace?" Danny spun around so quick his neck cracked.

"Not that Mrs. Wallace," Samantha assured him. "This Mrs. Wallace works as a seamstress in the village. She does all the kilts for the duke and his family."

"She's our Mrs. Wallace's sister," Dougal said with an evil grin. "They married brothers. Both widows now. Should I bring her here?"

"No, tell Mrs. Wallace we'll come down. I don't want some little old lady to have to climb all those stairs," Danny said.

Dougal's expression dropped from happy-go-lucky to terrified in a split second.

"What?" Danny glanced at Samantha and then back at Dougal.

"You never say a Scotswoman is too old to do anything, sir. Ever. Especially not either one of our Mrs. Wallaces." He crossed himself. He actually crossed himself. "The last man who did still walks with a limp. Do ye kin?"

If kin meant understand, Danny got it. "I have a Creole grandmother, Dougal. Of course, I understand." This time when he looked at Samantha, she was laughing behind her hand.

"Yes, Dougal, please bring her up," Samantha said, and started to follow the valet.

Danny took two long strides and caught her elbow. "Do *not* leave me alone with her."

"What on earth? Are you afraid of a sixty-year-old Scots seamstress, Mr. Action Star?"

Great. She was getting a kick out of this.

"I'm afraid of any woman related to the duke's house-keeper, especially one who sounds like my Maw Maw. Hell, even the duke's afraid of his housekeeper."

"He actually said that?" Samantha joined him at the window and tucked her hand into the crook of his arm. "What else did you and His Grace talk about?"

"Mostly about how much he hates having all these people here for the boot camp. Apparently, his dad pissed all the money away, and now the duke has to rent out his home to make money. I can understand that." Danny stared out the window. Fields of green divided by hedges and stone walls and dabbed with dots of white he knew to be sheep stretched into hills of trees and stone.

"You can?"

"I grew up in New Orleans. I understand what it's like for people to look at your home and see an amusement park instead of a place where your soul can finally rest."

"You're a poet, Dante Arneaux." She squeezed his arm.

The way she studied him made him nervous as hell. The last thing he needed was for her to see him as anything other than what he was—an actor from Louisiana who got by on his good looks and his ability to convince people he was some muscle-bound player. If she ever saw more than that in him, expected more, he'd have to live up to her expectations. He wasn't sure he could do that. In the week and half since he met her, Samantha Higgins had given him a set of ideas. Ideas that scared the hell out of him. Ideas that had nothing to do with a role in a movie or saving his career. He couldn't afford those kinds of ideas.

"The rest of the time the duke talks about how much he cannot stand Miss Witherspoon," he said.

"Really? I like her very much. She is so enthusiastic and helpful."

"I think so too, but the duke thinks she's…." Danny stood ramrod straight and looked down his nose at her. *"Too bossy by half, completely ridiculous, and has no idea of her proper place."*

"Oh, bravo. Your accent was perfect." Samantha's delighted smile made him feel ten feet tall.

He executed a snappy half-bow. "Thank you, Dr. Higgins. Your praise is much appreciated."

"You really are catching on." She frowned. "Eleanor talks about the duke as well. She finds him pompous, over-bearing, and stuffy. She talks about him quite a lot."

"He talks about her all the time. Wait." He exchanged a startled look with Samantha. "You don't think…."

"Couldn't be. Could it?" She bit her lip, but it didn't hide her smile.

Danny started to answer but was struck by the sudden overwhelming scent of something earthy with a hint of lavender—Maw Maw's favorite scent. He'd smelled it before, in his room, and when he was out riding.

"Do you smell that?" he asked.

"Yes, it's—"

An eerie wind rushed up the gallery from the fireplace, flipping up the corners of rugs and rattling heavy picture frames against the stone walls. It shook the windows, then died to nothing. Samantha shuddered, and Danny put his arm around her.

"You were saying?" He tried his best to keep his expression and tone of voice normal.

"The scent is heather. Where did that wind…." She looked left to right, following the path the wind had taken.

"I have no idea, but this isn't the first time," he murmured.

"What?" She looked up at him.

"First night I got here. Then right after Grenadier dumped me on my butt. And a few nights ago, when I conversed with the duke in the pool room. Not that he noticed it. I just thought I'd had too much to drink."

A commotion on the stairs forced Danny to step away from her, but not before he gave her a quick wink and tucked a strand of hair behind her ear. Definitely worth it when he caught the secret little smile on her lips as she turned away and went to kick down the flipped-up ends of one of the rugs.

Dougal and Robbie stumbled into the room, their arms loaded with bolts of fabric. They lurched over to drop the stuff on a long, very old wooden table beneath a painting of some hunting dogs and some guy wearing a hilarious wig riding a fat-butt horse. Danny's mind was still half on Samantha kissing him, and her telling him they might be able to explore their mutual attraction. This was turning out to be a pretty damned good day.

"Well, where is he?" a female voice bellowed from the staircase.

Hell's bells. The woman who marched through the arched doorway and into the gallery was the spitting image of Mrs. Wallace, Rosemount Manor's housekeeper, but as impossible as it might seem, she looked even meaner and tougher than her sister.

Danny swallowed hard.

Samantha glided past him in her little, short leather boots and whispered, "Brace yourself."

He stepped into the middle of the gallery. "I think I'm the one you—"

"Och. Aye, ye are. And I see she's been here to see ye." The stonewall of a woman dropped a large wooden box, kind of like an oversized tackle box, at her feet. She sniffed the air and followed the line of rumpled rugs with her gaze.

"She?" Samantha asked.

She glanced at Danny. He shrugged.

"Aye. The Innes Witch, of course." Mrs. Wallace looked at him. "Shall we get started?"

Chapter Eight

SAMANTHA KICKED A FEW MORE RUGS INTO PLACE AND SIDLED her way between Dougal and Robbie, who stood next to a table against the interior gallery wall. She kept her expression neutral, but her two companions were deriving a great deal of pleasure from Mrs. Wallace's treatment of poor Dante. Apparently, all the Wallace women were quite strong and very efficient. This one wrenched him out of his morning coat, out of his waistcoat, and was untucking his linen shirt before he had a chance to speak. At least with his mouth. His eyes were carrying on an entire conversation with Samantha.

Help me!

What the hell is she doing?

This isn't funny!

"Do either of you lads want to tell me about the Innes Witch?" Samantha asked as she watched Dante try to remove Mrs. Wallace's hands from the waistband of his buckskin breeches.

"Nae," Dougal said in unison with Robbie's, "No, miss."

Their answers wouldn't bother her so much if they

weren't looking at each other and not her—and if they didn't look as guilty as the devil.

"One of you lads bring me that bolt of Innes plaid. The Sassenach is shy." Mrs. Wallace stood, hands on hips, and glared at Dante who had his hands locked at his waistband as if his life depended on it.

"I've got this." Samantha took the fabric Dougal had picked up. "And when I get back, I expect you two to start talking or I'll take my questions to His Grace." Her announcement had an immediate and desired effect—abject fear followed by resignation that indicated they'd sing like canaries. As she strode to where Dante and Mrs. Wallace stood, she could hardly suppress her amusement. "What seems to be the trouble, *Mr. Arneaux*."

He cocked an eyebrow and flattened his lips into a line. "She wants me to strip to my drawers."

"And?"

"I'm not wearing any drawers. Dougal says I'm not supposed to."

"Ye'v got nothing I haven't seen before, lad," Mrs. Wallace assured him as she measured out the blue, black, and gray plaid wool fabric.

"Your sister said the same thing when she hauled me out of the bathtub like a sack of potatoes, but I'd rather not show what I do have to every woman in Scotland with the last name Wallace, if that's all right with you."

She cackled, and Samantha had to turn away to keep from joining her. Dante was so damned cute in his indignance. Oh, he'd hate it if she told him he was cute. Handsome? Yes. Hot? Yes. Cute? Probably not. She was still trying to sort out why she'd kissed him and why she'd agreed to continue to explore what was about to be an affair and maybe more.

Mrs. Wallace whipped the fabric around Dante's waist a few times then draped it over one shoulder. It looked like entirely too much fabric in Samantha's mind, but this woman had been making kilts and dressing Scotsmen and Scotswomen for nearly fifty years.

"Now strip," the seamstress ordered Dante.

The skin above his perfectly tied neckcloth turned bright red. Behind Samantha, Dougal and Robbie snickered. She crossed her arms and looked at Dante expectantly. He toed off his boots and kicked them aside. His gaze never left her face. He narrowed his eyes, reached under the makeshift kilt, wiggled about a bit, and drew his breeches out to toss them directly at Samantha. She caught them one-handed. Dante let loose a short laugh. Mrs. Wallace shook her head and took a tape measure from her dress pocket.

"Let's see what we have here," the seamstress muttered as she drew the tape around Dante's waist. "That costume lady wants me to make three Lowlander kilts to fit ye. Says they're easier to work with, whatever that means." She ran the tape from his ankle up under the kilt, and from the way Dante jumped, all the way to his crotch.

"There's a difference between kilts?" Dante asked, his voice a little tight.

"Oh, aye," Robbie said. "A true Scot wears his kilt of whole cloth, wrapped around him and belted to hold it on, pleat it, and give it shape. Mrs. Wallace makes the kilts we wear so we don't have to do all that." He hooked his thumbs in the waist of his kilt and did a slow turn while Dougal rolled his eyes.

Mrs. Wallace pulled out a ready-made kilt and a pincushion full of pins. "Step into this one and I'll fit it to you. Once I have that done, I can make as many as you need."

"I don't want one like that." Dante eyed a larger-than-life portrait hung high on the stone wall next to the doorway to the stairs. "I want one like his."

"That's the first duke. He fought at Bannockburn," Dougal said, his voice laced with reverence.

"Are only dukes allowed to wear a kilt like that?"

"Dante, I really think you need to let Mrs. Wallace fit you for what Miss Stepford ordered." Samantha nodded at the older woman to continue. A sudden rush of icy wind raced up the gallery—flipping rugs and banging paintings against the walls. The faint scent of heather whirled around them. "Or…perhaps not?" She glanced at Dougal and Robbie who were elbowing each other mercilessly.

"I don't know about you, Mrs. Wallace, but I make it a policy never to argue with a witch." Dante winked at Samantha and untied his neck cloth.

"Be it you're afraid of the witch or afraid of Mrs. Wallace and her pincushion?" Dougal asked.

Samantha pursed her lips and stared at Dante.

"Little of both, Dougal. A little of both. What do you say, Mrs. Wallace? Will you fit me for a proper kilt and show me how to wear it? Then maybe you can tell Dr. Higgins and me about this witch of yours since Robbie and Dougal are too chicken-hearted to talk about her."

Mrs. Wallace dropped the ready-made kilt back into her box and marched to the table the footman and the valet leaned against, mumbling in Gaelic the entire time. She shoved the two young men aside and began to dig through the items they'd deposited on the table.

"I think you made her angry," Samantha muttered as she stood next to Dante, but faced away from the rummaging seamstress.

"How can you tell? Ouch!" He flinched as she elbowed him in the side. "Look, would you want her poking you with pins around your…private parts?"

"Private, Mr. Arneaux?" Samantha couldn't believe she was actually flirting with him—and enjoying it.

"Well, for you, Dr. Higgins, nothing of mine is private. You can have as much access as you like. I'll write you an all-access pass if you like."

"So now you're a one-man Disney World?" Her entire body flushed with red hot arousal from merely flirting with him. If she ended up in his bed she might spontaneously combust.

"There's only one way to find out," he whispered in her ear before he straightened and gave Mrs. Wallace his full attention as she reached him and draped a length of tartan over his shoulder.

The seamstress placed a variety of belts and sporrans on her workbox. She reached for the tartan. "Are ye going to be sissy about this, or will you let me show you how to wear a proper kilt?"

He folded his arms across his chest. "Are ye going to tell me about the Innes Witch?" His Scot's brogue was spot on and brought a fierce grin to Mrs. Wallace's face.

"*Aontachadh.*" She threw the excess fabric across her arm and began to wind the rest around his waist. "Means we have a deal, lad. Here, miss." She handed Samantha a swath of the plaid. "You might as well learn how to get him in and out of this."

Samantha choked on her reply. A wicked light shone in Dante's eyes. She couldn't do anything about Mrs. Wallace's suggestion or Dante's typically male response, but at least she managed to cut off Dougal and Robbie's snickering with one incendiary side glance.

"Ye'll do a better job showing it to that Sassenach costume lady than meself'."

Why on earth would Mrs. Wallace assume Samantha would do a better job.... She suddenly had the distinct suspicion she was being set up by a matchmaking Scotswoman.

"Ye'r nae a Scot, but ye'll do in a pinch," Mrs. Wallace said as if she'd read Samantha's mind.

"Oh. Of course." Samantha's voice took on a strangled tone, half in laughter at the woman's machinations and half in anticipation. The idea of dressing or undressing Dante Arneaux sent all sorts of liquid sensations firing through her body. "Excellent idea, Mrs. Wallace."

The seamstress grunted and held the last layer of plaid together around Dante's waist with her thumb and forefinger. She tugged and snatched at the fabric to position it against one of his hip bones, then walked around him, wrapping the fabric as she went. Then, she started to talk as she pointed out lines and angles to Samantha.

"The first duke was near death after Bannockburn. They brought him back here and sent for the local midwife, a young woman named Elsbeth Dunhome. She was known as a powerful healer. She saved his life and 'tis said he fell in love with her. Some folks said she bewitched him." Mrs. Wallace took Samantha's hand and tucked it into the waist of the kilt. "Hold this. Now wrap this around him three times."

When Samantha pressed her fingers into the hard flesh of his stomach, she had to suppress the desire to slide her fingers along his skin. Instead, she reached around him and tucked the plaid in as Mrs. Wallace instructed. All the while, an electrified hum rose between her and Dante. A quick check of his face raised the temperature in the room considerably. Apparently, her touch had a similar effect on him—at least that was what the heat in his green eyes said.

"What happened between this Elsbeth and the duke?" asked quietly.

Mrs. Wallace chose a belt and fastened it around his waist to hold the kilt in place. She folded another layer over the belt and showed Samantha how to arrange the pleats at the back of the kilt. "He wanted to marry her, but his mother and others in the clan were against it. There were whispers Elsbeth was a witch. But the duke did marry her. When the old duchess had enough kinsmen to do her bidding, she had the lass tried for witchcraft. They tied her to a chair and threw her into the loch."

"Jesus," Dante muttered.

"Where was the duke?" Samantha asked as she fumbled to fasten the sporran around the final layer of the kilt. "I thought you said he loved her. He married her."

"He did." Mrs. Wallace arranged the rest of the plaid over Dante's shoulder and fastened it in place with an elaborate shoulder pin in the shape of a thistle with a sword through it. "But they locked him in yon tower before the trial, and all he could do was watch through the bars of the window as the water closed over the lass's head when they carried out the old duchess's sentence."

"What the hell kind of sentence is tying her to a chair and dropping her in the lake supposed to prove?"

"If she floated, she was guilty. If she sank, she was innocent." Mrs. Wallace kissed the little gold cross around her neck and shook her head. "And dead."

"Then she wasn't a witch," Dante said.

"No one truly knows. There's more than one kind of witch in the world, lad." Mrs. Wallace tucked her cross back into the neck of her dress. "People have sworn they've seen her since the first duke's time, wandering the loch and the parapets of the old castle. She's been called the Innes Witch ever since."

Samantha blinked furiously against the sting of tears. She drew her fingers from the waist of the kilt and worked to tuck Dante's linen shirt into place. "What a terrible story."

"They say you can hear the duke screaming her name from the tower at night," Dougal declared solemnly.

"Oh, aye," Robbie said. "And you don't dare walk the loch

at night for fear of running into the duke looking for her." He dropped his voice to a dramatic whisper. "Legend says he never found her body. She's still out in the loch somewhere."

"Has anyone ever seen him?" Samantha stepped back to take in her handiwork. "The duke? Or the witch? Has anyone actually seen them?"

"These days the Innes Witch only shows herself to the duke, or so they say. To anyone else she's a cold wind or the scent of heather or—"

"Laughter when no one else is in the room," Dante said, his voice just above a whisper.

Sudden silence hung in the room like a wet blanket. Samantha rubbed her hand up and down his arm. He braced himself against her and pulled on his boots. When he finally straightened, Mrs. Wallace took a step back and, hands on hips, gave him a thorough inspection.

"Ye'll do, lad. Ye'll do." She closed her work box and dropped her tape measure and the index card with his measurements into her pocket. "I'll have the kilts that costume lady wants ready in a week or so. But I think this one suits ye."

Samantha couldn't tear her eyes from Danny. What had the blonde attendant on the plane called him? Six feet of chai latte? The description was like comparing, well, Kermit the Frog to a bronze Highland god.

Her stomach did a somersault. *Not. What. You. Are. Here. For!* That was too bloody bad because the man looked good enough to—

"You keep looking at him like that, lass, and he's going to need a bigger kilt." Mrs. Wallace nudged her with an elbow and winked.

Samantha blinked. "What are you…oh. Oh!"

Mrs. Wallace bustled over to Dougal and Robbie and barked out orders for them to gather up everything on the table and come along. The faint scent of heather lingered in the air. The clatter of footsteps and Mrs. Wallace's commanding voice retreated, and Samantha was left alone in the gallery with a man she found hotter and sexier by the minute. A man who stared at her like she was the last piece of Scottish tablet on the plate. She cleared her throat, which didn't help a bit.

"What did you think of the ghost story?" Samantha asked in the hope of cooling down the heat between them.

He stepped forward and took her hand, his grip casual but warm and welcome. "Broke my heart," he said. "If ever a couple had the right to hang around and scare the hell out of people, they do." Dante looked up at the portrait of the first duke, his expression suddenly unreadable.

"A cold breeze and a stray scent aren't terribly scary." Samantha studied the portrait that held Dante so captivated. "Do you think this was painted before or after Elsbeth was killed?"

"After."

Samantha considered the skillfully rendered portrait. "I think you're right. His face. It's so sad. And there's something about his eyes." She shuddered.

"His face says heartache, the kind that never goes away. But the eyes? I damned sure don't want to meet him walking along the loch at night." He drew her arm through his and took a step toward the doorway to the stairs.

"What about the eyes?" Samantha focused on that small feature of the portrait once more. She had the sensation of falling, falling into something vast and burning. "What do you see?"

"Rage." With an odd little smile, he tugged her along. "Let's go show off my *proper* kilt. I'm not freezing my privates for nothing. The updraft under this thing is no joke."

Even as she gave the portrait one last look, Samantha had

to laugh. She'd laughed and smiled more in the last week than she had in years. Five years to be exact. Cedric had turned her love of the Regency into a trial, something to be hammered into the heads of others and painted onto the canvas of each film like scenery. A perfectly crafted, historically accurate facsimile, but with no more heart or understanding than a Hollywood backdrop. Something had changed.

"No wonder the Scots were such crazy fighters." Dante leaned into her as they crossed the landing and started down the stairs to the entrance hall. "Icicles hanging off the family jewels would make any man want to stab somebody with a sword."

Samantha snorted then let loose an unabashed belly laugh. Dante laughed with her all the way down the stairs. Tears leaked from the corner of her eyes.

"There you are, Mr. Arneaux. Did you forget about your Regency arms lesson?"

Teddy and Miss Randolph walked toward them. Dante stiffened, and Samantha instinctually rubbed her free palm up and down his forearm. A mistake as both of their observers focused like one of his bloodhounds on that very act.

"Well, I can certainly see why you're so late," Teddy said with his signature snotty sneer.

"No, Teddy, I didn't forget." Dante turned to Samantha. "Want to watch me shoot somebody who needs shooting?" This last he said in an attempted whisper. She suspected the weapons instructor heard it anyway.

Squabbling voices drew everyone's attention to two women arguing as they exited the downstairs drawing room.

"Ye cannae tell me he'll look any more handsome in one of those fancy-dress kilts than he does in what he's wearing now," Mrs. Wallace said as she pointed directly at Dante. "If the lad were any more handsome it'd be a crime."

Dante, of course, struck a defiant pose—hands on hips and chin in the air. Samantha rolled her eyes and elbowed him in the side.

"That is not the concept I sent to Mr. Wentworth," Bella Stepford said as she flipped through a large spiral sketch pad. "And it's nearly impossible to duplicate exactly if we have to reshoot back in California. You really don't…."

As the argument continued, Dougal and Robbie slid out of the drawing room and gave the women a wide berth.

Teddy took a step or two closer. The actress followed like a bramble on his *arse*. "We won't be shooting anything today, Mr. Arneaux. I thought we'd work with the swords today. *If* that is acceptable with you."

"You're the weapons master, Teddy. How about it, Doc? Feel like watching me?"

"I think I had better intervene before Mrs. Wallace punches poor Miss Stepford in the nose. If you'll excuse me."

Samantha couldn't help it. She and Dante had decided to indulge in the powerful attraction between them, but she wasn't interested in the whole house knowing it. People like Teddy would always call her expertise into question, but there was no need to provide him with ammunition. All the while, Lily Randolph followed Samantha's every move. She didn't know what the woman's game was, but Samantha damned sure didn't want to play.

Dante caught her arm as she started to walk toward the dressmaking combatants. "Tell Dougal to put five on Mrs. Wallace for me."

"You're horrible." She smiled, despite trying not to.

"How sweet," Miss Randolph said.

Samantha walked away.

"Can it, Lily," Dante said behind her.

"Fuck you, Danny."

"Not even at gunpoint, sweetheart."

Chapter Nine

Samantha took another surreptitious look at the lady's pocket watch pinned to the bodice of her slate blue kerseymere walking dress. She'd picked a spot at the far end of Rosemount's main library, away from the other guests, in order to conduct Dante's lesson in relative privacy. At least she gave herself the privacy excuse. In the three days since his kilt fitting and those passionate kisses, she'd had very little opportunity to spend time alone with him. A good thing for her professionally. Emotionally, not so much. She wanted…more of him unfettered by the necessity to default to the roles they wanted people to see them play.

She huffed an exasperated sigh and turned her attention back to the handbook and film script spread out on the end of the library table where she sat facing the library doors. Despite the lack of privacy, she and Dante had spent a great deal of time together. In that time, she'd learned much more about him. The Hollywood action star was actually quite the scholar. Anything she gave him to read he devoured overnight and remembered nearly every word. He dedicated himself to absorbing every lesson, hers as well as those of

Urquhart, of the dance master, and even those of the master swordsman and all-around pain in the arse, Teddy Rousseau.

Dante had asked her countless questions about the life and behavior of a Regency gentleman. More than that, he'd asked her countless questions about herself—and she'd answered those questions because he listened to her. Samantha had dealt with actors and film people for years. She was no fool, at least she hoped she wasn't. His interest was sincere. He made her think. He made her laugh. He….

She shivered at the ripple of awareness that slithered through her. Before she even raised her head, she knew he had entered the library. After a quick glance at the double doors across the opulent room full of books, she confirmed her ability to sense his presence was all too real. His gaze met hers, and he smiled. He never stopped looking at her, but he did stop at the different little groups of people seated at a card table or on the group of sofas and chairs in front of one of the two hearths long enough to say hello. A treat for her as she got to admire exactly how handsome he was in full Regency Scots regalia.

With a jacket of blue superfine, a silver waistcoat, a crisp white linen shirt, and his Innes plaid kilt, Dante looked like Captain Rothgate stepped out of the pages of Anna's book. The period lighting in the library gave the deep brown hue of his skin the sort of glow found in the gorgeous oil paintings of the Regency. His soft black leather Scots knee boots made little sound as he crossed the library to offer her a precise bow.

"Good afternoon, Miss Samantha. You look lovely this afternoon if I am permitted to say so." He did a creditable job of greeting her until he added the wink at the end.

"Good afternoon, Dante. Please do sit down." She tried to appear stern but had serious doubts as to her success.

"Alone at last," he said softly as he sat in the chair next to hers.

"We are *not* alone, sir. We are in a library full of people. Let's begin your lesson."

"A library the size of the Superdome with a mile of expensive antique carpet between us and that crowd of people you are so worried about." He propped his elbows on the table and rested his chin on his clasped hands. "We could probably get away with a few quick kisses, and they'd never even notice."

"Dante Arneaux." She leaned back in her chair, checked to see if the others had heard what he said, and opened the film script. "A gentleman does not participate in quick kisses in a library where he can be seen by at least half a dozen people or more."

"You're not giving me much incentive to be a gentleman."

"Aren't you the man who said you would do anything to play Captain Rothgate?"

"I…well, yeah, but I didn't realize there'd be no kissing involved." His face had gone a shade pale. He appeared almost startled by her question. She nearly asked him about the sudden change in his demeanor, but decided she was being silly.

"There is kissing involved. You'll be kissing Lily Randolph a great deal in this film."

"Way to kill the mood." He shuddered, then looked across the room to where Lily and Teddy sat together on the cushioned window seat at the other end of the library. "I'm thinking of asking Teddy to be my stand in for all the dangerous scenes."

"Kissing Lily is dangerous?"

"You have no idea." He turned his full concentration on Samantha. "Not nearly as dangerous as kissing you, though."

"Yet another reason for you not to kiss me." She had to

admit the idea of never kissing Dante again didn't sit well with her at all.

"I'll risk it. Kissing Lily, I might lose a lip. Kissing you, I think I'll lose my heart."

Her heart jumped to a gallop. "Dante—Mr. Arneaux—you can't keep saying things like that. I don't want people to think—"

"Samantha." He sat up and lay his forearms on the table in front of him. With one hand, he pulled the script toward him. With the other, he hooked his pinky finger around hers. "I know how important your career is to you. Nobody knows better than me how hard it is for a woman to survive in a business run by men."

His reference to his mother always started a sort of odd rhythm to her heart. They'd talked about her career and how hard she'd worked to get where she was.

"I promise you I will never do anything to compromise your position on this film," he said. "I will never give anyone a reason to doubt why you're here except for the fact you are so damned far past qualified for this job that you passed qualified about five miles back. I know we have to be careful." He glanced back at the rest of the guests. The ones at the card table had grown loud in an enthusiastic way. None of them even acknowledged she and Dante were in the room. "But I don't want to miss a chance to see where this thing between us leads. Do you?" His eyes glittered with an intensity that shook her and turned her on all at once.

That sensation of jumping off a bridge came over her once more. "Yes. I do, Dante. I truly do, but…."

"I kind of like the idea of sneaking around with you, Dr. Higgins. Adds another level of excitement to everything, and when it comes to you, that's saying something." He'd lowered his voice so as not to be heard, but his tone was a deep, erotic rumble that threatened to drain every ounce of common sense from her body. The heat generated from the small spot where their fingers joined sizzled along her nerve endings.

"Oh, I think we agree on that count, Mr. Arneaux, but if you don't stop talking right now, my ability to sneak may be in doubt." She'd never played the siren before. She rather liked it, especially when she noted the rapid speed of Dante's breathing and the hungry way he looked at her. She slipped her finger free of his very slowly, then sat back so as to observe the rest of the room. "And that would be, in Regency terms, quite the scandal."

He sighed dramatically and sat up straight in his chair. "Can't have that, can we?" He nodded slightly toward their fellow boot camp attendees. "We don't want them thinking we are anything but proper." This last he said in his newly minted English accent.

"Indeed. Although I don't think anyone will pay any attention to us with what Teddy and Lily are up to on the settee. He makes Regency rakes look like monks."

Dante laughed softly, watched the couple in question a moment, then leaned closer to Samantha. "According to our friend Robbie, Teddy is not the playboy he seems."

"What do you mean?" Samantha was intrigued or perhaps she simply enjoyed the warmth of Dante's breath on her neck and the trace of his cologne mixed with the exotic scent that was all him.

"Robbie thinks Teddy is gay and chases women to hide his true colors, so to speak. And Robbie would know."

Robbie made no secret of the fact he was gay. Still.... "Teddy? Gay?" Samantha leaned slightly around Dante to peer at Teddy and Lily laughing and flirting shamelessly. "Robbie's missed this one. Trust me, I've known Teddy a long time. He is many things, but he is most definitely not gay."

Dante widened his eyes. He clasped her wrist. "Wait. Please tell me you haven't—"

"What?" She realized too late how her statement sounded. His reaction indicated he was quite jealous. A nice bonus.

"Oh no. I've kissed him, or rather we kissed each other, but…."

"Ewww." He attempted to cover his all too male reaction with juvenile humor. She wasn't buying it.

"Oh, alcohol was involved. Enough for some heated kisses. Not enough for me to land in his bed. But you can understand why I want to appear professional. That happened when I was much younger and first started in this business, and way before I realized what an arrogant arse he is." She suddenly couldn't think of what else to say. There was no comparison between what happened with Teddy and what she felt for Dante. No comparison at all.

"Trust me, I know all about young and stupid." He rubbed her wrist then clasped her hand. With one more hasty glance at Lily and Teddy, Dante slowly lowered his and Samantha's joined hands beneath the library table. A ridiculous and juvenile thing to do, but she found the idea endearing. "People sometimes do things when they're young they'd never do once they're old enough to know better."

"Like sleep with an eighteen-year-old girl?" Samantha hadn't meant to ask him. Something about the beautiful, glamorous Lily and Dante together made her want to slap someone. Someone with long legs, big boobs, and an annoying laugh. She knew the answer, but she still wanted him to say the words. "You never slept with her. That's why she's so angry with you."

A whole host of emotions crossed his handsome face. Surprise. Resignation. And sadness? He squeezed her hand under the table and flipped a few pages of the script with his free hand for the benefit of their distant companions.

"Lily's angry about a lot of things. My not sleeping with her is just one of them. And don't make me some kind of hero because I turned her down. I wanted to. She was hot as hell, and I was the big powerful movie star then." He shook his head. "That's what she was after, or rather her mother was. The power."

"I don't understand." She wanted desperately to understand. The hurt in his words was palpable, and she wanted to soothe that hurt.

"I grew up around women who used their bodies to make a living. My Maw Maw ran a safe house. She did what she could to make sure the women who worked there had a fighting chance at getting out of the business if they wanted to. A lot of them did."

"If they wanted to? Why would any woman want to…."

Maw Maw said there were two kinds of women who came to work for her. Some women sell sex because they think they have no power over their lives and never will. They sell themselves because they believe it's the only way to get the attention of the people with the power."

"Men."

"Yep."

"And the other kind?"

"They think because they have something men want, that they have all the power. And they'll use sex to get what they want because they think it gives them more power. Their whole lives are spent getting even with the first man who ever made them feel weak. The more power they take, the safer they think they'll be."

"Which one has it right?"

"Neither. And if they're lucky, they figure that out before it destroys them." He turned his head slowly to look at Lily.

"Which one was she?"

"Neither. I hope. Her mother was a—" He smiled a little. "She wasn't my Maw Maw. Lily hooking up with me was her mother's idea. I don't know how many men she pimped Lily out to before me, but not long after I turned Lily down, she fired her mother as her agent and broke all ties with her, or so they say. She's run through a lot of men since then, but on her terms. I hope Lily finds someone who will teach her what sex is for, what it means when two people really care about each other."

Lily suddenly laughed so loudly, Samantha and Dante both jumped.

"Teddy, you are so bad," Lily said as she tapped the sword master with her fan.

Everyone in the room grew silent for a moment, but almost immediately went back to what they were doing and discussing.

Samantha met Dante's steady gaze.

"Whatever happens between us, Samantha, it won't be about power or manipulation. I promise you. There is too much good in whatever this is and for what we feel to ever be about that."

"Because we care about each other?" She hoped he didn't hear the breathless need in her voice.

"Aye, lass, we do indeed." His Scots accent was horrid and made her laugh.

Perhaps he'd attribute the sheen of tears that burned her eyes to laughter. This man surprised her at every turn, and he had no idea the power that gave him. Samantha began to believe her inability to resist the lure of a man like Dante Arneaux might be her undoing. Or it might be the one thing she'd been missing for as long as she could remember.

"Before we cause a scandal, let's go over these rules of introductions once more, shall we?"

He leaned over and whispered in her ear, "Only if you promise I can steal some kisses later on."

"You have a deal, Mr. Arneaux." She opened the boot

camp manual and placed it in front of him. "Robbie really thinks Teddy is gay?"

"Apparently, there's a betting pool on the subject."

"How much did you bet?"

"I put five against. Lily doesn't flirt with gay men. When do I get my kisses?"

Samantha covered her mouth with her hand, but not quickly enough. A short squeak of laughter escaped as Danny Arneaux straightened from his ridiculous example of a bow. He fisted his hands on his hips and his huff of disgust at her amusement only made matters worse.

"What?" he finally asked. "What the hell was wrong with that? I stood up when you pretended to enter the room. I bowed when you curtsied. What did I do wrong this time?"

"I'm sorry." She waved her hand to keep from dissolving into gales of laughter. "I shouldn't make fun. I keep forgetting you Americans watch entirely too many princess films."

The action film star dropped onto one of the garden benches before a long, neat hedge of holly and glared at her, his bottom lip poked out like a petulant child. He looked adorably disgruntled and entirely too kissable for her or any other woman's good.

"What's wrong with princess movies? My Maw Maw and I watch them all the time when I manage to make it home for a visit."

She rolled her eyes. "With all due respect to your grandmother, those films give people very unrealistic ideas about manners, royalty, aristocrats, and little girls finding their prince and living happily ever after." Samantha bit back a curse. She shouldn't have said that last bit. "First and foremost, the bows and curtsies they portray are extreme even for the Regency period."

"Extreme? How can anything be too extreme for the Regency?" He said the last word with an exaggerated but somewhat improved British accent. "The rules about men and women are ridiculous. And don't get me started on who gets to sit first at the dinner table. Hell, no wonder those guys spent all their time fighting wars. They were hungry, trussed up in clothes like a prize turkey, and horny as shit. I'll never learn all this." He propped his elbows on his knees and dropped his head into his hands.

Not good. Not good at all. Samantha sighed.

"Of course you will. Your table manners are already perfect. And you have stood every time a lady enters the room from the very first night."

He sat up and rested his palms on each of his muscled thighs. If ever a man was born to wear the buckskin breeches and boots of a Regency gentleman Danny Arneaux was the one.

"That was easy, Doc. I've been doing that since I was old enough to stand up. My mother and then Maw Maw drilled that into my head, literally."

"Literally? Really?"

"Yes, as in they slapped me in the back of the head every time I forgot. I do know what literally means. My mother was a college professor, remember?"

"Well, I hope I won't have to resort to slapping you in the back of the head. Sounds rather painful." She didn't mean to insult his intelligence, though she did so on a regular basis. Working with Cedric Wellesley-Smythe had rubbed off on her and not in a good way.

"Prepared me for playing football, but it's also the reason I went into acting instead of sports medicine. I think half my brains got knocked out onto Maw Maw's living room floor." He grinned.

"Keep trying to sell that dumb football player routine, Mr. Arneaux. I'm not buying it."

"Well, damn. I was hoping you would, and that it would make you feel sorry for me."

She snorted. "Not a chance. Now, stand up." He did as she ordered. "Let's work on a proper bow this time." She stood beside him and placed one hand on his upper chest and one on his back. Using slight pressure, she inclined the top half of his body forward just enough to execute a decent general bow. "See? In most situations that's all it takes."

"Most situations? Let me guess. More rules." He rolled his eyes.

"I'm afraid so. There is a whole section on this in the boot camp handbook I wrote. It's all very simple. For people of higher rank than you, you bow a little lower. For those of lesser rank a simple inclination of the head or a bow like the one I just showed you will do."

"And what about when I want to kiss a lady's hand?"

He shifted to stand in front of her, took her hand, and bowed exactly as she'd shown him before he pressed his warm lips to her hand, which had been cold a moment before in the Highland air. Now the space between her knuckles and her wrist burned and little darts of heat shot all the way up her arm.

"First of all, you never kiss a lady's bare hand, so I hope you have a taste for silk, cotton, or leather. And second, try to make certain you are looking up at a lady's eyes when you do so. Looking at…anything lower than that is rude and more than a bit scandalous."

"That's me," he said. "Rude and scandalous."

She returned to the bench across the pebbled path from his and sat down. "Yes, but Captain Rothgate is not."

Samantha retrieved her copy of the script and her consultant notebook.

Danny sat on the bench opposite her and gathered up his copy of the script, his copy of the boot camp handbook, and the legal pad he had persuaded Eleanor to allow him to use to take notes. "How did you learn all of this stuff, Doc? How does somebody become a period film consultant?"

Now there was an interesting question. What would he think if he knew this was her first film in this position, and she'd only acquired the job on a bet with the film's director? "I have degrees in nineteenth century British literature with an emphasis on women writers, and I have degrees in British history with an emphasis on the Georgian and Victorian eras. My parents were terrified I'd never find a job except perhaps as a part-time history professor."

"I can imagine. College professors barely make a living. My mother got by, but we lived with Maw Maw, and then Mama got sick…. Your parents were probably worried you'd starve."

"I was lucky, I guess." She broke a twig from the wall of abelia behind her. "A film company came to our little village in Suffolk to make a period film. I was just out of university and made a nuisance of myself correcting clothing mistakes and the like. One of the assistant directors suggested I try being a consultant." She shrugged, concentrating on the waxy leaves of the twig in her hand.

"But do you like it? I mean, sounds like you fell into it, kind of like I did with acting."

She glanced up and met his gaze. His question was a sincere one. There was no mockery or disinterest in his expression. He really wanted to know.

"It hasn't been easy. Women as period consultants is a new thing. I've had to work hard and put up with a load of arrogant, insulting pompous old…."

"Assholes? Or, excuse me, pompous old arses." He used his newly acquired British accent again. "But do you like doing it? The actual work dealing with actors and actresses and directors and all of these movie people, do you enjoy it?"

"Actually, I love it. I love being able to help film makers express the author's vision of the story. I love making certain all the little details are right. Jane Austen may not know I'm protecting her work, but authors like Anna Chase do. And I do like being the one who knows all of the answers, at least where the proper bow and the appropriate clothes are concerned."

"Aha!" He pointed at her with mock severity. "I knew it. You love being in charge and teaching us ignorant Americans the proper way to behave."

"You've caught me out," she agreed with a laugh. "What about you? How did you decide on acting after football? Do you love the work or does it just pay the bills?"

"Actually, I decided on acting because I got tired of seeing myself on billboards in nothing but my drawers everywhere I looked. At least in movies I wasn't naked for more than a scene or two. I got to drive great cars, shoot guns without hurting anyone, and blow stuff up. It was like being paid to play video games in real life."

"And do you love it?"

"I did. For a long time. But now, I kind of want to tell stories with more…I don't know. More real people and more real emotions. I want to do something grown up." He gave her a sheepish half-smile. "Silly, right?"

"Not at all. Our reasons for doing this are the same. We want to tell stories that matter, that people will remember." They sat together in the duke's elegant gardens and listened to the wind and the sound of the sheep in the distance.

"I think your parents should be very proud of you, Dr. Samantha Higgins. You've worked your way up in this business, and you're the lead consultant on one of the biggest period films to come out of Hollywood. Not bad for a little girl from…Suffolk, is it?"

"Yes, well." She took a breath to steady her voice. "The proof will be in the pudding, Dante Arneaux. Neither of us will have a job if I cannot set your British accent in stone in that brain your grandmother tried to smack out of your head. Back to work." She opened her script and looked for some dialogue for them to practice.

"Damn. That backfired on me, big time. I'll practice, but if you have me recite the rain in Spain stays mainly on the plain, I'll lay down on this nice grass and kick and scream like I did when I was five years old." He got up and stretched out on the strip of grass before the holly hedge with his script clutched to his chest.

"And what did your Maw Maw do about your kicking and screaming fits?" The man was entirely too enticing lying in the grass, and he knew it, damn him.

"She did what any self-respecting Cajun Maw Maw would do. She spanked me." He rolled onto his side to face her and gave her a suggestive leer. "How about it, Doc? Wanna give me a spanking?"

"Regency gentlemen do not ask ladies to spank them." She handed him her script opened to a page of dialogue.

"No wonder they didn't bow low," he grumbled as he got to his feet and looked at the script. "A man can't bend over when he's suffering from a case of blue—"

"Mr. Arneaux!" It was all she could do not to fall onto the grass laughing.

"The rain in Spain stays mainly on the plain," he recited dutifully.

Chapter Ten

Samantha spent the next week helping Eleanor make adjustments in the boot camp routine, which included smoothing over the hurt feelings Lily Randolph's constant complaints caused with nearly everyone in the house, including Dante's dogs. That morning, Lily had managed a perfectly performed Regency fit of the vapors that landed her at the feet of the duke all because the dog, Marie, had dropped a stick beside her. The actress had screamed "snake" and fainted dead away. Samantha had to recruit one of the estate gardeners to help the duke carry Lily to her room. Dante had insisted he needed to take his dogs upstairs before his weapons lesson. She suspected he simply didn't want to be around when Lily decided to come out of her faint.

Once Samantha had taken care of that crisis and assured Rosemount's cook, Mrs. Gordon, that eel pie was indeed a perfectly acceptable Regency dish to serve, though not a terribly appetizing one, Samantha sought out the butler, Abercrombie, to determine where Teddy might be conducting today's Regency arms lesson.

"Allow me to escort you, Dr. Higgins," Abercrombie said, small hamper in hand, as he led her down the steps from the back terrace and through the formal gardens at the rear of the house. "His Grace is observing Mr. Arneaux's instruction and has sent for libation."

Libation?

What about Dante's first shooting lesson had turned it into an event for which they required libation? Samantha held that question on the tip of her tongue, the need to know caused her to purse her lips. Butlers like Abercrombie didn't answer questions as to their employer's reasons for doing what they did, especially when that employer was a duke. Once they'd left the formal gardens behind and crossed a gated walkway across a wide ha-ha ditch that separated those gardens from the undulating emerald sheen of the estate's pastureland, the reports of gunfire reached them.

"No need to worry, ma'am," Abercrombie said at her slight jump. "They will not be firing in this direction. His Grace has a firm policy against shooting in the direction of the house."

"An excellent policy." Samantha flinched again despite knowing what to expect. She'd been on plenty of movie sets with live gunfire. Something about the tender serenity of Rosemount made the day's gunfire more...violently intrusive.

"Here we are, Dr. Higgins." Abercrombie conducted her to a cluster of expensive camp chairs arranged around a bale of hay onto which the butler spread a white cloth from the hamper. In moments, he had a tray of cheeses and fruits, small china plates, and delicate silver forks, accompanied by brandy snifters and a bottle of expensive brandy set out as beautifully as any formal dinner table.

She started to lower herself into one of the chairs when she spotted the duke standing several yards ahead of her.

Abercrombie strode to his side and leaned close to make himself heard above the report of the Baker rifle Dante fired at the target attached to a thick wall of hay bales. The duke turned and offered Samantha a slight bow. He waved her forward, and she complied. Of course, she did. Twenty-first century or not, he was a duke.

They stood side by side and watched as Dante took each of the firearms handed him and fired round after round into the bullseye of the target. Teddy's voice droned on and on, filling in the smoky lulls between shots. Either the weapons expert's instruction was so clear as to produce immediate results, or Teddy wasted all that hot air on lessons Dante didn't need.

What Samantha didn't need right now was the sight of Hollywood's favorite lady's man standing out there like something out of a Highlander movie. Not even her hottest teenaged fantasies had conjured up the weak-in-the-knees hunger Dante Arneaux in a kilt did. In anything, actually. Or nothing at all. *Damn!*

To hell with *Regency* boot camp. For the sake of her career, she'd been stuck at a *sex slimming* camp for the past five years, and just a few feet away stood a five-course come-to-mama sizzling buffet. She sneaked a peek at the duke, thankful he wasn't able to see the steam she imagined boiling out of her every pore.

"Dr. Higgins, your student is quite the marksman." His Grace stood with arms crossed and feet braced as he watched Dante take aim and fire again. "His skills with the claymore and the cavalry saber are rubbish according to Mr. Rousseau, but his talent with firearms has left the man speechless."

"Teddy? Speechless?" Samantha pulled her wool shawl more tightly around her shoulders. How could she be cold and on fire at the same time? "Or do you mean what he is saying is not fit for mixed company?"

The duke let loose a short bark of laughter. The man was handsome in an austere sort of way when he wasn't frowning at everything and everyone. Most especially—

"Miss Witherspoon," the duke announced as the young American woman came up the hill to join them. "Come to see the show?"

Samantha had seen Britain's finest thespians slip into a character with less speed. The duke became positively severe at the sight of the gorgeous redhead. Miss Witherspoon either hadn't seen the change or didn't give a damn. Samantha's money was on the latter.

Dante, Teddy, and a pair of ghillies, the young men's arms loaded down with antique guns, were now trudging their way.

"Is Mr. Arneaux finally showing up that horse's rear of a sword instructor?" Eleanor said. "How about it, Dr. Higgins? How is your boy doing? Oh my. He's impressive as hell in that kilt, isn't he?"

Samantha blinked. Eleanor had given the duke the *cut direct* better than any nineteenth-century chick had ever dared. She'd turned away from the man and acted as if she didn't know him better than any British actress playing a dismissive character in any period drama Samantha had ever seen. She made a note to have Eleanor show the women in Wentworth's film how to deliver the cut correctly.

Eleanor looked at her, and Samantha realized she hadn't answered her question.

"Mr. Arneaux decided he wanted a proper kilt after seeing the portrait of the first duke, your ancestor, I believe, Your Grace?" Samantha replied in a neutral tone, and looked at the duke. She hadn't missed Eleanor's reference to Danny as "your boy."

"The portrait in the gallery?" His Grace replied, his cold scrutiny fixed on Eleanor. "Yes, I am a direct descendant of that gentleman. He fought at Bannockburn."

"So Dougal and Robbie said. But it was Mrs. Wallace who told us about the Innes Witch," Samantha said.

The duke turned toward her, very much the laird of all he surveyed. Including her presumptuous self. "Indeed." Never had one word conveyed so much disdain.

Eleanor rolled her eyes, which made Samantha want to laugh. Then she caught a glimpse of Dante striding up the hill in his kilt and boots, his shirt open at the throat and a Baker rifle in the crook of his arm. *Impressive as hell* didn't begin to cover it. The last rays of sun covered the green fields as it sank behind him. The waning glow touched his dark hair and brought out the mahogany highlights struck by the fading light. He turned from his discussion with Teddy and, as he spotted Samantha, her blood turned to lava, slow and bubbling in her veins.

"Oh my," she and Eleanor murmured almost in unison.

"I should have known." Teddy's voice carried as the shooting party neared. "I cannot hope to have this man ready for filming if he continues to be distracted by you, Samantha."

"I beg your pardon?" A sudden chill caused goose bumps to pop up on Samantha's arms and across her shoulders despite the coverage of her Regency walking dress.

"Losing the light, my ass. The minute he saw you watching him, Arneaux decides he's done shooting. I see now why Wentworth hired you."

"Hold this, Your Grace." Dante handed the duke his Baker without breaking stride. The duke took the weapon without question.

Teddy prattled on as he continued toward the refreshments Abercrombie had arranged. "I should have known with this one's appetite for pretty girls. Seduce him on your own time, *Dr.* Higgins, if you—"

Dante caught up with him. Samantha gasped as he clapped a hand onto Teddy's shoulder, swung him around, and drove his fist into Teddy's jaw.

Crack!

Samantha and Eleanor shrieked and sprang apart just in time for Teddy to come flying between them and slide several feet back down the hill. The ghillies continued up the hill as if nothing had happened. The duke waved them toward the house. The two young men tugged at their caps and didn't give Teddy, sprawled in the grass, a second look. They did, however, give Dante a nod as they walked past him. Samantha swiveled her head from Dante to Teddy and back again. Several times. It didn't help. She still had no idea what had just happened, or why.

"Nice one," the duke said. "Abercrombie, see to Mr. Rousseau."

"Of course, Your Grace."

The butler strode down the hill and hauled Teddy to his feet. He practically dragged the poor glassy-eyed fellow, jacked up by one elbow, down to the ha-ha, across the bridge, and into the gardens toward the house. Neither Dante nor the duke spared the injured man a glance. In fact, Dante now stood over the tray of food, popping cubes of cheese and pieces of cut up fruit into his mouth. In between, making a muck of trying to check out Samantha's expression. He was about as subtle as…a sock to the foremost Regency weapons expert's jaw.

Bloody damned hell!

Samantha wanted to smack herself upside the head. Her ability to think had gone to Ibiza. Pity she couldn't join it. What just happened? Other than her professionalism and most of her reputation going up in smoke.

"I guess I should go and check on Mr. Rousseau." Miss Witherspoon marched around the duke without acknowledging him. "After all, I am in charge of this little adventure."

"So I've heard," the duke said to no one in particular.

Miss Witherspoon stopped mid-stride and turned back to where Samantha, the duke, and Dante stood. "Idiot man."

Whoa!

"I mean Mr. Rousseau, of course," she said sweetly with a half-assed curtsy.

"I'm coming too." Samantha's brain finally kicked into gear. "I'm supposed to be helping you. Not…." She waved a hand as any word she chose to finish that thought with would only make matters worse. If that was possible. Teddy wasn't the only idiot at Rosemount Manor.

"Samantha, this wasn't your fault." Dante walked toward her, hand outstretched. "He was being a horse's ass, um arse. He had no right to—"

She slapped his hand away and got close enough for the long skirt of her dress to cover the toes of his boots. "Teddy is always an ass, um arse. You should have ignored him. Now his suspicions are confirmed and everyone in the house will know it. Do me a favor. Start acting like a damned professional actor instead of an action star with a hot body." She turned and ran to join Eleanor. Samantha's eyes burned, and her throat felt like she'd swallowed hot coals. She didn't look back.

"Samantha, I—"

"Don't even think about it," the duke said.

Eleanor took her arm and guided her back toward the ha-ha. "Sonofabitch is smarter than he looks," she muttered. "For a duke. Want to tell me what that was all about?"

"Nothing." Samantha kept her focus on the French doors at the back of the house—a point on the horizon, like when she'd gone sailing with her father as a child. So long as she stayed fixed on that point, she wouldn't be sick. Talk about unprofessional.

"Know what you're going to do about it?" Eleanor asked as they stepped into the house.

"Fuck if I know."

"Well at least you have a plan."

Chapter Eleven

"Don't even think about it, lad."

The duke's accent didn't go from Brit to Scot often, but Danny had figured out it usually did when the shit had just hit the fan. Now, if he could just decide if he was the shit or the fan. Or both. He ran a hand over his face and collapsed into one of the camp chairs. The duke claimed the chair on the other side of the hay bale table, grabbed a cube of cheddar, and chewed on it while looking over the endless pastureland. He offered Danny the bowl of strawberries.

"Thanks," Danny said.

"You *should* thank me. I just saved your life."

"I think I already proved I can take ole Teddy-boy." Danny bit into one of the strawberries and fought the urge to get up and go after Samantha.

"I was referring to Dr. Higgins." The duke stretched out his legs and crossed his feet at the ankles. "Not to mention her red-headed backup."

"True that. Thanks."

"You're welcome. That's my job," the duke replied, an unmistakable bitter weariness in his tone.

"Your job?"

"Taking care of everyone in the dukedom. Upholding the family honor. Sacrificing my dreams on the altar of defending the clan. Cleaning up my father's mess for the last two years. All that sort of rot."

"Damn. Don't you have some type of choice?"

"Not according to my family. This"—he waved his hand around to indicate the house behind them and the land in front of them—"was all perfectly fine while my father drank and whored himself slowly to death, but the minute the old man was in the grave, it was all destined to disintegrate if I didn't take up the reins." He rubbed the back of his neck and adopted a hang-dog expression. "Sorry. Ignore my rubbish. You've got the more immediate problem. You have at least two women ready to kill you."

Danny chuckled and picked up the bottle of brandy. He pretended to read the label. What the hell was he thinking? He knew better than anyone the stupidity of reacting to some gossip's suspicions. Teddy was probably pissed because Samantha wouldn't give him the time of day—and Danny had stepped right into it.

"I wasn't thinking," Danny said.

"Oh, you were thinking. Just using the wrong head. Are we going to drink that?"

"Should we?" Danny handed him the bottle.

"Hell, yes. At this point it's a moral imperative. Get the glasses."

The duke unwrapped the top of the bottle, grabbed the corkscrew and uncorked the brandy. Once they each had a snifter full in hand, they sat back and stared straight ahead at the setting sun.

"Want to talk about it?" the duke asked.

"Want to talk about the Innes Witch? Or family obligations?" Danny chugged half of his glass of brandy.

He waited for an answer but knew he wouldn't get one. Family secrets were worse than secrets between…. Hell, he wasn't Samantha's lover. Or her boyfriend. He was simply the guy who'd just decked a man for insulting her, and she'd handed Danny his ass for it.

He sucked down the rest of his brandy and stuck his glass out for the duke to refill.

"What the hell is your name? I know your title. What do your friends call you?"

"Most people call me Turra. You can call me Knox." He raised his glass, and the two of them made a toast. The touch of their glasses echoed in the silence.

"I'm Danny, but you know that. For a broke-assed duke you keep some fine damned brandy."

"I said my father pissed all the money away. I didn't say he pissed it all away on useless shite. Rosemount has a legendary wine cellar."

"All my father left me was an old pickup truck and a couple of shotguns."

"No debts?"

"Nope. No debts and no money. Not even a name, just my good looks."

"Which you've made lucrative."

"Eh." Danny shrugged. "I've been lucky. That's about it."

"A bit more than that I should think."

"Maybe."

Danny sipped his brandy and ran through the afternoon's events in his mind. He'd never been angry enough or in a position to punch a guy in defense of a woman before—except maybe Maw Maw when he was in the sixth grade. Nobody called his grandmother a whore and got away with it. Nobody. Granted, Claudine Arneaux had a right hook that had taken down thugs, gangsters, and even a few corrupt NPD officers, so him defending his

Maw Maw hadn't been necessary. She was perfectly capable.

Merde!

"I shouldn't have hit him." Danny leaned forward, forearms on his knees and brandy snifter balanced between his fingertips.

"Probably not. Especially in public."

"I take it the only British women who go for that whole knight in shining armor thing are the ones in the movies. Or in romance novels."

"News bulletin, Danny. No man, Brit or Yank, knows what the hell a woman goes for on any given day. It's like playing the bloody Lotto. Hell, even Elizabeth Bennett told Mr. Darcy to go bugger himself."

"I should have read *that* version."

Knox laughed. "Oh, you've definitely made a muck of it."

"I embarrassed her."

"Yes. And you all but took out an advert in the Daily Mirror declaring yourself her protector, so to speak."

Danny sat up. "It's not like that. We haven't…that is…. She would hate people thinking she needed a protector."

Knox waved him off. "I daresay that's not what has her knickers in a twist the most."

Danny snorted brandy through his nose. Damn that stung!

"Do tell," he finally said.

"You usurped her chance to knock the tosser arse over the teakettle herself. A woman like our Dr. Higgins…."

"Is definitely a do-it-herself kind of girl." God, he was an idiot.

"You knew that."

"I did."

"And you hit Teddy anyway."

Danny gave the duke a good old American *eat-shit* look. "I take it you've had a lot of experience with—"

"Mucking it up with women and making them think I see them as the weaker sex? On a daily basis. But I'm a duke. I'm supposed to be a horse's *arse*. It's in the handbook."

"I didn't rescue her because I think she's weak. Sometimes women need to be rescued because they're tired. After putting up with men like Teddy for years, I guess I just thought Sam—Dr. Higgins was tired."

"Hmm. Never thought of it like that. Dr. Higgins is a clever woman. She might consent to being tired. God knows I am." Knox stared down into his glass.

"How long have you been at this duke business?"

"Part-time, two years. Full-time, about six months when my father died."

"Doc's been dealing with men like Teddy for at least five years."

Teddy had also kissed her, which was a big part of the reason Danny wanted to beat the man to a pulp. Well, damn. That was a bad sign for Teddy, but a good sign that Danny had a real thing for Samantha. Very real.

"Well, when you put it that way, I'd say she's definitely got every right to be tired," Knox said.

They sat and watched the last of the sun's rays disappear behind the rolling hills of Rosemount. Danny got to his feet and stretched, brandy glass still in hand.

"Kind of like families getting tired. Sometimes families get tired of holding down the fort and they need someone to come along and take up that sword." Danny glanced at the duke who now stood at his side.

Knox raised his glass and touched it to Danny's. "To taking up that sword."

"To taking up that sword."

A couple of the footmen spotted them as Danny and the duke crossed the ha-ha and ambled toward the house. The servants met them at the foot of the bridge, offered the duke a bow then ran up the hill to retrieve the camp chairs and dishes.

"You're not as dumb as people think you are, Mr. Arneaux."

"And you're not as big an ass as people say you are, Your Grace. Although I am pretty sure I'm going to get mine kicked somewhere in the process of apologizing to my Regency coach. Got any words of wisdom?"

"Might want to give her some time to cool off. Even then, duck and cover, Yank. Duck and cover."

DANNY TRUDGED UP THE NARROW DIRT LANE AND DID HIS BEST to keep the ball-freezing Highland wind from blowing up his kilt and exposing his ass to anyone else who happened to be making the trip from the manor to the duke's brother's cottage. Not that anyone else likely would. It wasn't a really long walk, but long enough to make him wish he'd kept his breeches on after his morning ride. And if he hadn't already spent over an hour on horseback at the ungodly hour of seven o' clock he might have stayed on Grenadier and gotten this fool's errand over with much quicker.

That's what Maw Maw called it when someone went off on a quest for help that was not likely to be given. The kind of an errand only a damned fool would waste their time doing. As Danny had decided he was an extra-large economy size fool from the moment he stepped foot on Erik Wentworth's jet and flew to Scotland, he figured he was the right man for the job. Besides, he needed help or he was going to end up killing his weapons instructor, and he was pretty sure he'd enjoy it. Sadistic, hound dog asshole wasn't a good combination in a teacher who handled swords like his Great Uncle Prejean handled a toothpick.

The towering thick hedges on each side of the lane finally gave way to stone walls. About fifty yards on, he spotted what the duke had called the gamekeeper's cottage, a large, whitewashed building with a heavy thatched roof and stone chimneys on either end. The cottage was surrounded by a large yard, or garden as they called it here in Scotland, which was walled in on the sides and back. Those walls met the wall running along the lane at the front and there was a wooden gate that separated the cottage area from the lane.

A section of the wall just past the gate appeared to have fallen down some. Danny had seen the duke's brother, Lachlan, before but only from a distance. There was a man remaking the wall and if he wasn't Lachlan Innes he missed a good chance. It was freezing ass cold and this man was naked from the waist up and wore a traditional kilt and boots. He was hefting damned fifty something pound rocks like they were tennis balls. This should be interesting.

"Lord Lachlan?" Danny called as walked past the gate to where the Scot was fitting rocks together with no sign of cement or mortar. "I'm Danny Arneaux. Your brother and Miss Witherspoon said you might be able to help me?"

"Lachlan," the young Scot said as he lifted a large flat stone onto the wall and wedged it into place.

"Excuse me?"

"My name is Lachlan, just Lachlan."

Well, this conversation was getting off to a great start. "Okay. Lachlan. I'm in the film that's going to be shot here. And—"

"I know who ye are, Arneaux."

"Well, Knox said you might work with me on this sword stuff. The claymore. I suck at it."

"Knox?" Now Lachlan did look at him. "You call my brother Knox?"

"Yeah. That's his name, isn't it?"

Lachlan wiped his hands on his kilt and gave Danny a once over somewhere between amusement and suspicion.

"He told me to call him Knox."

"Hmmm." Lachlan went back to sorting through the pile of stones along the back of the wall.

Fuck this. Like Maw Maw said, a fool's errand. He'd been an idiot to think the estate's resident hermit would come out of hiding to help the Yank actor. "Okay, well it was nice to meet you. Lachlan." Danny turned to go back the way he came. "Have a good one." He flung up his hand and started to walk away.

"I thought Elle hired a sword master to teach you. Damned good one from what I've seen."

Danny stopped in his tracks, turned, and ambled back to the gate. "He is good. And the pompous bastard knows it too. Said I'd never learn to swing a claymore properly." He said the last word with his newly learned fancy British accent.

"Of course he does. He's a Brit. They're born arrogant and only grow more arrogant as they age. Good with a claymore though."

"Not so good with his fists," Danny muttered, but Lachlan definitely caught what he said.

He raised an eyebrow and waited for Danny to explain.

"He pissed me off. So, I punched him in the face."

"You punched him in the face because he insulted your claymore skills? Here, hold this." He handed Danny a thick flat stone over the gate.

"I punched him because he insulted Saman…Dr. Higgins."

"Ah. That'll do it. Give me the rock." Lachlan took the rock and fitted it on top of another.

"He treats women like crap. I don't know what they see in him. Must be the damned hair in a ponytail thing."

"Might be." Lachlan pulled his own long hair back and tied it with a thin strip of leather.

Danny winced. Nice. If he kept this up the Scot would punch *him* in the face.

"Come around." Lachlan motioned at the gate.

"He's a horse's ass." Danny held out his hands for the stone the Scot shoved at him.

"I thought you knew. Women like horses." Lachlan grinned. "But if Mrs. Wallace catches another of the maids creeping out of Rousseau's room at dawn, she's going to geld him or worse."

"What? Which maid? And what could be worse than Mrs. Wallace gelding a man? We both know she wouldn't stop to use anesthesia."

"Katie Grace. Upstairs maid. Yer too right about Mrs. Wallace, but if she tells Knox about Rousseau's shagging the help that Brit will be on his way back to London with a claymore up his arse. My brother has strict rules about that because of our whore of a father."

"Damn." Danny handed Lachlan the next stone and started looking through the pile for one that might fit next. "I thought Teddy was fucking, I mean shagging Miss Stepford's assistant, Abby. He one night stand's her, and Abby will make his life hell. She slashed a guy's tires and smashed his windshield with a baseball bat for dumping her. She's worked on one of my films before."

"Bloody hell. Give me that one." He pointed at the stone Danny had chosen.

"And the car was a 1966 Corvette."

"Och, now that was criminal."

They both paused in silence in deference to the Corvette.

"How did you find out about Teddy and Katie Grace?"

Danny asked as he walked around the spot where Lachlan was working and searched through another pile of stones. Then he thought about what he'd asked.

He and Lachlan looked up at the same time.

"Robbie," they said in unison.

Danny laughed. "That man should be working for the CIA."

"Or MI5," Lachlan agreed. "He has an idea about who Rousseau will try to seduce next."

"Who?"

"Miss Randolph." The Scot's tone was casual, but his attitude was anything but. He wiped his face and leaned against the section of wall they'd nearly completed.

"Lily?"

"Aye. Ye two have a history?"

The hair on the back of Danny's neck stood up. "No. We don't, but if Teddy sets his sights on her, he'll be history. Lily Randolph will eat him alive."

"That bad, is she? She's always been kind to me." Lachlan's expression made Danny's stomach hurt. Shit!

"Look, Lachlan. Lily's kind of like two people. And it really isn't her fault. Her childhood makes yours and Knox's, from what he's told me, look like a Hallmark movie. You have to be careful with her. Sometimes she's nice to people because she wants something from them, and that's the only way she knows how to get it. She was raised that way."

"What way?"

Lachlan was already jumping to defend her. Danny heard it in those two words alone.

"To believe that the only thing she has to offer is her body and her fame. Her mother was a four-star bitch. She used Lily for her ability to make money and her ability to get invitations to all the right parties and premieres. She trotted her around like a trained pony from the time Lily did her first breakfast cereal commercial. She robbed her blind and taught her how to use and abuse people. Lily despises me, but I've always felt sorry for her."

"Ye said she is two people. What is the other Lily like?" he asked quietly.

Danny sighed. He knew he was going to regret this because he liked Knox's brother. He seemed like one of the good guys. But even if no one else in Lily's life was fair to her, Danny had to be. Because that was the way he was raised. *Thanks a lot, Maw Maw.*

"She donates money to animal shelters, even when she hasn't had a film in years. When her fitness coach and his husband lost their jobs, she hired them to be her personal trainer and housekeeper and moved them into her house. She's a damned good actress, better than I'll ever be. She's been engaged five or six times, but I think it's because she really believes in love and romance. And she's never gone after any of them after they split, even when they sold their stories and some really disgusting pictures to the tabloids. I'd have sued their asses off. She didn't."

"Sounds as if she's a very confused lady. Can't decide who she wants to be. Or maybe people won't let her be who she wants to be." Lachlan picked up another huge stone and placed it into a long gap in the wall. "Happens to the best of us, I expect."

Danny opened his mouth to warn Lachlan against getting involved with Lily. Something stopped him. Maybe it was the way the Scot went back to work. Maybe it was the heather scented breeze that swirled around him, much warmer than the wind that had been chafing his bare ass under his kilt.

"So," Lachlan said as he straightened and pressed his hands against his lower back. "Ye'll come back tomorrow for some more training?"

"Training?" Danny glanced around at the piles of rocks and the nearly completed wall. "This has been training?"

"Aye. Ye've no hope of besting Rousseau with a claymore if you don't build up those arms. They're strong enough for Sassenach lifting, no doubt. But we'll need to do some work to make them fit for lifting a claymore. Tomorrow morning around eight?"

"Why not?" Danny said, his words a half groan. "Urquhart can bust my balls while I'm riding Grenadier from seven to eight, and you can bust the rest of me from eight to nine. Can't wait." He went through the gate and reached over it to shake Lachlan's hand. "Thanks, Lachlan. See you tomorrow." He started back toward the manor.

"Arneaux?"

Danny turned back.

"Nobody is ever what they seem. Showing people who you really are is hard. Rousseau may be a horse's arse, but he came down here to ask if I wanted him to move the shooting practice off the estate to a range in the village. He likely has his reasons for being an arse. Just like Lily Randolph has her reasons for being…."

"A difficult woman?" Danny offered.

"Aye."

"Hell, Lachlan, all women are difficult women, but its only because all men are complete idiots, Highlanders or not."

He waved and continued his stroll up the lane. Lachlan's deep, rusty laughter put a spring in his step. The Innes brothers had overcome a shitshow of a childhood. Maybe Lily could too. Easy compared to what he had to do next— unfuck what he'd fucked up with Samantha by punching Teddy in the nose. He'd rather go back and stack stones.

Chapter Twelve

DANNY SHUFFLED THE CARDS IN HIS HAND AND SNEAKED A peek at the antique clock on the mantel for the five hundredth time in the last hour. He didn't even try to check out the card table across the drawing room. The one where Samantha, the duke, Mr. McGinty, and Miss Stepford played whist with all the excitement of patients in a waiting room at the dentist's office.

Samantha had neither spoken to him nor turned her head in his direction since dinner. Even then, she'd only looked at him to immediately turn her head and walk to the other side of the land yacht of a dining table to sit between McGinty and Mr. Goode. He'd begun to understand exactly what the *cut direct* was all about. His whole chest burned like one big papercut.

She was so pissed at him she'd chewed through an entire plate of haggis without saying a word, which was fine since Lily had bitched about it enough for the entire table. Danny hadn't tasted anything. Not dinner, not dessert. Not a sip of brandy nor a puff of the cigar he and the other guys had lingered over before coming into the drawing room where

Miss Witherspoon, with her usual enthusiasm, had divided them all into pairs for whist. He glanced at the clock again and played a random card from his hand.

"Well done, Mr. Arneaux, we've taken the trick and the game," Mr. Goode announced while the other pair at the table groaned.

"You, sir, are a Captain Sharp," Miss Chase said.

"A who?" Danny tried to pay attention to the authoress even as he caught Miss Witherspoon bending to whisper in Samantha's ear.

"A *Captain Sharpe* is a Regency term for someone who feigns ignorance, but plays cards like a professional gambler," Miss Chase explained. "Are you certain you have never played whist before this week?"

He raised his hand. "Scout's honor. But I spent God knows how many hours at my Maw Maw's kitchen table playing Rook with her and her little old lady posse. You want to talk about some Captain Sharpes? I'm lucky I got out of there with my shirt."

The other tables of players broke up. Some went to the sideboard for a last tipple. Others stopped at the tea table for a final cup of tea. Lily and the guy in charge of set design stood in front of the roaring fire discussing life without cell phones. Samantha sipped her tea while Miss Witherspoon talked about the gardens. Miss Chase and Mr. Goode said their good nights then headed for the first-floor landing and the stairs.

"Join me in the library for a moment," the duke said quietly as he stepped to Danny's side.

"Um, sure."

Danny sought out Samantha across the room, but she deliberately focused her attention on Mr. McGinty. Miss Witherspoon, however, gave Danny a wink and the duke a stern nod. *What the hell?* Never in a million years would he have picked these two people as co-conspirators. Oil and water didn't even begin to explain the relationship between the duke and the Regency boot camp director.

In the library, Danny followed the duke to the French doors at the far end of the room where, leashed up and waiting, Marie and Laveau lay unusually still, save for their wagging tails. The doors led to a terrace then the gardens. Danny gazed out to take in the length of the terrace.

"Miss Witherspoon is going to persuade Dr. Higgins to take a stroll," the duke said. Right on cue, the doors at the far end of the terrace opened, and the two ladies headed into the lamp-lit hedges and flower beds. "In a minute or two, the headmistress of this little experiment will make an excuse to come back inside." He glanced down at the dogs whose tails reached Keith Moon drum solo status. "At which point you will take these two creatures out for their evening constitutional and accidentally come upon Dr. Higgins."

"I see." Danny picked up the leashes and scanned the steps for Eleanor's return.

"I bloody well hope so. You have no idea how lowering it is for me to play matchmaker." He gave a William Shatner worthy shudder.

"Almost as lowering as having to take orders from Eleanor?"

"Bugger off."

They both watched as the red-headed event planner hurried inside, but not before she waved at them and gave them a thumb's up.

"Don't fuck this up, Yank. I only participate in about one romantic notion every decade." The duke tapped two fingers to the side of his head and headed to one of the library chairs.

"Hey, Knox," Danny called.

The duke turned his head, eyebrow raised.

"Thanks."

"Good luck."

Danny stared into the night and went over about seventeen different ways to start a conversation with Samantha. Seventeen ways to start without her ignoring him or kicking him in the kilt. He clicked his tongue at the dogs and opened the French doors.

"You two are no help," he muttered as they scrambled to their feet and bum-rushed him out the door. "She's been sneaking you two moochers sausage from the breakfast buffet every morning since we got here. She doesn't have to sleep with your farty asses."

He spent about fifteen minutes wandering around the hedges, fountains, statues, and flower beds like Moses in the damned desert before he figured out the best way to find Samantha was to go sheriff's department on her and loose the hounds. Once he unclipped their leashes, his two loyal companions left him like a chewed-up Nike, and in minutes all he had to do was follow the sound of her sweet-talking their traitorous hides.

"Hello, my darlings. What are you doing out here all alone? Your father will have Robbie's guts for garters if anything happens to you two. Daddy loves you very—oh!"

Samantha froze as Danny rounded the hedge. Kneeling between the two dogs, with an arm around each as she scratched their ears, she took his breath away. He'd heard and read that expression over and over all his life, but never really understood it until now.

In the combined light of the moon and the gas lights on posts all over the gardens, she was like one of those old-world paintings of a farm girl or a shepherdess. The cold night air might be responsible for her rosy cheeks, but everything else was pure Samantha Higgins. Her fondness for his slobbering pooches shone in her eyes. Away from the pressure of being the go-to Regency expert, she was just a happy woman, relaxed and enjoying a moonlit walk in the kind of gardens someone like her probably dreamed of on a regular basis. She was….

"Exquisite."

"Beg pardon?" She stood, and the dogs leaned into her in search of more petting. Smart dogs.

"I'manidiot." Great. Now he was speaking in tongues. Maw Maw would be so proud.

"Good night, Mr. Arneaux." She rose and stepped around him.

"I. Am. An. Idiot," he said, employing the English accent she'd so patiently taught him.

She stopped in her tracks, turned to face him, and crossed her arms over her breasts. "You have my attention."

Now what?

He took a deep breath—which didn't help because the air was like ice. Not to mention the night breezes up his kilt had him wondering how his family jewels could warm themselves.

"I shouldn't have hit Teddy."

"In that we are in complete agreement. All you did was—"

"I should have let you hit him."

Well, that shut her up for a minute. It even got a little smile out of her. A *very* little smile.

"You're perfectly capable of defending yourself, Samantha, and I acted like a damned redneck at a bayou juke joint. I embarrassed you, and I just gave that asshole more fuel for the fire he's trying to stir up."

"Yes. You did. Period film is a small world, Dante. Everyone knows everyone and they're constantly jockeying for position. This is my life." Her voice cracked. She sat on a wrought iron bench and hugged herself tightly, pulling the ends of the thick plaid shawl around her. Marie and Laveau settled at her feet. "I've worked hard to get here, and I can't afford to make mistakes no matter how much I…have come to care for you."

His nuts might be freezing, but his chest burned six ways to Sunday at her words. He'd heard the rest, but suddenly, that last little bit was all that mattered.

"He pissed me off, Doc. He had no right to spout that crap, and I just saw red. I wanted to clean his damned clock."

"Oh, I'd say you did that in spades." She smiled again, but it was a sad smile, and it hurt his heart to see it. "At least we didn't have to put up with him at dinner."

"Bonus," Danny muttered. He sat next to her on the bench. "Don't suppose I hit him hard enough to keep him in his room for the rest of the bootcamp *and* the movie shoot."

"I should think not."

"Should have hit him harder," they said together.

Samantha shook her head.

"I would have done it Regency style and challenged him to a duel," Danny declared. "But Knox said there'd be too much paperwork involved, and he hates paperwork."

"Knox?"

"The duke. That's his first name. Nobody ever calls him that, 'cept maybe his brother."

"I see." Samantha tilted her head back to gaze at the stars.

"I think those guys in the Regency had it right. Calling someone by their first name has a sort of power. It means you trust that person with…who you really are, I guess."

God, he had no clue what the hell he was talking about, but he knew he'd say anything to keep her sitting next to him. She warmed him just by being there, by her drive and passion for her work, for life. In that moment, he realized he'd spent a lot of his working hours with dead people. People just going through the motions for money.

Oh shit!

She was staring at him like he had two heads.

"I think you're right…Dante."

He took her hand and laced their fingers together. "I've decided I like it when you call me Dante. Does it mean you've decided to trust me? Even a little?"

"I want to, very much so, but…." She stole a quick look at the manor house, which had been their home these couple of weeks.

"I understand." God, those words tasted like vinegar.

She traced his mouth with the fingers of her free hand. "Do you really?" She smiled at the little shudder that went through him at her touch.

"Nope. But I'm pretty sure I have the luxury of having a love affair with any woman I want without it holding me back in my career. You don't."

"Love affair?"

She focused her gaze on his face like Laveau looking at a biscuit with gravy—which meant Danny had damned well better get what he next said spot-on. He needed to be damned sure where he was going with this. Easy, right?

"At the very least, Samantha." He gathered both of her hands in his and rubbed them to try and warm them up. "I can't say more than that."

"Why not?" She moved closer until their thighs touched, their arms, their shoulders.

He wasn't cold anymore. "Because if I say any more it's going to scare the hell out of me. And I'm thinking I'm going to need all the guts I can muster to convince you it's worth the risk."

"It?"

The stars in the endless Highland sky reflected in her eyes, and in that minute, she became as vast and mysterious and alluring as that sky. She became everything he'd ever won and lost, finally come back to him.

"Me, *mo chridhe*."

Clouds of icy breath had punctuated their conversation. Samantha's stopped for a minute. Then a minute more. "What did you say?" she finally asked, her voice soft.

Her expression. He wanted to catch it in his hand and never let go. His heart hammered against his ribs and every breath hurt like hell.

"Mo chridhe. Did I say it right? Knox taught me. He said it might come in handy. Said I should use it if I thought you were going to walk away, and I was bloody clever enough to know I didn't want you to walk away."

"Do you know what it means? Because I do."

"No, but if it makes you look at me like that, I'll never forget it."

"Like what?"

The dark, rough tone of her voice sent hot shivers all over his body, like fireworks over the bayou on the Fourth of July.

"The way I've wanted a woman to look at me all my life."

"Oh hell," she murmured.

"Oh hell, *I'm going to slap the taste out of your mouth*, or *oh hell, please kiss me?*"

"You're a silver-tongued devil, Dante Arneaux." She grabbed his head with both hands, pulled him down and planted a kiss so sudden and so hard on him his heart stopped for at least a hundred beats. She released him and leaned back enough to look him in the eye. "And I am a bloody fool."

"I love a matched set. Come here, woman."

Danny wrapped his arms around her and lifted her into his lap. He tilted her back against his arm so her face was bathed in moonlight. His hand was shaking, dammit. Didn't matter. He touched two fingers to her cheek. The softness of her skin went straight through him in fissures of heat and electric current so sweet he hardly breathed.

He walked his fingertips across her face in search of branding the memory of her expression, her beauty into his touch memory forever. Her eyes drifted closed, and he brushed his forefinger across her lids and eyelashes. When he bent and traced her lips with his tongue, her tongue darted out to sear his. He shuddered. She smiled.

Oh, hell yeah!

He captured her mouth in a kiss so fierce it frightened even him. Thank God she responded with a fierceness of her own. She gave as good as she got and then some. When she opened to him and wrapped her tongue around his, he groaned so deep he was pretty damned sure they heard him in Edinburgh. He hauled her up against his chest. No matter how hard he tried, she wasn't close enough. She sifted her hands through his hair and held fistfuls as if he might back away. *Not a snowball's chance in hell of that.*

His brain short-circuited, but other parts of his body came online with a vengeance. Samantha, wicked woman she was proving to be, moved against the ridge in his kilt to the point he had to break their kiss to gasp for air.

"Is that yer sword under yer kilt?" she asked, mimicking the Wallace sisters' brogue. "Or are ye just happy to see me?"

He loved her like this—eyes sparkling, well-kissed lips turned up in a sultry grin, cheeks flushed, and her hair tumbling from all the pins and braids.

"I don't know, lassie." He stuck with his newly learned British accent, with a hint of Dougal's Highland tone. "Why don't you reach up under there and find out?"

Her hand on his thigh made him jump, her palm steaming hot against his chilled flesh. The dogs leaped to their feet and ran toward the house.

Danny cupped Samantha's left cheek and touched his lips to her right. "You are so incredibly—"

"Bloody hell, get off me, you daft buggers!" the duke growled.

Samantha slid off Danny's lap so fast she almost landed on the cobblestone footpath. Danny grabbed her, dropped her on the bench, then stood to adjust his kilt. Damned near impossible to do with his cock ready to do a twenty-one-gun salute.

The duke came around the corner with his kilt turned sideways and what looked like a hedge branch in his hair, followed closely by two happy, slobbering bloodhounds. Knox tossed the leashes in Danny's direction.

"These two are a bloody menace. I'm going to have to deal with a highly pissed gardener when he sees where they knocked me into the boxwoods."

Danny gave his kilt one last tug. "They're not the only ones who are a menace. Your Grace."

"Dante," Samantha said in warning, a gentle hand on his arm.

"His timing sucks alligator ass."

The only thing more aggravating than icy Highland air on a man's dick was icy Highland air on his dick when it was hard as a brick bat. Danny ran his hand through his hair, then clasped the one Samantha had around his wrist.

The duke blinked a few times and cleared his throat. "Miss Witherspoon has informed me the lovely Miss Randolph is organizing a group to stroll the gardens before bed. Am I wrong to think the only exercise she is after is catching you two pretty much the way I did, or worse?"

"Shite." Samantha shot to her feet. "What?"

Danny stared at her like an idiot. Apparently, the duke did too.

"Oh, please, gentlemen, grow the fuck up." A buzz of voices filtered down from the terrace. "Now what do we do?"

"Exactly what I came down here to do," Knox said. He

offered Samantha his arm. "We stroll back to the house together, the three of us, and the bloody dogs, just like we've been strolling together since I left the house. Any questions?"

Danny took Samantha's other arm then whistled to the dogs, and they all started toward the house. "How'd you get so good at covering people's asses, Knox?"

"Caught my father shagging one of the maids on that very bench when I was nine. When my mother sprang out of the bushes, my father and I met her like nothing was amiss, and the maid hurried past us with a basket of flowers."

"Damn, Knox."

Danny thought he'd had a fucked-up childhood. Samantha squeezed his arm against her briefly. He bumped her shoulder.

"No worries. I made him pay me a hundred quid, and I still peached on him a week later."

"Peached?" Danny frowned. The duke was hard as hell to read most of the time. This was one of those times.

"He tattled on his father to his mother," Samantha explained.

They turned the last corner and nearly ran into the group made up of Lily Randolph, Teddy Rousseau, Miss Chase, and Miss Stepford. Lily's expression once she locked gazes with the duke told Danny all he needed to know. What a conniving—

"Good evening, Your Grace," Teddy said.

"Mr. Rousseau. Ladies. I've been showing Mr. Arneaux and Dr. Higgins the gardens. Quite lovely by moonlight. Enjoy your walk." He nodded and kept walking—which was pretty much the duke version of keep moving, peasants. Nothing to see here.

"That was nicely done," Samantha said as they reached the terrace.

"I despise people who insist on interfering in the lives of

others." Knox stared across the terrace at the other set of doors. Eleanor Witherspoon stood just outside, staring back at him. "People need to mind their own business."

Danny started to reply when a howling wind suddenly kicked up along the length of the terrace. An eerie howl and that scent of earth and lavender nearly overwhelmed him.

"What the hell?"

Samantha gasped, and when he turned to check on her, Danny realized why. The wind had snatched up the front of Knox's kilt and caught it on his shirt buttons. Wow. Even stuffy dukes went commando under their kilts. Danny looked up and spotted Eleanor with her hand over her mouth. But she sure as hell wasn't looking away.

"Dammit, Elsbeth!" Knox brushed his kilt down and stormed into the library.

"Elsbeth?" Danny and Samantha said together. The witch?

Chapter Thirteen

SAMANTHA ROLLED OVER AND GOT A FACE FULL OF bloodhound fur for her trouble. She gave the powerful canine shoulder next to her a shove. The sturdy four-poster canopied bed was big enough for six people, but Dante's two dogs insisted on sleeping so close to her and so sprawled out, she was lucky to occupy the edge of the mattress closest to the fireplace without landing on the floor.

"No wonder he didn't put up too much of a fuss when you two decided to sleep in here." She adjusted the mound of pillows and managed to scoot Laveau over enough for her to edge closer to the middle of the mattress. "He's got that huge bed across the corridor all to himself."

She smiled. They'd come up the stairs with Eleanor, discussing the duke's invocation of the name of the Innes Witch. The entire time, Samantha and Dante tried not to look at each other and failed utterly. Of course, she didn't have to meet his eyes to sense his presence, to feel the tenuous shimmering connection between them. However, when Marie and Laveau had gone to her door rather than his, Dante had put on quite the show of indignance and mortal jealousy. He'd muttered something about *traitors* and *mutts stealing my girl*. She and Eleanor had gotten a kick out of it.

But the way he'd stared at Samantha from the open door of his room after Eleanor wished them both good night and glided off down the hall in that elegant, ethereal way she had, Samantha had trouble believing his attention was on her instead of the long-legged, flame-haired American, but it was. His gaze had never left the spot where Samantha stood. He stood in that doorway for an innumerable amount of time. The light from the gas lamps up and down the corridor caught the gold flecks in his green eyes, and they burned. He had scanned her body and face like a script he wanted to memorize. She'd felt a heated touch everywhere his eyes lingered.

When "Good night, *mo chridhe.*" rumbled at her from deep in his chest, she nearly leaped across the corridor to shove him into his room and drag him to bed, which would have been a huge mistake. Or at least that was what she kept telling herself. Yes, she wanted him. Badly. Entirely too badly. And he wanted her. For more than a hook up, if she chose to believe what he said and did. She liked him. She liked talking to him, and arguing with him, and just being with him.

She'd spent a lot of time with actors over the last five years. Handsome actors who'd propositioned her as a matter of course. That was what actors did. Anyone with breasts was fair game. Dante wasn't like that, and she'd given him plenty of opportunities to be as rude, crude, and socially unacceptable as he wanted to be. Yes, he'd punched Teddy to defend her but had apologized for assuming she needed to be defended.

So much of her life, Samantha had fought for the respect of her colleagues—male and female, but especially the men. It started when she was at university and only grew more difficult as she entered the field of period film consultant. Being better simply to break even and putting up with the most belittling sort of condescension at worst and being utterly ignored in favor of Cedric or some other male historian at best. It wore on her and forced her to put her wants and desires when it came to relationships and passion utterly on the shelf.

Then along came Dante Arneaux with his movie star looks and a body out of every woman's pornographic dreams. Oh sure, her fantasies drew her to him. She'd have to be dead not to want him in her bed. All that did was slide her desires to the edge of that shelf, but it was all the rest that knocked her off and had her contemplating changing her entire philosophy on involvement with any man, let alone a man in this business.

The cliché of it all made it no less true and him no less irresistible. His self-deprecating sense of humor. His earnest desire to learn anything he could to play this role. The way he listened to the mousy little authoress, so intently others listened as well. His complete lack of filter. His ability to make people comfortable, from Robbie the footman to the arrogant and lonely duke. The way her toes curled in her Regency slippers when he kissed her and, cricket in a corset, the ways he looked at her as if she were a queen, a genius, a lover he desired like air, water, or Mrs. Gordon's cranachan.

Dammit, Safely Samantha was arse over teakettle in lo—

Samantha flung back the covers and sat up on the side of the bed. The dogs grumbled a bit then went immediately back to snoring.

What would happen if he found out *she* was the person who had the last word on whether he played Captain Rothgate or not? She'd told him from the beginning it would all be so much easier if he wasn't…him. But he was, and she was mad about him. Mad enough to throw her every caution and fear to the wind and embark on a smoking hot affair with no idea where or when it might end.

Her feet hovered over the wool mules Eleanor had provided them all *for authenticity*. The pretty blue robe draped across the foot of the bed tempted her. By now, everyone was asleep, and temptation on a cracker was just across the corridor.

A quick glance back at the sleeping dogs, who were no help at all, and Samantha jumped off the bed. She chased her slippers around with her feet and snatched the robe from the foot of the bed.

"This is the most dicked in the nob thing you have ever—"

A blood-curdling scream shot down the corridor outside her door. Doors slammed open. Running feet. Shouts. A fair amount of very un-Regency cursing. More running. More screaming.

"What the hell?" Samantha chased the sleeve of the robe around with her arm until she finally shrugged her way into the damned thing then tied the belt into a knot at her waist. Marie raised her head and opened one eye. Laveau didn't move. "No, don't trouble yourselves. I'll see to it." She stomped to her door and flung it open.

To utter mayhem.

Footmen and maids thundered up and down the corridor. Lily Randolph stood in the middle of the antique Turkey carpet runner in front of her room screaming at the top of her lungs—and the woman had some lungs. In addition to very flattering black silk lingerie and heeled mules with the obligatory black feathers on them.

"It's in there," she cried. "Why are you out here asking me when you should be in there killing it?"

Teddy and Mr. McGinty tried to calm her only to have her point her red, nail tipped finger toward her room and begin shrieking again.

At the far end of the corridor, Miss Chase seemed, with much hand waving, to be explaining something to Mr. Goode, Miss Stepford, and Eleanor.

"Shewasstandingovermybedlaughing.   Shelookedjust-likeyou,Eleanor."

The poor author spoke so quickly it took Samantha a minute to process her words. *She?* Lily was talking about an "it".

A small black something flitted out of Lily's room, swooped over Samantha's head, and flew back into the actress's room, who screamed like a banshee the entire time, even as she and the gentlemen ducked out of the way.

Samantha raised a hand to her hair. "Was that a ba—"

"A wee bat," Dougal said as he trotted past her with a fishing net in hand.

"Get yourself in there and take care of it, Dougal McPhee," Mrs. Wallace barked as she came up behind him. "And you lot, shut your gobs and quit acting like a bunch of blockheaded sheep." This last she addressed to a group of young maids just a few feet away from the landing, dressed in mob caps and Regency night clothes, and looking ready to bolt back down the stairs.

Samantha stepped toward Lily's room and peered in the door as Dougal chased the bat from one side of the room to the other, wielding the net like a claymore. "Don't hurt him," she cried. "He's frightened." She turned back to find Lily Randolph giving her such a look, Teddy and Mr. McGinty took a step back.

"Don't hurt it?" Lily said.

"Now, Miss Randolph, I'm sure the staff will have this all sorted in no time," Teddy said with what sounded like genuine compassion.

"It should have been sorted before we got here," she

snapped. "I am not paying a fortune to stay in a castle with bats in it. Oh my God!"

The bat flew out of Lily's room. She covered her head and spun in circles, wordless shouts punctuating every turn as the bat fluttered back and forth into the corridor walls.

Samantha looked around. Where was Dante? He was missing all the fun.

A cold, lavender-scented breeze swept down the corridor, an eerie whistling accompanying the scent, which set off the maids again. They ran up and down the corridor adding to the chaos. Mrs. Wallace chased after them like a flannel-robed sheep dog.

Another maid came around the corner from the direction of Miss Chase's room. "The witch! The Innes Witch! I saw her. She's in the young lady's room."

Samantha made eye contact with poor Eleanor who looked ready to knock heads together.

Miss Chase held the maid's hands and tried to calm her. "I'm sure I was dreaming. I didn't mean to frighten you."

"What did you see, Anna?" Eleanor asked, raising her voice to be heard above the noise of everyone talking at once. Not to mention the chaos of Lily Randolph still going on about a little bat.

Samantha sneaked a glance at Dante's bedroom door, still firmly closed. How the devil was he sleeping through all this?

"It's silly really," Miss Chase said. "I woke up to the smell of lavender and my room was cold. I thought I saw a lady sitting in the chair in front of the fire reading my book. She was laughing."

"The Innes Witch." The maid looked about frantically as if just saying the name would conjure up the poor maligned dead woman. "It was her ghost. I saw it."

The level of raised voices reached a level seldom heard outside a football match or a pub darts tournament.

"I was only half awake," Anna Chase shouted. "I'm certain—"

"Quiet!" The word was drawn out in a rich, steady baritone. The Duke of Turra strode along the corridor from the direction of the landing. An obviously expensive black velvet dressing gown covered him from neck to ankles and made him look like some Persian potentate. Silence fell like a stone. "There is no ghost at Rosemount Manor. Mrs. Wallace, will you take these girls in hand?" He waved toward the gaggle of maids gathered at the far end of the corridor. "Where the devil is Abercrombie?"

"Here, Your Grace."

Abercrombie? When did he show up? Hell, in all the confusion a full Scots Brigade could have shown up, which made Dante's absence even more strange.

The butler stepped out of Lily's room followed by Dougal, who had his hand squeezed tightly around the top of the fishing net. "We've caught an intruder."

The duke deigned to check out the creature fluttering in the net and shuddered. "Well for pity's sake get him out of the house so we can all get some sleep."

Dougal hurried toward the stairs to do just that.

His Grace turned to the crowd milling about the corridor. "The culprit is caught. I suggest we all return to our rooms and—"

"What about the witch?" the fresh-faced young maid, Tildie, asked.

Samantha had often read the phrase "his face became a thundercloud of anger." She'd never actually understood that phrase until now. In the glow of the antique gas lights along the walls, the duke looked very much the descendent of Celtic warriors. Everyone in his field of vision took a step back. Some people took two.

"Where's our intrepid hero, Dr. Higgins?" Teddy suddenly

asked. "Being a country boy, I'm sure he could have dispatched our winged invader with no effort at all. I believe they eat bats in Louisiana, don't they?"

She was going to punch Teddy in the face just as Dante had before this Regency boot camp was over, but for the moment, she was glad he turned the duke's focus away from the now white-faced maid.

"I have no idea, Teddy," she replied. "I can't believe he's slept through all this."

"Where exactly is he sleeping, Samantha, dear?" Lily swayed down the Turkey carpet runner, lowering the IQ of every man in sight in less than two seconds.

Who wore slippers with feathers and heels during the Regency? And how bad would it be for Samantha to knock the bitch off those heels?

"I assume he's in his room, Lily, dear. Why don't you check?" She hated that she was reduced to such a catty tone, especially with everyone in the entire damned house watching like it was a bloody tennis match.

"Yes, well, which one is his?" Lily sidled up to Samantha's door, pushed it open, and disappeared inside with horribly fake nonchalance. "Arneaux, you're missing all the— Noooooo!"

The room erupted into a deafening mix of bloodhound baying and spiteful actress screaming. Lily finally stumbled out and slammed the door so quickly, her silky robe caught in the door jamb. She grabbed the end of the caught fabric and pulled with both hands until Samantha opened the door —which resulted in Lily falling on her arse. Even better, when the duke went to help her up, he ended up with a handful of dog drool down the sleeve of his exquisite dressing gown. Lily was covered in it. *Poor thing.*

"I think this is Mr. Arneaux's room." His Grace indicated the door across the hall from Samantha's as he took the handkerchief Mr. McGinty handed him and attempted to wipe the drool off his arm.

"Then why are his dogs in *her* room?" Lily took the handkerchief Teddy offered her and swiped at her clothes and face. She'd known which room was Dante's all along. Teddy wasn't the only person Samantha wanted to punch.

"They like her," Dougal said as he returned from setting the bat free. "They like Miss Chase as well. They slept in her room last night, didn't they, Miss Chase?"

Samantha smiled. Well, Marie and Laveau were certainly making the rounds.

"They did, indeed, Dougal. I wish they'd slept with me tonight. Perhaps I wouldn't have let my imagination run away with me and awakened the entire house."

"T'weren't your imagination, miss," Tildie, said eagerly. "I saw her too. Big as day in the corridor outside your room. The Innes Witch—"

"There is no witch!" the duke shouted so loudly the dogs started baying from inside Samantha's room.

"Quiet!" McGinty barked, one hand raised for emphasis.

"Miss Witherspoon, will you please escort Miss Chase and Tildie back to Miss Chase's room and check for this spectral witch? It would be nice if we could all get some sleep sometime tonight." His Grace was well past not at all pleased.

Miss Witherspoon glared at him, a fake smile pasted on her face. She gave a really bad curtsy, beckoned to the other ladies, and marched down the adjacent corridor as if going to war.

"Did you hear that?" Mr. McGinty tilted his head at several angles like a demented foxhound in search of his prey.

"I did," Mr. Goode said. "Someone is calling out from one of these rooms."

A faint cry came from Dante's door. Everyone stepped

closer. With a simple hand gesture, the duke had Abercrombie dismiss the maids and all the footmen except Dougal. They scurried back toward the servants' quarters in one large clump, glancing over their shoulders as they went. Mrs. Wallace, Mr. Goode, Teddy, Lily, and Miss Stepford moved closer.

Samantha joined McGinty and His Grace at Dante's door, whilst the others lagged back a bit. Afraid of another bat, perhaps? The duke knocked softly.

"Arneaux? Are you awake?"

"Help. Me," Dante said softly through the thick oak barrier.

The three of them exchanged a puzzled look.

"Did he—"

"Did you hear—"

"Arneaux." The duke knocked more insistently. "Answer the door."

Quiet swept up and down the corridor like the lavender breeze of moments ago.

"I can't answer the door, asshole. Get in here and help me."

"Are you armed, McGinty?"

"Yes, Your Grace." The burly steward pulled a pistol from the pocket of his plaid flannel dressing gown.

"Armed?" Samantha put her hand on the door handle. "Why would he need to be armed?"

"Please step back, Dr. Higgins." The duke inserted himself between her and the door and pushed her hand away. "Just a precaution. The rest of you, step back, please."

Samantha turned to find everyone else right behind her. Dante wasn't going to like this. What the hell was he up to now? McGinty stepped into the room. The light from the fireplace and at least one oil lamp spilled out into the corridor. Some sort of artificial source of light was on as it moved across the doorway in short erratic bursts. Samantha followed the duke inside.

"If Miss Witherspoon catches ye with that flashlight she'll have your hide, Mr. Arneaux," McGinty said. He scanned the room as if he expected ninjas or at least the ghost of a Sassenach cavalry officer to come charging out of the shadows.

Samantha would find McGinty's actions funny if Dante weren't lying so stiff and still in his bed, a small flashlight on top of the covers next to his hip, or at least where she imagined his hip to be. Was he injured?

She wanted to run to his bedside, but between his expression and the slight shake of his head and the crowd of people who pushed in behind her, she squelched that impulse and quick. Why wasn't he moving? Except for the spitting and hissing of the fire and the shuffling of everyone's feet, the lack of noise was either surreal or completely comical.

"Well, now you have us all gathered together, Arneaux," Teddy finally said. "Care to tell us what—"

"There's a snake in my bed."

Teddy blinked. "I beg your pardon?"

Samantha shook her head. Teddy Rousseau wasn't the only one who needed a repeat of that statement.

Dante indicated a lump beneath the exposed sheet at the bottom of the bed. "There is a gigantic orange snake in this bed with me, and it wasn't listed in the amenities provided in this Regency experience. Boatloads of tea, yes. Quaint period lighting, yes. Humongous orange sherbet reptiles, no. I've been lying here for the last hour screaming for help," he said with a strained get-me-the-hell-out-of-this-situation look. "Well not exactly screaming. I didn't want to wake up the snake."

"A snake?" Teddy reached for the lump under the sheet. "Are you sure this isn't some sort of rubber snake someone left as a—"

The sheet began to undulate, then stilled. The silly git had the good sense to jump back.

"Thanks, Teddy," Dante said between gritted teeth. "Now the damned thing's awake."

"How does one tell if a snake is asleep?" Bella Stepford asked as she leaned over the foot of the bed. "Are its eyes closed?"

"I haven't actually looked it in the eyes, ma'am. Didn't want to encourage its acquaintance or get that close to the end with the teeth."

Samantha couldn't smile because if she did, she'd start laughing, which was really bad because Dante's eyes communicated so much to her.

Do you believe this?

Help me.

Could this be any more embarrassing?

"You're all being ridiculous," Mrs. Wallace pushed past Samantha and stepped between the duke and the bed. "Let's just see what we're—"

Dante grabbed the covers like they were the last life jacket on the Titanic. "Let's not," he said firmly. "Teddy's already upset the damned thing."

The duke took the housekeeper by the elbow and steered her a few steps back and away from the bed.

"Don't you all have somewhere else to be?" Dante asked as he tried to sit up higher against the headboard. "Your beds? A Highland fling? A county fair? Some other freak show where I am *not* the main attraction?"

"Oh, you're hardly the main attraction, Danny." Lily sidled next to the duke. "We're here for the snake."

"Next time you decide to hold a family reunion, Lily, make sure your relatives crawl into your bed, not mine."

"Asshole," Lily snapped, and stormed back to the foot of the bed.

"Perhaps everyone should return to their rooms and let McGinty and me handle this," the duke suggested.

"Great idea, Your Grace." Relief crossed Dante's face.

Samantha gave him an encouraging smile.

McGinty had crept on surprisingly quiet feet to the far side of the bed. He gently lifted the edge of the sheet. "Holy Mary, Mother of God. That's a big bloody snake." He dropped the sheet and stepped back.

Teddy, Lily, and Bella rushed to that side of the bed. The burly steward kept them from getting too close. They weren't going anywhere no matter what the duke said.

"Thanks for that incredibly scientific assessment, Mr. McGinty. Now could you do something to *help* me with the big bloody snake?" Dante's voice was demanding, though tight and strained.

Even in the dim light, Samantha could see he'd gone a couple of shades paler since they'd entered the room. Being torn between laughter and genuine concern had her stomach doing somersaults.

"I'm afraid snake removal is above my pay grade, lad." Never had a man sounded so relieved to make that statement as McGinty did.

"Why don't you simply slide out of bed?" the duke suggested. "You can't tell me you've never had to sneak out of a lady's bed without getting caught for some reason or other."

"And what reasons might those be?" Lily inquired in that patently not-so-innocent tone of hers.

The other ladies in the room snickered. The sound echoed against the high ceiling of the room.

The duke cleared his throat.

"Don't answer that," McGinty and Dante muttered in unison.

"Don't you think I'd have already done that and be down the pub for a pint by now if I could?" Dante asked.

Samantha had to refrain from praising his British accent on *down the pub*. Somehow, she didn't think he'd be all that receptive to her praise at the moment.

"Dougal, go down to Miss Chase's room and fetch Miss Witherspoon, if you please."

"Yes, Your Grace." The footman gave a short bow, then ran out of the room.

"There aren't enough women in my room in one of the most humiliating moments of my life?" Dante muttered.

"Probably," the duke said. "But in this case, we don't have a choice. It's her snake."

"It's what?" Dante shifted up in the bed, but immediately stopped, eyes wide and breath suddenly short.

The duke frowned. "That's what happens when you allow an American party planner to turn your home into Regency Disney World. The woman is a menace. Putting people in costumes. Disrupting my routine."

"Taking away cell phones," Lily declared.

"And traveling with a thirteen-foot albino python," the duke said. "Unless, in addition to a supposed witch and a few bats, we have another *humongous orange snake* slithering about the house."

"This is ridiculous," Teddy announced. "There are five grown men in this room. We are more than a match for a python no matter how large it is. Unless this is all a ploy for attention on Arneaux's part. We all know what drama whores actors are."

"Screw you, Teddy. Don't let the door hit you where the good Lord split you on the way out. I don't need your help."

McGinty let loose a deep belly laugh. Even the duke smiled.

"Oh, I wouldn't miss this for the world." Teddy crossed

his arms over his broad chest and planted his feet firmly on the thick Aubusson rug covering the stone floor.

"Mr. Rousseau is correct in one thing." The duke came to the edge of the bed. "There has to be a way to get you out of this without disturbing your scaly date. As much as Miss Witherspoon will hate it, I think we need to switch on the electric lights."

"Certainly, Your Grace." Mrs. Wallace went to the wall switch, and in an instant, they were all squinting at the glare of the chandelier-like fixture overhead. They'd been living so authentically the last couple of weeks that electric light was quite a shock.

"You ladies can leave if you like," Dante said. "It's after midnight, way past even your bedtime, Mrs. Wallace."

"You've got enough to worry about in your own bed, Mr. Arneaux. Keep your nose out of mine."

"Yes, ma'am."

McGinty snorted, and Dante threw him a glare.

"At least you're wearing a nightshirt," the duke said.

"Keeps me from freezing to death when my traitor dogs decide they prefer Dr. Higgins's bed to mine."

"One can hardly blame them," Mr. Goode said.

Teddy looked as if he wanted to say something, but one glance from Dante and he kept his mouth firmly closed. He wasn't a complete idiot.

"What the hell?" Dante flinched and nearly came off the bed.

"What's wrong with you now, lad?" McGinty asked.

"It licked me."

"Do we need to leave you two alone?" the duke asked.

"Screw you, Your Grace."

"As flattering as that invitation is, Mr. Arneaux, you are not my type, and you appear to already have a bed partner who is more than willing."

"I really hate you right now."

"What on earth is everyone doing in Danny's room in the middle of the night?" Eleanor asked as she breezed into the room.

"Apparently, we're about to watch *Danny* have sex with your pet," Lily said.

The room erupted into a chorus of coughing and muttering. Samantha changed her mind. Teddy had been at the top of her *I'm-going-to-smack-this-person-before-boot camp-is-over* list. He'd just been shoved into the second position by Lily Randolph, the queen of nasty, inappropriate remarks.

"Excuse me?" Eleanor narrowed her eyes at the actress.

"Your little pet has crawled into bed with Arneaux here and has been holding him hostage for hours," the duke said, his voice cold enough to frost a volcano's arse. "Were you aware this creature was on the loose, or do I need to appoint a footman to walk it along with Arneaux's beasts?"

"Oh, for God's sake, someone unplugged her warming lamp," Eleanor said. "She came in here looking for heat. You should be flattered, Danny."

"Your snake gets an electric heater?" Lily asked.

"She's not in Regency boot camp, Miss Randolph."

"I'd be more flattered if I hadn't woken up with her wrapped around my leg," Danny said.

"She's perfectly safe," Eleanor assured him. She stepped purposefully to the bedside, practically elbowing the duke out of the way in the process. "Move over here and I'll—"

"Uh-uh." Dante grabbed her reaching hand. "Do not try to move her."

"Why not?"

"Maybe Arneaux prefers his bed partners cold-blooded and stiff," Lily said.

He closed his eyes and started mumbling in what sounded like French. "An English gentleman would not say what I want to say more than I want this snake out of my bed, would he, Dr. Higgins?" He opened his eyes and focused on Samantha, a familiar wicked twinkle in his eyes.

"Probably not, Mr. Arneaux." Samantha refused to check Lily's reaction. She really wanted to slap the woman silly, which wouldn't take much.

Dante signaled the duke with a crooked finger. His Grace leaned in to hear what Dante had to say.

"Well," Eleanor said, tapping her foot. "What did he say?"

"Actually he…that is, there is a problem with…." The all-powerful Duke of Turra turned bright red.

"Great job there, Your Grace. The damned snake's head is on my…groin." Dante's last word came out as a nearly inaudible whisper.

"What?" Samantha blurted.

"Excuse me?" Teddy said.

"I beg your pardon?" Miss Witherspoon said.

"The snake has crawled up my shirt and is using my nuts for a pillow, okay? And, if it's all the same to you ladies and gentlemen, I'd rather she didn't get pissed off enough to bite me right now."

Samantha didn't know for certain, but she suspected the sudden low hiss was every man in the room wincing.

Eleanor snatched the covers out of Dante's hands. "Persephone is not going to bite you. She's probably asleep." She threw back the duvet, blankets, and sheet, then reached under Dante's nightshirt.

"Whoa!" Dante's eyes widened, and he tried to lever himself up the headboard on his fists. "Careful, Eleanor. That's not a snake you're grabbing."

"Sorry about that." She shot the other ladies in the room a quick glance. "Apparently those rumors are all true." She winked, which sent the duke into a flurry of determined motion.

He pulled Eleanor away and stepped into her place.

"Oh, for pity's sake, woman. You'd think you'd never had your hand on a cock before." He reached under Dante's nightshirt and pulled a few feet of snake out, head first.

"Shit!" Dante tried to move away. "Her bottom half is still wrapped around my leg, and she's squeezing now. Thanks a lot."

"Oh, let me help." Eleanor pulled the sheet off Dante's legs and began to tug at the coils of snake wrapped around his knee and thigh. "Come here, Persephone. Come to Mama."

"Bloody hell!" Now the snake had wrapped its coils around His Grace's hands.

"Your Grace!" McGinty stepped toward him, Mrs. Wallace at his side, and they tried to break him free.

Wide eyed, Lily, Teddy, Bella, and Mr. Goode offered suggestions like a demented Greek chorus.

"Just relax."

"Try not to struggle."

"Try not to make it angry."

"It's not going to eat him, is it?"

"Jesus, take the wheel." Dante closed his eyes and shook his head.

"Stop pulling," Eleanor ordered the duke. "You're upsetting her."

"How can you tell?" McGinty asked as he and Mrs. Wallace obeyed the duke's wordless command and stepped back.

The snake undulated her body from tail to head. Eleanor and the duke landed across Dante in a tangled sprawl of arms, legs, and pastel orange coils.

"You know," Dante said tightly. "My fantasies of a ménage à trois never involved a snake." He looked around the room. "Or an audience."

"Get. Me. Out. Of. This. Bed," His Grace demanded.

"Or a duke," Dante said. "McGinty, why don't you just go ahead and shoot me."

"Before or after I help His Grace?" McGinty wrapped a thick arm around the duke's middle and hauled him off the mattress, snake and all.

Samantha hurried to help Eleanor to her feet. The redheaded American laughed as she unwrapped the snake from around the duke's hands. Samantha worked to free Dante's leg from Persephone's powerful reptilian grip. While everyone else took a few steps back, she was able to exchange a few glances with Dante. His embarrassed grin and the shivers that coursed through him every time she touched his bare skin had her body humming with awareness. Heaven if they were alone. Not so good when half the house was in his bedroom.

"See," Eleanor said as she pulled the snake across her shoulders and allowed its head to rest in her outstretched hand. "She's perfectly harmless. All this fuss over—"

The snake lashed out and sank its fangs into the duke's upraised hand—and held on.

"You were saying?" The duke lifted an eyebrow at Eleanor.

Thud!

McGinty had passed out cold.

The scent of lavender and a woman's spectral laughter floated through the room.

Chapter Fourteen

AT NEARLY TWO IN THE MORNING, AFTER THE NIGHT THEY'D had, Samantha had no illusions about the way she looked. Bats. Ghosts. Witches. Snakes. And an injured duke. She didn't dare ask what else for fear the universe might take it as a challenge. After a group expedition to the kitchens for cocoa and biscuits, and a bit of first aid for the duke and McGinty, everyone had drifted upstairs to their beds.

"A penny for them," Dante said once they reached the door to her bedroom.

She half raised her hand to check her hair, but let it fall to her side instead. "I was wondering what else could possibly happen tonight."

He pressed two fingers to her lips. "Shhh. Someone will hear you." He slid those fingers across her cheek and down the side of her neck to the spot where her pulse fluttered.

"I was thinking the same thing." She leaned against the door, her hand on the door latch. "But I thought you handled the entire episode with a great deal of dignity. Captain Rothgate would be proud."

"Captain Rothgate would have wrestled the snake into

submission and made boots out of its hide." He braced a hand on the door and toyed with a strand of her hair with his other.

"Eleanor might have objected to that."

Suddenly, she lost the ability to breathe. Or to think. He stood so close and radiated such heat she wanted to climb inside him and never leave. Her breasts grew heavy and tender all at once.

"She might have, but McGinty wouldn't. Did you feel the floor shake when he went down? I'm surprised he didn't crack the wood."

"Poor thing." McGinty fainting did nothing to the floor compared to how looking into Dante Arneaux's eyes made it shift beneath Samantha's feet.

"Poor thing, my ass. I thought we'd never get him up, especially with Knox trying to help while a snake chewed on him."

Samantha snorted. She covered her mouth. It didn't help. One breath and they both collapsed against each other in laughter. The deep vibration of Dante's laughter in his chest brushed her nipples and sent tiny fissures of lightning careening through her body.

"I don't know what was funnier," Dante said between gasps, "McGinty hitting the floor, Knox commanding the snake to let go, or Mrs. Wallace stepping over McGinty to pull the snake's jaws apart like some kind of Mary Poppins Steve Irwin."

Samantha raised her hand and mimicked the housekeeper dropping the business end of a highly indignant Persephone into Eleanor's outstretched arms. *In future do try to keep your pet from molesting His Grace and his guests, Miss Witherspoon.*

Dante touched his lips to her ear and whispered, "You're very sexy with a Scottish accent, Dr. Higgins."

A door slammed somewhere around the corner of the

corridor. He sighed against her neck, which sent a delicious shiver down her spine.

"I suppose we'd better say goodnight and try to get a little sleep. I have a British diction lesson early tomorrow morning, and my teacher is a real whip-cracker."

"She sounds like quite the nightmare," Samantha murmured as she tilted her head in a half-hearted effort to escape the kisses he trailed down to the neck of her Regency era nightgown.

"You have no idea." Dante finally straightened and stuck his hands into the pockets of his dressing gown.

They stood a few inches apart. Not speaking. At least not with words. The way Dante studied her, as if she were a foreign country he wanted to explore, said everything she'd ever imagined a man saying to her and more.

She reached behind her and grabbed the door latch once more. "Marie and Laveau have certainly had an eventful night. Would you like them to sleep with you? Perhaps make certain no more snakes wander into your bed?"

"Please keep them. My bed's seen quite enough animal action for one night." He glanced up and down the corridor. With a positively wicked grin, he leaned in and kissed her. Quite chastely at first, but that didn't last. Thank God.

The man was an artist when it came to kissing. He teased and tempted her lips, pulling nearly all the way back, then nibbling and nipping only to scorch her with a searing kiss that only got hotter when he parted her lips with his tongue and tasted every inch of her mouth. She wrapped her tongue around his and sucked softly. He groaned and started to reach for her. Finally, he gasped and stepped back.

"If we don't stop now, I will not be answerable for my actions." The last phrase was delivered with a near perfect imitation of the Duke of Turra's upper crust British accent. "Go to bed, Samantha. Sweet dreams." He backed slowly toward his door until his broad shoulders pressed into the wood and he fumbled around to lift the latch. "Good night." He didn't move to go into his room, and she realized he was waiting for her to go into her room first.

"Good night, Dante."

She raised the latch and hurried inside, then pushed the door slowly closed behind her. Then immediately collapsed against the thick oak wood. The sweat she broke out in had nothing to do with the fire in the hearth and everything to do with the man across the corridor. She'd been dancing around these feelings since she'd met him. *They'd* been dancing around these feelings. There was no doubt in her mind Dante Arneaux wanted her. Almost as much as she wanted him.

A soft *woofle* drew her attention to the bed. Both dogs, heads slightly raised, fixed their soft brown gazes on her.

"What would you do?" she asked.

Of course, they didn't answer, merely continued to watch her expectantly. She'd taken this job in a blind leap of faith in herself and in her desire to make a success of her career on her own. Now, she contemplated taking an even more dangerous leap that might cost her something, everything, or nothing at all. Was it enough? Was she? *Safely Samantha—* her university nickname had followed her even into her work with Cedric. Caution had marked every aspect of her life.

She recalled Dante's words, *"I'm thinking I'm going to need all the guts I can muster to convince you it's worth the risk."*

"It?"

"Me, mo chridhe."

She pushed off the door, shedding her robe as she did. Once the frilly dressing gown lay tossed across the foot of the bed, she opened the bedside table drawer and began to rummage through it. Samantha closed her hand around a small box and drew it out in her fist. She crossed to the bedroom door.

"Don't wait up," she said over her shoulder as she opened the door.

She looked up and down the corridor, closed the door behind her with a quiet click, then hurried across to Dante's room. She didn't bother to knock. Simply lifted the latch, slipped inside, and closed the door firmly behind her.

She couldn't breathe.

Dante stood at the fireplace, one arm propped on the intricately carved marble mantlepiece and one foot resting on the wrought iron fender. He still wore the ridiculous Regency nightshirt Eleanor had provided all the men. Only on him, it was the furthest thing from ridiculous. The fire-light made the fabric nearly transparent. It outlined his powerful body—wide shoulders, muscled back, narrow waist, glorious arse, thick thighs and...bloody hell, was that his—

"Samantha?"

She swallowed and licked her lips. "Still opposed to more animal activity in your bed tonight, Mr. Arneaux?"

He prowled toward her, steps slow, as if afraid she might run. Not that she didn't consider it—for about half a second.

"That, Dr. Higgins, is completely up to you." He raised his hand to touch her, a hand that shook slightly. "It always was."

She stepped into him, pressed her body against his from knees to breasts. She slid one foot between his and curled one arm around his waist. Standing on her tiptoes, Samantha kissed her way up his throat and nipped his chin before she found his mouth and kissed him with every ounce of pent-up desire that pulsed through her like electric lava. She dropped the box on the floor.

A dark, sexy moan rumbled in Dante's chest as he wrapped his arms around her and lifted her off her feet. He held her up with one arm while he cupped the back of her head with his free hand—his erection pressed into her thigh.

With a little cry of need, she wrapped her legs around his hips, and he moved both hands to cup her arse and draw her closer. Still melding their mouths together, he carried her to the bed then laid her down, her legs dangling over the edge of the mattress. He braced his hands on each side of her hips and loomed over her. She broke their kiss and pulled at his nightshirt, trying to drag it off him. He reached between them and yanked it over his shoulders, then tossed it behind her.

"Are you absolutely sure about this, Samantha?" Dante's eyes shone so bright they appeared emerald green.

"I've never been more sure in my life." She meant every word, a thought that frightened her and made her heart soar all at once.

"Me either."

Now propped on his elbows, he caressed her face and pressed soft, sweet kisses to her eyelids, her cheeks, her nose, her chin. He traced her lips with the tip of his tongue. She opened her legs to cradle his hips, which brought his cock exactly where she needed it—brushing against the sensitized place between her thighs, already hot and wet and waiting for him even through the thin cotton of her nightgown. She gathered handfuls of the soft fabric to pull it over her head.

"Allow me, milady."

Dante smiled slowly as he slid to his knees and ran his hands down her hips and legs until he reached the hem of the nightgown, then inch by excruciating inch, drew the fabric up her body. He tilted his head as he revealed her thighs, her hips, the vee of dark blonde curls, her belly, her ribcage, and her breasts. She raised her arms over her head, but he pushed the gown only as high as her neck then traced his fingertips across her collarbones, between her breasts and along her ribs. Samantha twisted and turned. She wanted his hands on her breasts. She wanted a strong, firm touch, not these teasing strokes.

As if sensing her need, he covered one breast with his palm, gently shaping and weighing it before he closed two fingers over her nipple, then plucked and brushed and tortured her to the point the sensation shot down to the tips of her toes. He closed his teeth around the other nipple, flicking his tongue across the very tip before taking as much of her breast as he could into his mouth and sucking hard.

He used the fingers of his other hand to slide up and down her slick labia in a slow, steady rhythm, dipping inside her just a bit then moving back to stroke and circle—which drove her crazy. Every few caresses, he'd lick her nipple and drag one finger across her clit. She jumped every time, working her legs to try and get him to relieve the steady pressure he built every moment he continued.

"Dante, please. Please."

He released her breast with one last kiss then raised his head. The passion and desire in his face roared over her like a tidal wave.

"We're just getting started, *cher*. I'm not letting you go until you're too exhausted to move." He burned a path of kisses down her rib cage, first one side then the other.

"Condoms. Box. On the floor." Already so breathless, she could hardly get the words out. His mouth curled into a grin against her belly. He raised his head, eyes wide in mock surprise.

"You brought your own condoms? Why, Dr. Higgins, how long have you been planning to take advantage of me?"

The entire time, he continued to play over the engorged, trembling flesh between her legs, bringing her to the point of screaming only to back off like an outgoing tide. Every wave of sensation grew higher and more intense.

"Dante," she said between clenched teeth as she fisted the bedclothes to keep from grabbing him and forcing him to do what she wanted.

"Tell me, sweet Samantha." He kissed her hipbone and nuzzled at the damp curls at the apex of her thighs. "When did you get the condoms? Hmm?" He tortured her with kisses that surrounded but never touched the one place she wanted them desperately. He laid his arms across her thighs to keep her from bucking against him.

Fiend.

"Eleanor put them…in every room and you know it…don't stop." Samantha closed her eyes, bit her lower lip, and hummed against the exquisite pains spiraling from her wet core. "Said it was because I'd written…Regency house parties…were notorious…for bed hopping. Oh God, Dante, please!" Chills and fever washed over her. She opened her eyes to lock gazes with him.

"You are so beautiful, Samantha." The rough, dark edge of his voice went through her, around her. The resonance touched her heart and settled in some secret spot she'd never known was there. "You are beautiful everywhere. You are beautiful in every moment, every breath, but right now you are gorgeous. I want to watch you. I want to watch you come for me."

The deep blush started at the soles of her feet and reached her hairline in seconds. He laughed. He laughed with his lips pressed to her labia, then he drew the tip of his tongue up the seam. She did scream then. She clapped her hand over her mouth to muffle the sound, but it didn't help much. He was merciless. Licking, sucking, nibbling, pushing her higher and higher. He slid his hands under her thighs and raised them, so she had no control over the lower half of her body. She was his, utterly and completely. Her efforts to increase the rhythm, to buck against his tormenting mouth only made the need worse.

A powerful tremble ripped through her. Her entire body shook as a heart-stopping orgasm shook her to her core. Samantha screamed his name and nearly shredded the bed clothes. Her sex life had never been something to write home about, but with this man, good God!

It took a moment or two for her to re-enter her body with any sense at all, especially as Dante kissed the inside of her thigh, her knee, then worked his way down her calf to the top of her foot. She couldn't even raise her head as he slid back off the mattress. The thud of a log landing in the fireplace and a brief increase in the room's illumination finally instilled enough curiosity in her to prop herself on her elbows.

Oh, my damn!

She hadn't really seen him completely naked before, and a good thing too, otherwise, she'd never have had the courage to cross the corridor tonight. His skin, deep bronze, stretched over lean sculpted muscles everywhere—his arms, his shoulders, his abs, his thighs, and he was sporting an erection that took her breath away, and had her hungering to know exactly what something that thick and heavy would feel like deep inside her.

Dante had the box of condoms in one hand, but he froze when he saw her looking at him. Since he obliged, she took her time and studied every line and shadow of his magnificent body. Finally, their eyes met. His expression—confident, yes but also almost shy, turned her heart over.

"Hey," he said quietly.

"Come here."

"Yes, ma'am."

He sauntered over, all Dante Arneaux now. "What can I

do for you, *mo chridhe?*" He put the box of condoms on the bed next to her.

Samantha sat all the way up and molded both her palms to his washboard abs. He sucked in just a bit. She ran her hands across his hard, hot skin, across his belly and along his ribcage. Then she walked her fingertips across his chest and shoulders and down his arms. She pressed a kiss to the center of his chest, and he cupped the back of her head to hold her against his skin. His heart pounded against her lips, fast and hard. His breathing rasped. His kissed the top her head.

"Tell me you want me, Samantha."

She pulled back enough to cradle his face in her hands. "So much." She kissed him. "So very much." She grabbed the condom box and opened it.

"Please tell me those aren't made of sheep's gut," he said as he stroked her breasts.

She shivered. "You really have read the Regency manual." She tried to keep her voice steady despite the fact he'd bent to lick her nipple then blow across it.

"I want to be teacher's pet."

Samantha took his cock in her hand and gave it a few long exploratory strokes. Dante moaned. Eyes closed and lips firmed, he was the picture of sexual concentration. Already she hummed with desire. She needed this, needed him. She'd never experienced such erotic fulfillment in her life, had never been so sexually aware and aroused. There was power in holding him in her hand and eliciting little gasps and groans from him with her touch alone.

"I'm not going to last if you keep that up," he muttered.

"Neither am I."

Samantha's hands shook as she rolled the condom over his hot velvety flesh then cupped his balls as she rose to her knees to kiss him again. He took control of the kiss in a swift branding of seeking lips and invading tongue. She scooted back as he climbed onto the bed, straddling her as he lowered her to the mattress. He continued to devour her mouth as he shifted the two of them across the mattress, so her legs no longer dangled over the side. She lay in the middle of the thick duvet and blankets and gripped his biceps as he braced himself above her on his hands.

He teased her with several long brushes of his cock across her clit. She wrapped her legs around his hips to try and force him inside her. He dropped his head to her breast, gave her nipple a sharp nip, then suckled the hard tip to the point of delicious pain. Samantha thrust up once, twice, doing her damnedest to get him where she needed him.

He raised his head. "Tell me what you want, cher. What do you want?"

"You. Inside me. Now." She was shocked at the raw, primitive tone of her voice.

Dante slowly rolled them over, so he was flat on his back, knees raised, and she straddled him. He cupped her breasts. "Take what you want, *mo chridhe*. I'm all yours."

Did he know what those words did to her? Did he have any idea the deep desires and dreams he awakened in her? She was so stunned she had to focus hard to lift herself into position and situate him so she could lower herself onto his cock. As he stretched and filled her, she had to look down, wanted to. She settled onto him slowly, determined to feel and enjoy every delicious, wonderful centimeter. Once she felt the poke of his hipbones against the backs of her thighs and the rough scratch of the dark, springy hair around his cock, she sighed and braced her hands on his belly.

Dante groaned and lifted his hips. "You feel so damned good, Samantha."

She tilted her head and stared into his eyes. Desire. Passion. Both shone brightly, but there was more. She raised herself up then down again. It took a few tries to get the hang of it as she'd never been on top before. She shifted her body forward to find the perfect angle. Dante put his hands on her waist and helped her set a rhythm. She moved her hands to his shoulders, which put her breasts in a great position for him to lick and suck each time she rocked forward.

A glorious tension began to build where they were joined. He grabbed her hands and laced their fingers together, raising his arms so their clasped hands rested on each side of his head. On her knees, Samantha rocked back and forth, pressing her clit against the hard planes of his abdomen. The friction was powerful, painful, and incredible. She bit her lower lip and increased her rhythmic thrusts, whining softly as each bolt of sensation sliced her erotic haze.

"Samantha. Look at me. Look at me, sweetheart."

She did. The scent of sweat, sex, the fire, and a combination of her perfume and his cologne wrapped around her. The chill of the room could not compete with the heat they generated inside and out. She reached for something just out of sight. His face filled her vision even as she struggled to keep her eyes open. His hands clutched hers so tightly they were nearly numb.

"Dante… Dante, I can't stop." There was nothing for her but the hedonist need to ride the kaleidoscope of sensations to the finish. "Dante."

"Don't stop. Don't. Samantha. Samantha. Oh God. Oh!" He shouted her name so loudly she just knew the entire house heard it. It didn't matter.

In the next moment, her entire being exploded in a cascade of lights, sounds, and a soaring pleasure like none she'd ever known. She collapsed against his chest, their hips still thrusting, slower and slower until they stopped, and she lay plastered on top of him, panting like she'd run a marathon. The sweetest part was the thundering of his heart beneath her cheek. Time seemed to stand still until he slid from beneath her and left the bed.

The sizzle in the fireplace told her he'd gotten rid of the condom. Samantha was exhausted, amazed, terrified, and utterly confused. With herculean effort she managed to crawl under the covers. She'd had the most exquisite sex of her life with a man who was technically her client. She'd risked the career she'd always wanted all for some incredible pleasure. Was there more to it than that? Was she out of her mind to wonder what—

"Samantha?" Dante wrestled his way under the various blankets and covers and pulled her on top of him.

"Hmm?"

"Stop overthinking. I can hear the wheels turning in your head."

"Mm-hmm." Was there anything more scrumptious than lying on top of over six feet of hot, sweaty male after having banged the hell out of him? She was so tired and so heavenly replete.

"Samantha?"

"Hmm?"

"I don't mean to scare you or anything, but I love you."

Samantha's heart stuttered.

Now I know how Elizabeth Bennett felt.

Chapter Fifteen

Now I know how Mr. Darcy felt.

Three fantastic days and three glorious nights had passed since he'd told Samantha he loved her, and she had pretended to fall asleep.

Danny smiled as he and Samantha strode up the crest of the hill. He paused to take in the magnificent view. Two magnificent views, actually. The endless primitive Highland landscape of the Rosemount estate and the beautiful woman who stood beside him, her little finger entwined with his.

Samantha, head tilted back to the sun and eyes closed against its bright light, reminded him of some romance novel cover heroine. Dressed in a simple ankle-length wool dress that buttoned up the front, for which he was very grateful, with a Scot's plaid shawl wrapped around her shoulders, she was so simply and ethereally pretty it took his breath away, which had happened a lot lately. In his bed. In front of the fireplace. In the big copper tub. On a bed of grass with the sun shining on them and the March wind chapping his naked butt.

"What are you thinking?" Samantha squeezed his finger.

"How gorgeous you are. How lucky I am. How much my ass is itching and burning."

She threw back her head and laughed. God, he loved it when she laughed. She'd been so serious when they first met.

"I'm sorry," she said. "I really shouldn't find that so funny."

"No, go ahead and make fun of me," Danny said. "But you could have *told* me about nettles before you rolled my naked ass into a patch of them while you were having your wicked way with me."

"You were the one who picked the spot."

"You were the one who couldn't wait until we got back to the house." He wrapped an arm around her and pulled her close. The wind teased the loose strands spilling from her elegant Regency updo. He used his thumb to push the hair away from her face. "Do you have any idea what you do to me?"

"Other than land you in a patch of nettles?" She touched the fingers of her free hand to his lips. "We need to get back. I'll have Mrs. Wallace give us something for the rash on your exquisite arse."

He kissed her. Hard. Bent her over his arm and plundered her mouth with lips and tongue. By the time he released her, they were both panting.

"Please don't turn me over to Mrs. Wallace," he begged. "I don't think I could take her doctoring my posterior again."

She reached under his kilt and pinched him.

He jumped. "Hey! Do that again."

"You like that?" She gave him a saucy side-eye as they walked down the hill toward the manor house.

The grass was high and dry as it whipped against their legs. They walked this path every day, and still the stark enchantment of the land struck him.

"Yes, ma'am."

"I'll be sure to tell Mrs. Wallace."

"You're a hard woman, Dr. Higgins. That's what makes you so good at your job."

She caught her lower lip beneath her teeth and shook her head.

"You are, you know. You're the only reason I stand a snowball's chance in hell of doing Rothgate justice."

It was true. She'd spent hours every day teaching him how to speak, how to move, how to behave like a Regency gentleman. The dancing lessons and weapons lessons helped, but Samantha lived and breathed this era, and she'd taught him to live and breathe it too.

"Urquhart sings your praises, you know. You've become quite the horseman. Mr. Goode says you've become quite *light of foot* on the dance floor. Or course, Teddy isn't quite so effusive in his praise." She wasn't looking at Danny, just walking beside him, hands behind her back and head down. What had he said?

"Teddy wouldn't say anything nice about me if his life depended on it. I've been sneaking in lessons with Lord Lachlan while you've been having your meetings with Eleanor and Miss Stepford." Danny wished he knew what Samantha was thinking.

"Lord Lachlan? The duke's brother?" Samantha stumbled on the rocky path. Danny grabbed her elbow and steadied her.

She looked at him with such longing in her eyes he nearly dragged her to the gardens to flatten some of the shrubs.

"Yeah. He's amazing with a sword and a damned good shot with a bow and arrow. Knox hooked me up with him. I don't think they get along, and Knox worries about him. He served in the Middle East. PTSD, like my cousin. He won't talk to Knox, but he talks a little to me."

Danny had told her the story of his cousin's suicide one

night while they lay in bed. She'd loved him so sweetly and fiercely afterward that he'd wanted to cry.

"You're a good man, Dante Arneaux. I hope you know that."

They crossed the cobblestone drive and walked around the fountain to the front of the house.

"I'm a work in progress, Samantha. Not much more to me than that."

Was *good man* the same as *nice guy*? Not that it mattered. He'd never seen himself as either. Women like Samantha married *nice guys*, not men like him. His heart stuttered.

Whoa! Where the hell did that come from?

One of the footmen opened the door, and Danny and Samantha stepped into the entrance hall. The sound of loud voices drew their attention to the downstairs drawing room.

"We're late. Everyone is already waiting to go up for luncheon," Samantha said.

"Good," Danny said as he offered her his arm. "I'm starving."

She hesitated. When she didn't take his arm, he dropped it back to his side.

"I need to tell you something, Dante." She frowned, putting little darts in the bridge of her nose. "I should have told you weeks ago."

Crash!

The sudden noise came from the drawing room.

"What the hell?" he and Samantha exclaimed together.

They rushed to the drawing room doors at the same time Robbie dashed down the stairs from the dining room.

The footman opened one of the double doors slightly. He peered inside, then turned to look at them. "Trouble brewing. Keep yer heads down."

Danny grasped the door and opened it wide enough for them all to step inside. Teddy sat in a high-backed armchair near the fireplace, eyes on Lily who stood in the middle of the room, her back to them, Eleanor's velvet bag hanging from her fingertips. Every time Eleanor reached for the bag, Lily stepped back. Apparently, she'd crashed into the dainty table that lay scattered around the drawing room. A broken vase lay on the floor. God only knew how much it was worth.

"I hate these clothes," Lily ranted. "I hate using a chamber pot. I ate eel for God's sake. Eel. I want my phones. I want electricity. I want Netflix!"

"You signed up for this, Miss Randolph," Eleanor said.

"I want to wear makeup and my stilettos," Lily shot back. "And I don't care what you're in charge of—you have no right to hide my phones separately from everyone else's."

"When did we eat eel?" Danny asked in the hope of diffusing the situation. He'd seen Lily in a full-blown tantrum. They'd never get to lunch if this kept up. "What's wrong with eel?"

As hoped, every focus in the room shifted to him. One of the French doors that led out onto the front terrace cracked open, and the duke's hermit of a brother stepped just inside the room. The breeze that followed him stirred the flames in the giant drawing room fireplace. A log shifted and sent sparks up the chimney. Lord Lachlan stared at Lily. Fortunately, everyone else stared at Danny.

"What? I'm from Louisiana. We eat gator and snake. Hell, we eat crawfish and barbecued nutria on the fourth of July."

"What the devil is nutria?" Teddy asked.

"Well, it's a sort of…it's…actually, it's a big rat, but don't take that personally, Teddy."

Teddy rolled her eyes. "Bugger off, Arneaux."

"There are ladies present, Mr. Rousseau." Knox used his duke voice. Never a good sign. That voice would freeze ice on a New Orleans's stripper's ass in August.

"I don't give a damn about any of that. I want my phones, you red-headed witch." Lily stepped closer to Eleanor but hid the bag behind her back. "Now."

"You signed a contract just like everyone else, Lily. Give me the bag so we can all go to lunch. It's roast beef today, not eel."

"That's *Miss Randolph* to you, Eleanor." Lily glanced around the room. When she saw Danny and Samantha, an eerie smile twisted her lips.

Not. Good.

"Fine." Eleanor folded her arms across her chest. "Miss Randolph, give me the fucking bag of phones so we can all get on with our lives."

Teddy leaned forward in his chair. Samantha stepped closer to Eleanor, and Danny followed.

"I want my phones." Lily shouted so loudly everyone in the room jumped, except for the duke's silently watchful brother.

Danny had had enough. Not to mention he was hungry as hell. "For God's sake, Lily. Stop playing this tired old cliché. Child actress has a terrible life and becomes a spoiled diva so difficult nobody wants to work with her. Give it a rest. Grow up."

The trouble with stepping into a hole was he would never knew how deep it was until he fell on his ass. Danny had the scariest falling sensation he'd ever had in his life.

"A cliché? A cliché? How about the cliché of the Holly-wood bad boy who screws every hot actress in town but walks away when they get too serious? What can you expect from a guy raised by his grandmother who ran the most infamous whore house in New Orleans?"

Samantha gasped and put her hand on his arm.

"You leave my Maw Maw out of this," he murmured. "At least she didn't pimp me out to every director and actor in the business to boost my career like your mother did. And then run off with most of your money and your latest boyfriend when your career crashed and burned."

He'd made a mistake. A bad one. Like a stunt about to go horribly wrong he saw it coming and there wasn't a fucking thing he could do but brace for impact. Lily pulled the velvet bag from behind her back. She rifled through it and pulled out a cell phone. Danny's cell phone.

He was trapped in the burning car with no way out.

"No, your agent is the pimp." She tossed the phone to Samantha who caught it.

The screen flared to life with her touch. The sinking feeling in Danny's stomach told him he would have taken Jackie's advice years ago and put a lock code, or better yet, fingerprint lock, on his phone. Samantha's forehead wrinkled. Danny opened his mouth. Samantha raised her hand, palm out.

"Miss Randolph, this has gone far enough. You had no right to come into my room. Give me that bag," Eleanor said.

The breathy edge of panic to her voice set off alarm bells in Danny's head.

Lily nearly purred. "You really should call your agent, Danny. She's anxious to know if you've managed to get our Dr. Higgins into bed."

"Shut up, Lily," Danny snapped.

Shock became a living, breathing presence in the room. Danny stopped breathing in an effort to hear what was going on. There was no need as everyone else's breath was so damned loud his breath didn't matter. Samantha kept staring at his phone as if it held the answers to every question in the universe.

"We've been deceived, ladies and gentlemen," Lily practically crowed. "It seems this is little Miss Higgins's very first job running the show. Her boss wouldn't take it."

"Lily, I've felt bad for you for a long time. It sucks to have a mother willing to pimp out her daughter then steal from her. But there's no excuse for this cruelty," he said.

Eleanor rushed forward like a linebacker and tried to get the bag back. The duke stepped in and took it from Lily.

"I suggest you end this, Miss Randolph." The duke handed the bag to Eleanor and set his hand on Lily's wrist.

Lily threw him off, eyes on Danny. "And Wentworth has so much faith in her, the final decision as to whether Danny-boy gets the part of a lifetime lies in her amateur hands. Danny wasn't supposed to know that, but his agent tells him everything, doesn't she? That Amazon bitch ordered him to seduce the lovely teacher to make sure he got the part. Even if it means sleeping with her. Who's the pimp now, asshole?"

Danny stared at Samantha, willing her to speak. He caught movement out of the corner of his eye and took a surprised step backwards as the duke's quiet brother, Lachlan, threw Lily over his shoulder. She gasped as he slipped out the French doors. Good, because if Samantha didn't say something soon, Danny was going to have to strangle Lily on general principle.

As if she'd heard his thoughts, Samantha finally looked up. "If you all will excuse me, I suddenly find I am not hungry. Enjoy your lunch." She strode toward the drawing room doors. Robbie ran to open them for her.

"Samantha, wait." Danny took a step toward her.

She turned back and her face stopped him dead in his tracks. Danny's heart shriveled up so tight he could swear he heard ribs crack. She was the one who had the right to be hurt, but he was the one whose chest throbbed like he'd been skewered on one of Lachlan's claymores.

"Don't." One word, but it was the only one she needed. She left the room with all the dignity of any Regency grande dame.

For a moment all Danny heard was the snapping and popping of the fire and his own harsh breathing. When had he drawn enough air in his lungs to breathe?

"Well, that was certainly—"

"Say the wrong thing, Teddy." Danny whipped his head around, fists clenched to glare a hole through the weapons instructor. "Say the wrong fucking thing."

The man was smart enough to stop talking.

Danny couldn't seem to move his feet. He glanced around the room and took in the various expressions of the others. It was like being at his own funeral. Only Miss Chase didn't look at him as if he'd just died.

"Go," she mouthed, her eyes bright. "Go."

He ran to the foyer and nearly slipped when his boots hit the marble floor. He searched frantically and found Samantha at the top of the stairs to the first-floor landing.

"Samantha, wait." He took the stairs two at the time. "It isn't what it looks like, I swear it."

"I was right the first time, Mr. Arneaux," she said, her voice so rough his own throat hurt in sympathy. Her eyes were hard beneath the sheen of tears. "If only you weren't you. But you are, and I promise, I will never forget that again."

"*Mo chridhe*, please."

"You might want to call your agent and tell her—mission accomplished." She threw the phone so hard it bounced off his chest and crashed down the stairs onto the foyer floor in a million pieces—kind of like his heart. Then she strode up the next set of stairs to the second floor and out of sight.

Chapter Sixteen

HAD ANYONE EVER DIED FROM AN OVERDOSE OF SCOTTISH tablet? Samantha stared at the nearly empty porcelain china plate. She didn't remember eating the stack of neatly cut squares of the rich, sugary confection, but since she'd sent Marie and Laveau back across the hall, she had no one to blame but herself. She dug her fist into her chest, but the pain there didn't ease.

Actually, she blamed Mrs. Wallace. Someone had reported the details of that little scene in the drawing room to the housekeeper. An hour later, the tall Scotswoman had knocked once on Samantha's door and barged into the room carrying a tray of food, tea, and a bottle of wine. Once she'd arranged it all on the tea table in front of the high-back, overstuffed fireside chair she'd looked at Samantha, *harrumphed* once, and marched out without saying a word.

The hot scones, jam, and clotted cream had disappeared first. Followed by a plate of cheese and a bunch of grapes. Followed by the tablet washed down with the wine. She owed the consuming of all that food in an hour to...having her heart broken by America's number one action hero.

"Stupid, stupid, stupid," she muttered as she shoved out of the chair and began to pace.

She'd done quite a bit of that since she'd made her dignified exit from the drawing room. Pacing and berating herself. Interspersed with having a good cry face down on the bed a time or two.

Samantha scrubbed her hands over her face. She went to the washstand and poured some water from the pitcher into the matching basin. Cupping the icy water in her hands, she doused her eyes and cheeks over and over again. Didn't help. Her eyes burned. They'd swelled and now they itched. Her cheeks? Heated with anger.

At Dante Arneaux. At Lily Randolph. Most of all at herself. She'd thrown her chance to have a career out from under Cedric's thumb to the devil. Lily had probably broadcast her little discovery to every tabloid in America by now—which meant the London papers would carry it in the morning. Lovely.

What the hell had made her think someone like Dante was honestly interested in her? She wasn't a naïve young girl. She'd seen the film business from the inside for years. She knew how it worked. She'd worked with dozens of handsome actors. Never as intensely or one-on-one as she had with Dante, but still. She wasn't the sort to be taken in by a handsome face and a glib tongue.

No, she *hadn't* been taken in by the superficial things other saw in him. There was more to him than that. A woman didn't spend nearly every waking hour with a man for weeks on end and not learn something of his character. Nobody was that good an actor. Or was he? Samantha sat down on the side of the bed. Hard.

"You have lost your bloody mind," she announced to the beautifully decorated bedchamber.

That was what it was—a Regency bedchamber in a stately

home in Scotland. She'd landed in every Austenite's dream. Her job was every Austenite's dream, and she'd thrown it all away for some hot kisses, great sex, and…beautiful green eyes. In those eyes she'd seen genuine desire to learn what she had to teach him, genuine pain over the loss of his mother and his cousin and so many things, and what she'd still swear was genuine desire and even more for her.

Mistake.

Instantly, an image came to mind of the two of them lying on top of his plaid and making love. The things he did to her. The sensations he tempted and teased and demanded from her entire body. For so long she'd decided sex just wasn't going to be that big a deal for her. *Wrong!* With Dante it was an obsession. She'd never been with a man who cared so much about her pleasure.

Pleasure.

Desire.

Love?

No, no, no, no, no!

Sex was not love. Not even mind-blowing, name scream-ing, ankles-locking-behind-his-back sex. Love was respect and laughter and caring and a sincere appreciation of who the beloved was as a person. And…*shit!*

But he'd told her he loved her. Why had he done that? He didn't need to go that far. He had her in bed, had her right where he wanted her. Why such a terrible, cruel lie? Why had he made her believe?

She fell back across the bed, arms wide. "Dante Arneaux, why are you…you? Who are you? Dammiiiiiiit!" Samantha beat against the thick duvet with her fists.

"That settles it," a familiar American voice declared. "No more tablet for you, girl."

Eleanor closed the door as she entered and did a careful visual assessment of the room. Samantha sat up and did the same. Open luggage sat on the blanket chest and the settee on the other side of the room, and scattered clothes hung out of drawers and on the floor.

"I see you made good use of Mrs. Wallace's eat-your-way-through-bad-news tray." Eleanor pushed around the remains of Samantha's feast. "Who knew somebody your size could pack away so much food."

"Bad news? Is that what you Yanks call total public humiliation?" Samantha slid off the bed and settled into the armchair before the fire. She poured herself half a glass of wine and offered Eleanor the bottle.

"Yes, thank you." The event planner grabbed the bottle with one hand and Samantha's glass of wine with the other. She downed the wine and put the bottle on the mantel. "From the sound of it you've had enough, sweetie."

"How much of that did you hear?"

"Enough to know you are more than a little confused about Danny Arneaux." Eleanor sat in the chair opposite her. "Want to talk about it?"

"Not particularly. Do you want to talk about the most idiotic thing you've ever done in your life?"

"Not particularly." Eleanor gave her a sad little smile. "I would offer to kill Lily Randolph for you, but Lord Lachlan hustled her out of the drawing room the minute Danny bulldozed back in with murder in his eyes."

"Lord Lachlan?"

"Yes, I think he has a thing for America's little sweetheart. He was looking at her like our Danny looks at Mrs. Gordon's cranachan."

A sharp pang stabbed Samantha right in the solar plexus. "I hope he's prepared for a bad case of indigestion." She wanted to feel bad about taking a cheap shot at the actress. She didn't. "What does His Grace think about his brother and Lily?"

"Oh, Teddy made his usual subtle remark about it afterward. The duke's response was short and sweet."

"Oh?"

"And I quote 'Not bloody likely.'"

"How angry was Dante with Lily?"

Pitiful. Samantha wanted to kick herself for asking.

"Furious. That Louisiana upbringing and McGinty are the only things that stopped him from decking her."

"Dante would never hit a woman. It's not in him." Samantha wasn't sure of much, but she was sure of that.

"No, it isn't, is it? I suspect there are a great many things that aren't in your Cajun in a kilt." Eleanor picked up one of the last pieces of tablet and popped it in her mouth.

"He's not my anything." How bitter those words tasted. "And you'd be surprised what someone would do for the chance of a lifetime."

"Hmm. Like take on artistic direction of a major motion picture for the first time *and* guarantee to turn an action hero into a serious actor in a matter of weeks?"

"I didn't guarantee. I hoped. I also had the power to take the role away from him if I decided he couldn't do it." She sighed and shook her head. "But yes, it was my first job running the show."

"Was?"

"Come on, Eleanor. You and I both know Lily has blasted this story to every tabloid in the world by now. Regency Coach seduced by the famous *Danny* Arneaux. Wentworth has probably already called my cell to fire me. One of the advantages of living a Regency lifestyle is bad news travels slowly."

"Well," Eleanor pulled the velvet bag out of her dress pocket. "I've checked. She hasn't made any calls from any of these phones, and her phones are locked in His Grace's safe."

"You knew she wouldn't play by the rules." Samantha

didn't know why she was surprised. People underestimated Eleanor because she was beautiful. Just like they underestimated Samantha because she was a history nerd.

"I suspected. I just didn't anticipate how deep the mean went in that woman."

"It doesn't matter." Samantha stood and started to gather up the clothes she'd tossed onto the floor. She clutched the oversized LSU t-shirt and closed her eyes. She'd always thought women who talked about a tearing sensation at the loss of…what? Love? Please, not love. Anything but that. She thrust the shirt toward Eleanor. "Return this to him, please."

Eleanor got up slowly from the chair and took the shirt, then draped it over her arm. "Okay. Is there anything of yours that you want back from him?"

Samantha's eyes burned. Her throat started to close. "Whatever he has of mine is going to take a while to get back, I'm afraid."

"What are you going to do?"

Excellent damned question. What was she going to do? Thinking about it was driving her mad. Worse. The more she thought about it, the weaker she became.

"Talk to him, Samantha. Give him a chance to explain."

"I can't afford to do that, Eleanor. Not if I have any hope of salvaging my career."

"I see." Eleanor held Samantha's gaze, her expression compassionate and a little sad. "You want me to have Robbie or one of the other footmen to bring you a tray for supper?"

"Please." Samantha didn't have the power to think beyond the next few minutes, but supper downstairs with everyone else was a definite no. "Eleanor?"

"Yes?" She'd reached the door but turned to face Samantha.

"I…need my phone, please."

To her surprise, Eleanor reached into her bodice and

withdrew the iPhone in the *Pride and Prejudice* skin, then handed it to her. Once the door closed behind the far-too-wise redhead, Samantha curled her hand to her chest, pressing the hard phone into her breastbone in the hope of relieving the pressure there. Didn't work.

A sudden chill swept through the room. Samantha plucked her plaid shawl from the back of her chair and wrapped it around her shoulders—and immediately regretted it. The fabric smelled of Dante's cologne and the winter grass of the Highlands. The drapes across the windows suddenly undulated as if blown by a breeze. There *was* a breeze, a lavender scented breeze with the hint of a feminine sigh on it. Trouble was, all the windows were firmly closed.

"That's all well and good, Elsbeth," Samantha said as she glanced around the room. "But I could really use a bit more help deciding what the hell to do now."

❧

DANNY STARED OUT OVER THE LOCH AND WATCHED THE evening fog roll in like an old quilt spread across the top of a too-big bed. The sun wasn't setting, but the time wasn't far off. The afternoon had turned dreary and cold in more ways than one. He'd come out here to clear his head or at least that was what he'd told McGinty. The man might be up in years, but his size gave him a definite advantage even against someone Danny's height. The steward had wrestled Danny out of the drawing room, out the front doors, and around the corner of the house before he knew what hit him. Good thing too. After Lily's *announcement*, Lord Lachlan had grabbed her and dragged her off in the opposite direction.

Danny wouldn't have hit her. He wanted to in the worst possible way, but he'd been raised by a couple of powerful women who'd instilled in him from an early age you didn't use your strength to harm others, especially not women or children or animals. He just hoped Lachlan was wearing a cup.

The desire to find Samantha, to talk to her and try to explain pulsed at his temple like the world's worst headache. But here he sat and had been sitting for hours. Too damned chicken-shit to go back to the house and even try to see her. He knew her well enough to know there was no way in hell she'd let him in her room, let alone give a damn what he had to say. He'd told her to trust him. He'd told her nobody would find out about them and there'd be no chance their relationship would screw with her career.

He'd blown that all to hell and back.

The look on her face. It hurt to breathe. It hurt to even think about it. His hands still shook—with rage or fear or maybe a combination of both. Her career was so important to her. She worked so damned hard at it. She'd spent hours teaching him and more hours working with everyone else to get ready for production of this film. She deserved every bit of success the film might bring her, and now….

From down the loch where the old tower stood, the mournful sound of bagpipes floated to where he sat. Not loud, but soft enough to force him to listen. Eerily the disembodied melody rode the mist and suddenly surrounded him, notes just out of reach, but there. So very there, the hurt seeping out of his heart into his blood and bones like a slow-burning fever.

He had it bad and had no idea how to fix the fuck up he'd made of his life with Samantha. The role of Captain Rothgate no longer seemed important. Ironic as a kick in the nuts and a helluva lot more excruciating. The pipes played on, and he told himself he'd get over it, get over her. He'd move on whether he starred in *A Matter of Honor* or not. He could blame Jackie for encouraging him to create the bad boy action star he'd been living the last ten years. Bullshit. He played the part because he'd enjoyed the hell out of it. Then he'd continued to play the part because it had become easier to pretend to be what everyone expected him to be. Not because it was fun, but because he'd so immersed himself in the role to the point he could practically sleepwalk through his life. Easy. And Danny had always been all about easy. He'd traded on his looks, his physical abilities, and his brains all his life. None of which he'd earned. He'd been lucky as hell, and he'd ridden that luck until today when it finally ran out. When it mattered the most, his luck had run out.

The pipes soared high and shook his soul to its core. He didn't know who was playing, but they damned sure knew how to cry. Danny lowered his head into his hands.

"Dammit, Samantha, I am so damned sorry," he whispered.

"I used to hate the sound of those bloody bagpipes."

Danny raised his head to see the duke walking down the path out of the mists like the ghost of his ancient ancestor. In one hand, he carried a long, thick staff, similar to a walking stick but a foot higher than his head. In the other, he had a couple of bottles of ale by their necks. He stopped next to the bench. Danny slid over to let him sit.

"And now?" Danny asked as he took the bottle Knox handed him.

"Now?"

"You said you used to hate them."

"Aye. I guess they've grown on me. Times like this I think they serve a purpose."

"What purpose is that?"

"Saying what we can't."

"Hmm." Danny couldn't argue with him there. He twisted the cap off the ale then took a long drink.

"So, what are you going to do now?" Knox asked.

"Do?"

The duke swallowed his own sip of ale. "About the fair Dr. Higgins. Miss Randolph has cocked things up quite nicely."

"I had a hand in it in the first place. I never should have agreed to my agent's suggestion."

"Probably not."

"Are you always this helpful?" Danny rubbed a hand across his eyes.

The glow of a light flared in the top window of the old tower. The music of the pipes came just a little closer. Something caught his eye on the loch in the fading sunlight. The wind had picked up and that damned scent of lavender and earth came to him on that wind.

"Asking the men in my family for help with a woman is not necessarily a good idea," the duke said.

Danny turned to look at Knox. The duke gazed out over the loch, and Danny almost thought the man clearly saw what to Danny looked like only a hint of a figure on the water.

"Why is that?" he asked.

"According to the storytellers, there's a curse on the men of the Innes family. Has been since Elsbeth Dunhome met her end in this very loch. Supposedly, she and my ancestor are destined to wander the loch, her in the water and him on the shore in search of each other, doomed to love eternally from afar. There hasn't been a happy marriage in my family in seven hundred years. Each one has been more miserable than the last. Of course, it could be that the Innes men are all arses and have terrible taste in women."

"Damn. That sucks. Does it have something to do with the witch that doesn't exist?"

"So they say. The legend states until there is a happy

marriage, the witch and her laird will wander the loch in search of each other."

Knox raised his bottle and saluted the loch. Or at least that was what it looked like to Danny. Except for that weird shape out in the mist.

Danny stood and took a step closer to the bank of the loch. "I thought there was no witch."

What the hell was that out on the water? Or who? A feminine laugh twined with the melody of the bagpipes. He whipped his head around to see if Knox noticed it.

Bastard sat there like a sphinx. "There isn't. It's…just a story."

"Uh-huh. You don't believe in curses or witches or—"

"Ghosts or eternal love. None of it."

"That's a shame." Danny hurt with a physical ache like no broken bone or wrenched muscle had ever given him, but he wasn't sure he was ready to give up on love even if it meant no immunity to the pain that came with it.

"Do you believe in it? A love so powerful you'd give up your place in heaven to search for it for all time?" the duke murmured.

Damn. For a man who said he didn't believe in love or forever, Knox Innes, Duke of Turra, had a pretty good handle on what love was supposed to be. Danny had always thought he knew what love was, would recognize love when it came along.

"I used to believe. Now, I just don't know." Danny finished his ale and glanced back at the loch. He couldn't be seeing what he thought he was seeing.

"I think you might want to figure it out before it is too late."

"Do you see…." Danny looked at him. "Figure out what? What do you mean, 'too late?'"

"Love. Figure out if you believe in it or not. Decide what

you're willing to do, how far you're willing to go to keep it. Let's get you back to the house." Knox took Danny's arm and practically bum-rushed him up the hill toward the back gardens. Not up the path they'd both taken to the loch earlier.

"I thought you didn't believe," Danny said as he kept trying to look over his shoulder.

"Oh, I don't. But every now and again I want to."

Danny stopped and stared at him for a moment. He couldn't read his face in the last light of the day. In a few more steps they reached the gardens, and the gaslights lining the path to the back terrace showed Knox had put on his duke face again.

"Want to believe in what, Knox? In ghosts or in a love like that?"

"Good night, Dante." He took the empty ale bottle from him then slipped inside the doors from the terrace into the library.

Decide what you're willing to do, how far you're willing to go to keep it.

The walls of Rosemount Manor rose in front of him. Samantha was in there somewhere, probably in her room, across the hall from his. There was no way in hell she'd see him. Not tonight. That whole scene in the drawing room had kicked the shit out of his confidence, and there was no way in hell he wanted to see any of the players in that soap opera. If he felt like that, he couldn't imagine how she felt. Then again, he didn't even know if she loved him. Maybe she was glad to be rid of him. Yeah, and maybe he was looking for reasons not to see her again, because he was a coward.

The wind whistled down the terrace and blew up under his kilt. He turned. The mists from the loch had crawled up into the gardens. Danny sat down on the steps then rested his elbows on his knees and his head in his hands. He thought about those lonely bagpipes and Knox's ancestor wandering the shores of the loch looking for the woman who'd been taken from him.

Decide what you're willing to do.

"Elsbeth, honey," he said into the night, "I need a sign or something. Help a dumbass American out?"

THE FIRE HAD GONE OUT IN HIS ROOM. THAT HAD TO BE IT. Danny was cold as hell, and the damned dogs had stolen all the covers. Every bone in his body ached like a toothache. Was he hungover or had Samantha sneaked into his room while he slept and beat him with a baseball bat?

He'd been dreaming, hadn't he? About misty lochs and a woman walking out of the fog. She'd come right up on the terrace and bent over him. Spoken to him in a lavender-scented whisper.

What wid nae ye do for a once in a lifetime woman? What wid nae ye do?

"Samantha." He sat up.

His body sounded like a bowl of Rice Krispies. What the hell? It took a minute, but he finally realized he lay on the steps of the back terrace just outside the library. The sun was just coming up, and unless he'd gone to bed and then gone sleepwalking, he'd slept out here all night. The last thing he remembered was…Samantha.

He'd made a decision. He needed a phone. Movement from the French doors into the library caught his eye.

Knox.

Good.

He'd have a phone.

Danny stood, then pushed one of the doors open and stumbled into the elegant and, thank God, warm room.

Knox and McGinty sat at a desk passing papers back and forth. The way they looked at him, like he was a bastard arriving at a family reunion, made him wonder if they'd even help him.

"Arneaux?" McGinty got up first. "What the hell are you doing out there, lad?"

"Did you sleep on the terrace?" Knox unfolded from his chair then headed to the closest fireplace. "What the devil possessed you?" He waved Danny into one of the chairs.

McGinty, bless his grumpy ass, poured a big mug of coffee from the sideboard then handed it to Danny.

"B-b-bless you." The coffee was nearly scalding hot, but he didn't care. It was nectar of the gods as far as he was concerned.

"I realize you're a country boy at heart, but is there a reason you slept out of doors in the Highlands in March, instead of the nice warm bed upstairs?" Knox asked.

"I was thinking about what you said, and I guess I fell asleep." Danny wrapped both hands around the heavy coffee cup and held his face over it between sips.

McGinty gave the duke a *what-the-hell-did-you-say* look. Knox shrugged. The light bulb must have lit up because the steward gave Danny a slow, sad smile.

"Didn't want to sleep across the way from the lass?" McGinty asked as he topped off Danny's cup.

"Something like that," Danny muttered. "I didn't trust myself not to go all pitiful and bang on her door in the middle of the night to beg her forgiveness."

"Poor wee Sassenach is a romantic," McGinty said with a grin.

"Poor wee Sassenach has embarrassed the lady enough,". Danny said between sips. "Lily Randolph is across the same corridor. I didn't want to give her more ammunition. Or start up World War III."

"Wise choice," Knox agreed. "But there are a couple of dozen unoccupied bedrooms in this house at least."

"I had a lot of thinking to do." It all came back to him now. For better or worse he'd made a decision. "I need to use a phone. One with international calling."

"Bring him mine," the duke ordered his steward.

McGinty went to the desk and brought his boss's cell phone to Danny.

"Would you like some privacy?" Knox asked.

"Nope. I'm a firm believer that career suicide should be a spectator sport."

Danny punched in the phone number. In a few minutes he was talking to the person he needed. Watching Knox's and McGinty's expressions made him want to laugh. Hysterically, probably. Once he hung up and handed Knox the phone, the duke and the older Scot just stared at him until Danny finally pushed himself out of the chair and ran a hand through his hair.

"Are you sure about what you just did?" Knox asked in that quiet, direct way of his when he knew the answer to a question but asked it anyway.

"I guess I'll find out in the next few minutes." Danny didn't see any point in wasting time. He strode toward the doors into the rest of the house.

"Where are you going?" Knox called after him.

"To talk to Samantha. I've put it off long enough."

"You've put it off *too* long, lad," McGinty said. "She's gone."

Danny turned back slowly. He couldn't actually feel his body. All his blood had drained to somewhere beneath his feet. "Gone? Gone…where?"

"She's on her way to the airport," McGinty said.

"She called Wentworth last night and quit," Knox said. "She's going back to London."

"She— Oh, fuck no she is not." Danny fumbled with the door handles. "How long has she been gone? Knox, dammit, how long?"

"Here now." McGinty stepped toward him.

Knox waved the steward off. "I had my personal driver pick her up in one of my cars a few minutes ago. I'll call him and tell him—"

"Tell him to slow down and wait for me," Danny said, an insane idea coming into his head. "McGinty, can you call Urquhart and have him saddle Grenadier for me?"

"Grenadier? What the devil for?"

"Just do it, McGinty." Knox looked at Danny and shook his head. "The Sassenach's run mad as a hatter."

"What else is new?" McGinty grumbled as he went to the intercom on Knox's desk.

Knox followed Danny out of the library and across the foyer to the front doors. "Are you sure about this?"

"Absolutely not. I'll probably fall off and break my neck." Danny ran down the steps toward the stables.

"Try not to, if you please. You know I hate the paperwork," Knox called after him.

Danny looked over his shoulder to see the duke with his phone to his ear.

By the time Danny reached the stables, Grenadier was prancing in place, and every man who worked with the horses had gathered around him. Danny grabbed the reins from the groom. Without a word, Urquhart gave him a leg up.

"Why did I choose today to wear a damned kilt?" Danny grumbled.

"You had that kilt on yesterday, guv," Urquhart reminded him.

Danny gave him a dirty look. "I had a bad night and had no time to change."

"Aye, I suppose you did."

"Riding in this kilt is going to chafe the hell out of my nuts, isn't it?"

"Oh, aye, Yank. Something chronic." Urquhart grinned and shoved Danny's foot more securely into the stirrup. Never had he thought he'd be grateful for those daily early morning riding lessons.

"What shall I put you down for, Yank?" one of the lads asked as Danny directed the horse to the front gate of the stable yard.

"Put me down for a fiver," he called back.

"Staying on or falling off?"

"Getting the girl!" Danny goaded the horse into a gallop, cut across in front of the fountain, and headed up the cobble-stone drive.

Chapter Seventeen

Samantha tried her damnedest not to look out the windows from the roomy back seat of the Duke of Turra's Rolls Royce. He'd been incredibly kind in putting the car and his personal driver at her disposal. She could have taken the train from the village to Aberdeen, but His Grace had insisted. Thank goodness he had. In her present state she was in no mood to see other people, let alone talk to them over a long train ride.

Still, she wished the driver would speed up down the long tree-lined drive. The rhythmic *bump, bump, bump* of the drive's surface beneath the tires didn't bother her, though her head had continued to ache since she'd forced herself to get out of bed. Not that she'd experienced it before, but she supposed headaches happened after spending the night alternating between crying and swearing. She rummaged through her bag in search of her phone. No messages. Of course not. She'd spoken to Wentworth and told him her decision was final. Why would he bother to get in touch with her? And as for anyone else....

Why were they moving so slowly? She leaned forward to knock on the divider glass between the driver and her, but the view out the window she'd tried to avoid caught her attention. She'd grown to love Rosemount Manor and the Highlands. Seeing it for the last time would only remind her of everything she was leaving behind and…everyone.

Don't go there. Dante Arneaux was the last person she wanted to—

"What the hell?" Samantha tapped violently on the divider. "Stop. Stop!"

Across the glorious green and wheat carpet of Rosemount's front acreage, a streak of black raced toward the Rolls. *Grenadier.* In the saddle, with his kilt and white shirt blowing in the wind, Dante Arneaux rode out of the glittering Highland sunlight toward the drive.

She stared, mouth agape, as they neared on an intercept course. Dante pushed Grenadier to breakneck speed. The fool would kill himself and probably lame the horse in the bargain. Still, she couldn't tear her eyes from the sight. Dear God, why hadn't he left her alone? She would never forget the feel of his arms around her, him inside her, his mouth on hers, or the way he looked, wild, fierce, and all Dante Arneaux. And this—

The driver slammed on the brakes. Samantha surged forward and the seatbelt locked her into place with a snap that had her seeing stars for an instant. Dante pulled Grenadier to a sliding stop right next to the window where Samantha stared, open-mouthed at the—

"Idiot man!" She mashed the button to lower the window. "Are you out of your bloody mind? You might have been killed."

He was bloody damned magnificent. Even if he wore the same clothes as yesterday. He sat on that horse, hand on his hip, hair a completely delicious mess, and looked every inch the romance novel hero. Damn him to hell.

"What are you doing, Dante? Why are you here?"

"I need to talk to you." He jumped down from the horse, held the reins in one hand, and came to the window.

"You couldn't call?"

"Not part of my Regency experience. Besides, someone broke my phone."

A searing heat started at the back of Samantha's neck and crept up her face to her hairline. His bland, innocent expression didn't fool her one bit.

"I'm sure your agent can arrange to have a new one sent to you even out here."

"I'll be lucky if she doesn't come out here to murder me once she finds out what I've done. Can I join you in there for a few minutes? I'd rather not have this conversation standing out here in the cold."

She blew out a frustrated breath, then said, "Go ahead and turn off the car, Seamus. We won't be long."

"Yes, miss." The duke's driver killed the engine and got out of the car. Dante handed Grenadier's reins to him, and Samantha swore the Scot muttered, "Good luck" as he led Grenadier a few steps away to the grass.

Samantha slid all the way across the seat to the opposite window, which gave her a great view of Dante's long, muscled bare legs as he climbed into the car and settled onto the spot she'd vacated. She shouldn't be noticing his legs. Or the way he moved so comfortably in a kilt. Or the slight British accent that came out on certain words when he spoke. He'd used her, dammit. Made a fool of her.

"I have a plane to catch in Aberdeen, Mr. Arneaux, so let's get on with it. What can I do for you?" Her Dr. Higgins mantel settled over her. Better. Safer.

He reached over to pull her phone out of her hand. "You can call Wentworth and tell him your evil twin called him and you have no intention of quitting this project." With his free hand he scratched his hip.

"I don't have an evil twin, and I have no intention of embarrassing either of us by continuing to work on this film with you."

"Bugger embarrassment." His accent was spot on. Would she ever stop taking pleasure in the things she'd taught him?

"I beg your pardon?" She folded her hands in her lap and tried not to clutch them.

"No, *mo chridhe*," he said, his voice a dark, husky rumble. "I beg yours."

"Don't call me—"

"I should have told you about my agent's crazy plan the minute I fell in love with you. I should have told you everything."

She couldn't take her eyes off him. He was lying. He had to be. He had become too good an actor. She'd see it. She would. Any minute now.

"I knew the moment I met you there was no way in hell I'd ever be able to fool you. Then I fell in love with you, and I didn't want to fool you even if I could."

"Dante, stop."

"The only person I fooled was myself. I wasn't seducing you for a damned part. Everything I did, I did because I wanted you to love me as much as I love you." He shook his head and grinned that little boy grin of his. "Still do. More than anything I've ever wanted in my life."

Samantha's heart took off like a runaway horse. She could barely breathe. What was he doing? What was *she* doing? She'd made up her mind, and she didn't want her anger at him to leach away. Her anger was the only thing keeping her safe. That and her self-respect.

"I can't…I accept your apology, but I don't see this going anywhere. It just can't. I wish…."

He raised a hand. "I understand. I really do." He cleared his throat. "I'll get used to the idea that you don't love me. Eventually. But I can't let you sacrifice your career over the reputation I was too damned lazy to fix. And I don't ever want you to think that a single moment of our time together was anything other than the most honest and beautiful relationship of my life."

Samantha's eyes clouded over. She swallowed several times against the ache in her throat. "I don't…I don't know what to say." She did. She really did, but to say it was the most dangerous thing she'd ever do. Dangerous, and wonderful.

"You and this place have changed me, Samantha. You made me believe in me, the real me." He put down her phone, reached across the seat, and took her hand between his. "Maw Maw says there are people and places that have this power. The power to perfectly put all the broken pieces of a person's life together again so not even he can see the seams. You, and this place, this experience, have done that for me. I'll never be able to repay you, but if you call Wentworth and take your job back, maybe it's a start. I talked to him this morning. I know he wants you to continue with the project." He scratched at his hip once more.

"You called to get my job back?"

Perhaps the most ridiculous question she could ask when all she really wanted to know was if he meant what he said about loving her.

"Actually, I called to tell him I was backing out of the project. I didn't know you'd quit until this morning after I woke up on the terrace. But he did say—"

"You what? You could have frozen to death." No wonder she'd heard his dogs pacing the floors last night. "Wait. You gave up Rothgate? Are you mad? This is your chance. You're going to be amazing in this role."

"Not without my Regency coach, I won't. It's okay. The next guy Wentworth hires will be a Brit. You won't have to teach him a thing." He raised her hand to his lips, kissed her fingertips, and gently placed her hand back on the seat. "Call Wentworth," he said as he handed her the phone. "Please. You deserve to do this film. Don't allow a couple of raunchy Americans to fuck up your life." He opened the car door and turned to slide his booted feet out onto the drive. "Samantha?"

"Yes?" Her breath caught despite the fact he wasn't looking at her.

"I love you. I probably always will. And I'm probably the biggest dumbass on the planet for asking you, but…I'm only going to ask you this once. You tell me to shut up and get the hell out of your life, and you'll never hear from me again." He looked slowly over his shoulder at her. "Do you…could you ever have loved me?"

Samantha's whole life flashed before her eyes, which was only supposed to happen when on the verge of dying, but most of her life experiences involved the last few weeks and this man whose green eyes stared into hers and showed her everything in his heart—if only she hadn't been so blinded by self-doubt to see.

How the devil had Elizabeth Bennett ever have turned down Mr. Darcy?

"Samantha?"

"Shut up, Dante." Her voice cracked on the last word.

"Okay, I guess I'd—"

"Shut up and kiss me this instant."

He blinked. His forehead wrinkled, and he slowly got back into the car. "Um, excuse me?"

She slid across the seat and ignored the sense of freefall

rolling over her entire body. She captured his face between her hands and kissed him so hard he fell back into the corner of the seat, arms flailing. She rose up onto her knees and proceeded to plunder his mouth like a marauding pirate. He finally managed to wrap his arms around her and squeezed so hard she had to gasp for breath.

"By the way," she whispered. "I love you, you daft American lunatic. I don't know when it happened, perhaps a little bit every day, but I do. More than anything in the world." She used her thumb to brush away the single tear that rolled slowly down his cheek.

"Say it again," he said hoarsely. "Say it again, Samantha."

"I love you, Dante Arneaux. God help us both."

He touched his lips to hers, lightly at first in kisses and brushes. Then slowly and surely in a building of passion she'd come to crave from this man. She shouldn't have doubted him. She shouldn't have doubted herself. He never did. Not when it counted.

Suddenly, he stopped and sat up, still holding her in his arms. "I've got an idea."

"I hope it's to call Wentworth and get Rothgate back." She caressed his cheek and brushed his hair from his face. "I meant what I said. You're perfect for the part. I knew it as soon as I saw your screen test. That's why I took the job."

"Marry me." His expression said he was as surprised as she was, but then he smiled. "Marry me, Samantha. Today."

"You have run mad." He wasn't the only one. The instant he asked, her heart had nearly broken free from her chest.

Dante leaned out the window. "Seamus, how far to Gretna Green?"

Gretna Green? Oh. My. God.

"About a five-hour drive, sir. More or less. Whoa! Stop that, you nasty bugger. Wait!"

The sound of receding hoofbeats indicated Grenadier had

grown tired of waiting and had headed, no doubt, for the stables.

Dante settled back into the seat. He drew Samantha closer and brushed his lips across hers with a feather light touch. "Marry me, *mo chridhe*." He kissed her with tender touches and soft sighs across her lips. "Don't think about it. If we think about it, we'll do the sensible thing and not get married. I don't want to be sensible. Marry me."

She kissed him back because she couldn't think of what else to do. It struck her she'd only had this sensation once before in her life—when she'd watched the screen test of an actor she'd never seen in a single one of his movies and bet her entire future on being able to turn him into a romantic hero. More fool she, he already was one. That same sensation came over her. She'd thrown caution to the wind and offered to take Cedric's place based on her faith in the man gazing at her with such love and hope in his eyes she wanted to burst into tears. She was free falling, but this time, she knew where she'd land.

"Grenadier is on his way back to the stables," she murmured against his lips. "How would we get to Gretna Green?"

"Is that a yes?" He kissed her, a hard buss that seared her mouth. "Is that a yes, Dr. Higgins?"

"Yes. I'll marry you, Dante Arneaux. We'll be in every tabloid on both sides of the Atlantic, but I will marry you."

He threw his head back and gave a loud inarticulate cry. "Seamus." He nearly climbed out the window. "Start the car. Give me your phone. I need to call the duke."

He landed back in the seat and nearly squashed her. She wriggled her way out, but he grabbed her and dragged her across his lap as Seamus started the car and they rolled down the drive.

"Hey, Knox," Dante said into the phone. "I'm borrowing your Rolls. Yeah. Gretna Green. About a week."

Samantha's eyes began to burn. She searched through her bag and found a handkerchief. Ridiculous. Utterly. Deliriously. Ridiculous.

"Well, you asked me how far I'd go for a forever kind of love. All the way to Gretna Green, apparently. Take care of my dogs." He paused for a moment and rolled his eyes. "No, that does not mean serve them on toast. We'll be back. And at some point, we're going to want to book Rosemount for a big wedding and reception. Yeah, yeah, I know Eleanor will charge me a fortune." Dante kissed Samantha's hand and then pressed it to his heart. "It'll be worth it. Bye, Knox. And thanks." He opened the partition just enough to slide the phone through to Seamus.

"Now," Dante said as he pulled her against his chest and raised his eyebrows. "What are we going to do for the next five hours?" He reached under the back of his kilt. "How long does the damned nettle itch last?"

"Oh!" Samantha emptied her bag onto the seat and searched through the contents until she found the distinctive pink bottle. "I told Eleanor I wanted to drive a high-perch phaeton before I left. She and I caused quite a stir tooling into the village in that sporty carriage with those matched grays in the traces. I bought this for you. I intended to leave it outside your door, but I was in such a hurry to leave, I forgot."

He took the bottle of calamine she'd bought and rolled it around in one hand. "You were mad as hell at me, and you still worried about my itchy ass." He shook his head.

"Yes. Well, it *is* a very fine arse."

"So, you're marrying me for my arse," he said, his tone teasing. "Or maybe in spite of it."

"Let's get you out of this kilt, Captain Rothgate, and I'll make good use of this calamine."

"Whatever you say, ma'am. In or out of a kilt, this Cajun's arse is yours."

"And his heart?"

"It always was, *mo chridhe*, and it always will be."

SNEAK PEEK AT SASSENACH IN STILETTOS

Sneak preview of the next Rosemount Manor Love Regency Style series

Chapter One

28TH FEBRUARY
Los Angeles, California

THE CAR SERVICE WAS LATE. PAR FOR THE COURSE AS FAR AS Lily Randolph was concerned. One last disaster in a month-long series of disasters. The way things were going, she might not make that plane to Scotland at all. Why tempt fate? Or whoever was running the shitshow her life had become.

"We could drive you, sweetie," Derek said from behind the kitchen island where he cleaned up the remnants of the fruit smoothie he'd made for her breakfast.

He'd started out as her personal chef, but now served as chef, housekeeper, personal shopper, and friend. When she'd had to cut back on staff, Derek and his husband, Raphael, had stayed. They told her they had nowhere else to go. A lie, but one the three of them had tacitly agreed never to admit, at least not to one another.

"You just want an excuse to get behind the wheel of my Maserati." Lily checked the driveway of her Hollywood Hills home for the tenth time. Nothing. Dammit, her credit was bad, but not that bad. She had enough to pay for car service to the airport.

"There is that," Derek said with a grin.

His lithe body and blond surfer good looks made him appear much younger than forty. He'd hooked up with body-builder and personal trainer Raphael, eight years his junior, six years ago—about the same time Lily had hired them both in the hope of giving her failing career one last try.

"And how would you suggest we load all my luggage and the three of us into the 'Rati? Raphael would have to ride on the hood."

"He would make a show-stopping hood ornament." Derek gave the island's marble top one last swipe then draped the dishcloth over the edge of one of the sinks. "Or I could run down to the gatehouse and hotwire *he-who-shall-not-be-named's* Hummer."

"Only if you promise to park it at the airport and leave the keys in it," Lily said as she dropped onto one of the cream-colored couches in the great room and rummaged through her carry-on.

She dragged out her copy of *A Matter of Honor* and tucked it into her Kate Spade purse. The most anticipated film of the year was about to start production. Based on a novel by an obscure romance writer, the female lead role had been fought over like the last pair of size six Jimmy Choo's the night before the Oscars. And somehow, Lily had come up Cinder-fucking-ella. She still had trouble believing it.

"Ouch!" Derek flopped down on the oversized ottoman in front of her. "Tell me how you really feel."

"Doesn't matter." She pretended to check the tags and locks on her Louis Vuitton carry-on. "They picked up the Hummer last night." She handed Derek an index card. "New security codes. I sold the car, along with everything else he left in the gatehouse. And I changed the gate and house codes so he can't come on the property."

"Wasn't he supposed to come back tomorrow and pick up the Hummer and his possessions?"

"Was he?" Lily checked her phone with her patented expression of pretend innocence.

"That's my bitch," Derek said with a laugh.

"I learned from the best. Where is that damned car?" She sprang from the couch and stalked back to the front door, phone still in hand.

"He didn't deserve you, Lily," Derek said in that firm, *I-know-what-I'm-talking-about* voice. Not to be confused with his *I'm-trying-not-to-sound patronizing-because-you're-sad* voice.

"I don't know about that, Derek. But I do know I didn't deserve to walk into *my* sauna and find him banging *my* personal assistant." Oddly enough, saying it out loud only hurt a little today. In a month or so it wouldn't hurt at all, especially now.

"Do you want me to have Raphael kill him? There's room in the rose garden for at least one more scumbag ex before we have to start burying them under the jacuzzi."

"Before I kill anyone, there's a limo out front," Raphael said as he sauntered in shirtless, with his sweatpants riding low on his hips. "And the driver does *not* look like the type who loads luggage." He hefted two suitcases under each arm and headed for the door, which Lily held open even as she stood on her toes and kissed his cheek.

"You are so lucky," she told Derek as he grabbed her carry-on and handed her the Kate Spade.

"So are you, sweetie," Derek replied as they trekked out to the limo. "You just landed the biggest role in the biggest film of your life. This is the one. I can feel it. Everything is going to be wonderful from here on out."

"From your lips to God's ears, my friend." She stood next to the open limo door while Derek situated her carry-on and purse inside. Raphael made two more trips from the house, then finally closed the trunk of the long, black stretch.

"You're all set," Raphael said as he hugged her and kissed her on both cheeks. "Maybe you'll meet some handsome Highlander in Scotland and bring him home as a souvenir."

"I have no idea why Wentworth is insisting on us spending all this time in Bumfuck, Scotland before filming starts. And I have no interest in men in skirts, thank you very much."

Lily's nerves hummed like a thousand stage lights. Derek saw this role as the start of a revived career. He didn't realize it could be the end of one. Or if he did, he didn't say so.

"Don't knock men in skirts until you try one." Derek helped her into the limo. "And I do recommend you try one."

"I love you both," Lily said as Raphael put his arm around Derek. "I'll call you when I land. Take care of each other."

She knelt in the seat to peer out the back window as the limo rolled slowly down the drive. Once her friends disappeared from view and the driver merged onto the road into the heart of LA, she settled onto the soft leather seat and checked her phone again. She'd missed a call.

From her mother.

How the hell had she gotten this number?

She deleted the call and blocked the number. Mommy Dearest probably got it from Lily's latest ex. Now that she'd booted him out, he was desperate for money. He'd sell his own mother, let alone Lily's private cell number. She could count on one hand the number of people who had it and whom she hadn't blocked—Erik Wentworth, the director who had given her the role of a lifetime, Derek, Raphael, her agent of the last five years, and her hairdresser. Pathetic if she thought about it, which she tried hard as hell not to do.

She had bigger fish to fry. The flight from LA to Aberdeen might give her just enough time to fire up the grease.

THREE HOURS LATER, LILY HAD TO ADMIT GRATITUDE FOR TWO things. The first? She had restrained herself from getting shitfaced while she waited in British Airways' VIP lounge. The second? Her agent hadn't only booked her a flight on British Airways, but he'd booked her in first class. She was in her own luxurious little pod of a seat and there were only three other passengers in this section of the plane. They had all recognized her, as had the flight attendants. So, either they'd decided to show some class and not disturb her, or they all knew her career was a dumpster fire and wouldn't lower themselves to associate with, let alone fawn over, a now B-list actress who hadn't had a major movie role in years.

Whatever the reasons, Lily now had time to think through this latest turn her life had taken. Rumors about the casting of *A Matter of Honor* had been circling Hollywood like the mechanical shark from *Jaws* for months. Even now, Erik Wentworth, the hottest new director of period films, hadn't made an official announcement, though he'd told Lily the entire cast was pretty much a lock at this point. That was the source of her angst and irritation at the moment—one of the sources at least.

It was a good thing she'd already signed the contracts before Wentworth told Lily who her leading man was going to be. Of all the actors in the business, of all the actors in the world, what the hell had possessed this supposedly brilliant director to cast an action star in the lead role of the most anticipated period film of the decade? Not just any action star. No, in keeping with the shitshow theme her life had adopted of late, Wentworth had cast Danny Arneaux as Captain Rothgate.

Lily had read the damned book twice. If Danny I-Don't-Screw-Children was a Regency romance hero, her mother was Mother Teresa. And Lily's mother was no damned Mother Teresa. Danny Arneaux was no saint either. He'd hooked up with every starlet in Hollywood six years ago. She'd been eighteen years old and not a child by any stretch of the imagination. He'd turned her down anyway. His last two films had crashed and burned spectacularly, which meant she was going to have to carry him in this film.

Like hell she would.

They were both flying to Scotland to participate in some kind of Regency boot camp, but Wentworth had hired a special Regency tutor for Arneaux. That meant the director *knew* the Cajun Ken doll didn't have the chops for the job. Lily intended to make sure Wentworth never forgot it. With luck, he'd dump Arneaux and hire a real actor for the role.

"Are you reading *A Matter of Honor*?" the flight attendant with the cute British accent and sort of old-fashioned uniform asked as she delivered Lily's elegant meal tray. She indicated the book Lily had been trying to read again. "I love that book. I've read it three or four times."

"Why?" Lily fiddled with the contents of the tray—draped her napkin across her lap, organized her silverware, then buttered the fluffy roll. "Why do you love it?"

She didn't normally engage with the people who waited on her. Most saw it as her being too snobby and self-absorbed to bother, which was fine with her. Over the years, she'd come to understand that if people hated a celebrity, they tended to leave them alone. However, she really wanted to know the appeal of this romance novel that had come out of nowhere and become a bestseller so monumental Erik Wentworth had snapped up the movie rights.

"Really?" The flight attendant sounded suspicious, as if Lily were either making small talk or looking for a reason to tease her.

"I really want to know." Lily put down the silverware and gave the woman her full attention.

The flight attendant stepped closer and said in a low voice, "Because he does the right thing. Captain Rothgate. He has every chance not to, every chance to escape a terrible situation. He's been hurt, betrayed, traumatized by war, and he still does the honorable thing. He has no idea if it will work out for him and his wife. Neither does she. Life has been awful to them. But in the end…." She shrugged. "I guess I like the idea of someone doing the right thing even if they don't have to, and in the end it's the one thing that works out. Because of love. Silly, when I say it out loud like that."

"Not at all," Lily replied. "Life never works out like that, but it's nice to think it might."

"Exactly." The woman smiled and went back up the aisle to the first-class galley.

Well, that was monumentally not helpful. The flight attendant's reasons for loving *A Matter of Honor* were the same as those in every review of the book Lily had read. Hundreds of them. The same as those of everyone she'd asked from her hairdresser to the girl that did her nails to… hell, even Derek had rattled off words like *right thing* and *honorable man* and *love wins*. Lily didn't get it. She truly didn't. Intellectually, her lack of understanding made her a cynic. Emotionally, it scared the hell out of her. Lately everything about acting scared her.

She'd won an Oscar at the age of twelve. In a period film, no less. That was why she'd latched onto *A Matter of Honor* as her chance to revive her career after a couple of years of lackluster young adult films followed by ten years of television movies and offers of projects one step above porn. The role she'd played at twelve had been easy because she understood the character and the story. She wasn't one of those actors who could portray a role she didn't understand through technique, method, or talent. She had to…step into the character's soul.

She glanced at her worn copy of the novel and shook her head. Time to eat. She could do that. It was instinctual. When it came to opening herself up enough emotionally to deliver an Oscar-worthy performance in the part of a woman like Captain Rothgate's wife, she didn't know where to start. Those instincts had taken one helluva beating in the past five or so years. Her biggest fear of all? That those instincts might never come back.

Chapter Two

Lachlan Innes leaned against the worn stone corner of the west wing of Rosemount Manor and folded his arms across his chest. The perfect spot to watch his brother's worst nightmare unfold in the front drive of their ancestral home. Then again, since their father's death six months ago, Knox had dealt with a whole series of nightmares, each one worse than the last. It had started with him inheriting the title of Duke of Turra and had sped downhill ever since. Lachlan tried to muster a bit of sympathy for his older brother. The man damned sure didn't make it easy.

"Think Himself will make an appearance?"

Urquhart, Rosemount's wiry horse master, eased up next to Lachlan without so much as disturbing a blade of grass. The man would've made a damned fine assassin had MI5 been clever enough to lure him away from the Highlands. Nothing short of a Holy Edict or a ducal command would do that.

"Not so far," Lachlan said. "Is he supposed to?"

"'Tis said that Miss Witherspoon ordered him to be there to welcome the Sassenachs to the manor."

'Tis said meant someone on Rosemount's staff had over-heard Knox arguing with Miss Witherspoon, or Elle, as she'd asked Lachlan to call her, and had delivered a blow-by-blow description of said argument at the staff dining table. Elle would also have words with Urquhart if she heard him call their visitors Sassenachs—his word for anyone not born in the Highlands, and not a particularly flattering word at that.

"I'm sure that went over like Irish whiskey at a High-lander's wake," Lachlan remarked. Whoever these people were, they traveled with enough luggage for a general's staff setting up headquarters. The familiar twitch that image evoked only lasted for a second this time. Lachlan was having a good day for a change.

"Don't know about that." Urquhart nodded toward the front of the house. "There he is."

"Well, I'll be damned."

"Never happen. Mrs. Wallace lights a candle for the both of us every Sunday. Not even the Almighty would cross that woman. We're doomed to an eternity of playing harps and singing hymns."

"You need to shag that old woman and get it over with, Urquhart." All hell had broken out on the front lawn. Two large black and red dogs wreaked havoc with the footmen. This whole Regency boot camp might be a bit of fun after all.

"I will if you will," the old man shot back.

"'Fraid I'm not man enough to shag Mrs. Wallace."

Urquhart laughed and elbowed Lachlan in the side. "You've been wandering these hills too long, lad. You need a bonny lass to keep you warm in that hut you've holed your-self up in and no mistaking it."

"Now you sound like my brother. He's the one that needs a woman so he can breed an heir for all this. Though little good it's done him to take on Rosemount. Little good it did our father."

"Your father didn't take on Rosemount. Himself is the only duke in my memory to try and save this place."

"Despite hating every minute of it?"

"He doesn't hate Rosemount, lad. He'd not be letting the American lass do all of this if he hated it."

"Time will tell." Lachlan straightened and took a step closer to the front drive, closer, but not close enough to be seen. "Who is that?"

A dark-haired woman in a bright green monstrosity of a coat launched herself out of the ridiculous luxury coach looking vehicle and appeared to give the other two passengers what-for. She had the pale sort of skin that would look incredible in moonlight. God only knew what her shape might be, but those legs. Lachlan had never seen legs like those in his life. Or if he had, maybe he just hadn't noticed. He damned sure noticed them now. His cock was hard enough to jump out of his kilt and cross the lawn all by itself.

"Humph." Urquhart pulled an ancient pipe out of the pocket of his tweed jacket and lit it up. He looked Lachlan up and down.

"What?"

"Didn't say a word." He nodded toward the fountain in front of the manor's double doors. "This don't look good."

Knox stood in front of the fountain. Miss Legs in the ugly coat sauntered toward him. She curtsied for God's sake. Lachlan rolled his eyes. Another American looking to become a duchess. Knox extended his hand about the time the two huge dogs arrived and reared up to....

"Bloody hell," Lachlan choked out.

"Aye," Urquhart said solemnly.

Lachlan snorted. He couldn't help it. It hurt too. He planted his fists on his hips to keep from covering his mouth with his hands. Didn't help. Suddenly he was bent double laughing his arse off. His throat hurt. His ribs hurt. It had been so long his entire body seemed to say *What the hell do you think you're doing?* In a few more minutes, he regained his composure, though it still hurt to breathe.

"I don't know whose dogs they are, but I'm having Cook serve them two of our finest game hens for dinner," he said.

"For knocking your brother into yon fountain? Shame on you, Lachlan Innes."

"For knocking His Grace, the Duke of Turra, on his arse into yon fountain in front of the entire household, Elle, and a coachload of Yanks." Lachlan brushed a tear from his eye. "I'd give my left nut to see Knox's face."

"You might have seen his face if you weren't staring at that lass's legs when she went arse over teakettle into the fountain."

"And you didn't look, old man?"

"Didn't say I didn't. Said you did."

A gust of wind whipped around the corner of the house— wind that smelled and tasted of heather, lavender, and earth as the footmen helped Knox and the woman in question out of the fountain. Elle hurried everyone into the house.

"Well, I'm not dead yet," Lachlan said as the two of them turned and strolled toward the stables.

"Couldn't prove it by me these two years since you got back."

Lachlan had no intention of starting this conversation with Urquhart yet again. It served no purpose and triggered nightmares. Nightmares far worse than anything the Duke of Turra suffered.

"You don't need to be worrying about me. You need to worry about teaching the Sassenachs how to ride horses and drive carriages. Seamus said Miss Witherspoon has you signed up for this little charade as well."

"I'm more than a match for the Sassenachs. You're the one who needs to be worried." Urquhart touched the brim of his cap and opened the gate to the garden in front of his little cottage next to Rosemount's impressive stables.

"Me? What have I got to worry about?"

The horse master's rusty laughter followed Lachlan like a Highland mist as he strode down the unpaved lane from the stables across the sheep fields and on to the gamekeeper's cottage, which he'd called home since he'd returned from Afghanistan. He opened his door, but an odd sensation kept him from going inside just yet. There was that scent again of heather, old lavender and newly turned dirt. He turned back toward Rosemount Manor.

Elle, the American event planner who his brother had hired to come up with ways to use Rosemount Manor's ancient house and remote location to attract high-priced clients, had said the Regency boot camp would last at least three months, and if the Hollywood director who'd set it all up had his way, these first people and others would invade Rosemount for as long as a year or more while making a film. Knox hated the whole idea, but thanks to their father, they needed the money to keep the estate going and to pay off inheritance taxes and debts. Lachlan hated the disruption of the peace he'd found in this place that hadn't changed a great deal in the last hundred or so years.

He'd have to avoid the house and the guests, that was all. An image of dark hair, pale skin, and long slender legs came unbidden to mind. His cock stirred.

"None of that," he said as he entered his cottage. "Keep that up and we'll be going for a swim in the loch, March or not."

THIS WAS LACHLAN'S FAVORITE TIME OF NIGHT, NOT QUITE midnight, but late enough the manor had settled. His only companions as he hiked the fields, his staff for aid, were the night calling birds, some sheep, and the scrap of fur he'd brought back from Afghanistan with him. Black and white like the estate's sheepdogs, but no bigger than one of his late mother's lap dogs, Leonidas thought he was a mastiff.

Lachlan refused to argue with him. The dog had survived at least a year in a country where dogs were seen as vermin, unclean, and targets for marksmen's practice. Even after he'd attached himself to Lachlan and the other men in his unit, Leonidas had dodged roadside bombs, artillery fire, and military regulations.

"Come on, lad," he called as the dog's white flag of a tail disappeared behind a hedgerow. "I'm for home and a toddy. Freezing my *magairles* off out here." With luck the past few hours roaming the hills would wear them both out enough to sleep. Sleep without dreams.

Where the hell had the dog gone?

A flash of white caught Lachlan's eye. Headed toward the manor. Leonidas had honed his begging skills on the streets of Baghdad. He needn't have bothered. Rosemount's cook was a soft touch when it came to dogs and young boys whose parents' only talent was for hurting each other or their sons.

Lachlan shifted the heavily carved seven-foot staff in his hand and headed down the hill toward the ditch they called a ha-ha between the fields and the formal gardens at the back of the manor. If he hurried, he'd head Leonidas off before he crossed the bridge over the ha-ha.

"For pity's sake, 'Nidas, you've been eating all day." Lachlan started around another hedge and stopped in his tracks. He took a step back.

"She took my phone, Derek. Seriously. These people definitely drank the Regency Kool-Aid."

Derek? Lachlan didn't see anyone with the woman seated on the stone bench on the other side of the hedge. She *was* an

American. Maybe she was like Knox's *imaginary friend* when they were children.

"Well, of course I had a spare phone. I'm not stupid, I just play stupid on TV." She paused, he assumed to listen to this Derek person. Boyfriend? Husband? "Oh, don't even ask," she continued. "Arneaux is being a horse's ass and then some. I slapped the hell out of him to remind him who he is dealing with. At the airport in front of his Regency coach. I'll fill you in later. I'm freezing in this idiotic costume. Kiss your hubby for me and I'll talk to you soon."

Aha! Most definitely not a boyfriend or husband.

Lachlan peered through the branches of the neatly trimmed boxwoods. It was her, the woman who'd landed in the fountain with his brother. She wore a costume evening gown with no sign of a coat or shawl. He'd been right. Her skin took on a mother-of-pearl glow in the moonlight. Her hair was so dark and thick piled on top of her head the light glinted off it in little sparkles.

His breath grew thick. His vision began to curl at the periphery. Perfect time for a panic attack. He needed to get back to his cottage. Leonidas would find his way home, he always did. Something brushed across his forehead, a gentle sweep of his hair like a mother's touch. Lachlan straightened and turned to leave.

"Great. How the hell am I supposed to get back across this ditch?"

The sound of the woman slapping against the hedge and stumbling on the pebbled path along the ha-ha made Lachlan turn and edge back to the end of the row of boxwoods. She mumbled some very unladylike curses and stalked up and down the edge of the deep, wide ditch that separated the fields from the grounds of Rosemount Manor. The more she paced the more creative her language became and, unfortunately, the closer she got to falling into the—

"Oh, shit!"

Lachlan dropped his staff, crashed through the hedge, and in two strides grabbed the woman around the waist just as she started to slide down the embankment. He earned a flailing elbow in the nose in the process. Stung like hell.

"Hey, watch it, buddy."

Once Lachlan set her back away from the ha-ha, she wiggled out of his grip and batted at his hands.

Lachlan backed away arms raised. "Maybe I should have let you fall in the ha-ha. Good night." He gave a sharp whistle. "Come, Leonidas." Out of the dark, a white streak flew from the direction of the bridge, circled Lachlan's ankles, and ran back toward the woman. Lachlan looked over his shoulder to see his furry friend sitting at her feet, his head cocked to one side.

"Wait a minute. Is this yours?"

"He is, and the bridge across the ha-ha is up that way. Come on, lad. Home with you." Lachlan strode on in the hope the woman would cross the bridge and leave him alone.

The wind kicked up and pushed against him. *What the devil?*

"Is everybody in this country rude as hell?" she demanded.

Lachlan turned just as the woman stepped into a wide swath of moonlight. *Damn!* She had the face of a fairy queen from one of the stories Mrs. Wallace used to read to him and Knox when they were boys. High cheekbones, a delicate nose, dainty ears, full lips, and eyebrows like birds in flight. Her eyes were dark in the moonlight, perhaps brown? And while he was staring at her like an idiot, she rubbed her arms and shivered.

"Is everyone from the States stubborn enough to freeze to death just to make a phone call?" He shrugged out of his coat and wrapped it around her. She waste no time in slipping her arms into the sleeves and buttoning half the buttons. "This way." He took her hand and tugged her toward the bridge. He loosened his grasp, terrified he'd crush such tiny fingers.

"Excuse me? Hello? My name is Lily Randolph, and yours is?"

"Lachlan Innes. Here you go." He stopped at the foot of the bridge and dropped her hand. He clenched his fist around the place in his palm burned by her touch. "Cross this, and you'll be in the gardens. Go straight up the path between the rows of gas lights."

"You want your coat, Lachlan Innes?" She started to unbutton the black wool overcoat that nearly drowned her.

"Keep it. One of the footmen can bring it to me tomorrow. Next time, wear that green puffer. If it's dried out by then."

By the light of the gas lights at the far side of the little footbridge, it was obvious her eyes were brown—big brown eyes like a doe. This particular woman, however, wouldn't like the comparison. He was nearly certain of it, especially as those lovely brown eyes narrowed and currently had murder in them.

"You saw that."

He gave a curt nod. "I did."

"I didn't see you there."

"You were rather busy at the time."

"Busy?"

"Shrieking. Falling. Legs in the air. Head in the fountain. Shrieking some more. Dripping all the way to the house."

"I suppose you thought it was really funny. Seeing someone like me humiliated that way."

She was a great deal more upset about the entire episode than her stony expression let on. He'd learned to mask his own emotions well enough to recognize that state in another person.

"Someone like you?" he said.

Her brow folded into a series of wrinkles, which made her look confused, and cute. "You don't know who I am, do you?"

"Should I?" Probably not a good answer, but these days he tended to speak first and think about it later. Much later. Most days his brain had trouble making connections.

"Well." She paused as if to give him time to come up with an appropriate response. Whatever that may be. "I'm glad you enjoyed the show. Thanks for the coat." She stepped up onto the bridge.

"Miss Randolph?"

"Yes?" Her response reeked of suspicion.

"I was standing at the far corner of the manor. That's why you didn't see me. And the only part of the show I enjoyed was seeing His Grace get a good dunking."

Leonidas stopped beside her, and she surprised Lachlan by bending and scratching the dog behind his ears. "You're not the first person to say so. That far away at least you couldn't see well enough to get in on the bet the footmen had."

"Bet?"

"The color of my panties."

He waited until she'd crossed the foot bridge. "Lime green," he called after her. "To match your skirt."

He walked to the hedge, picked up his staff, whistled for Leonidas, and trekked back across the fields toward his cottage. The complete outrage on her face kept him warm all the way to his front door. Well, that and the brilliant way she wove *rude, asshole,* and *in a skirt* into a tapestry of profanity every one of the regulars down the pub would stand up and applaud. There were United States marines who didn't curse like this woman.

Once he'd built up the fire in the sitting room, and

Leonidas had burrowed under the quilts and sheepskin rug on Lachlan's bed, he fired up his computer. While it booted, he made himself a hot toddy with a hefty dose of the local whisky, some honey, and some mulling spices.

Elle had warned him not to allow any of the guests participating in the present event to use his computer. Something about ruining their Regency experience. Silly warning as not even Knox had been in the gamekeeper's cottage for the last two years—which was exactly the way Lachlan wanted it.

He dropped into his desk chair and pulled up Google. "Let's find out who your latest lady love is, shall we?"

Leonidas thumped his tail but didn't bother to open his eyes. There wasn't a housemaid, shopkeeper, or barmaid in the county who could resist Lachlan's little furry lothario friend. Miss Lily Randolph was no exception.

The windows rattled under the sudden onslaught of the March breezes from the hills. Lachlan scrubbed his face with his hands to rid his nose of the latent aroma of heather and lavender. This was not happening. The enigmatic scent of lavender only happened to Knox, usually when Knox was dead drunk or close to it, which was not very often.

Leonidas yipped in his sleep. All he had to do was roll over, snuffle, and sleep returned to the fuzzy beast immediately. Lachlan should be so fortunate. The long walk in the cold was meant to wear them both out to the point they'd collapse into bed and not wake up until the fire went out and the room grew too cold to sleep. Tonight, his encounter with the American beauty had his nerves humming and his mind racing. Among other things.

He turned back to his computer. His monitor screen was filled with an image of *Lily Randolph – America's Sweetheart, All Grown Up.*

"Jesus, Mary, and Joseph." He'd seen sticking plasters bigger than the bikini she wore in the photo.

She stood on the bow of some millionaire's yacht and smiled like...a woman who'd rather be anywhere else. He recognized that smile in an instant. It was the one he wore anytime he had to go up to the manor and hold it together for the sake of the clan.

In addition to her glorious legs, she had a lithe, but athletic build, except for a pair of beyond memorable breasts. Her hair was longer than he realized, but it was the smile that got him. The smile that wasn't a smile, *and* her grip on one of the mast ropes of the yacht.

Bloody fucking hell.

The blurry sound of feminine laughter wafted past the closed cottage door.

Nothing for it. He'd have to stay holed up in his hermit hole for as long as the Yanks invaded Rosemount. He glanced at the bed where Leonidas now sat up, head tilted, looking at him with a question in his liquid brown eyes.

"We're screwed, my friend. There is no way in hell I'm going anywhere near Lily Randolph ever again."

GET YOUR COPY HERE

Rosemount Manor

LOVE REGENCY STYLE

Cajun in a Kilt
Sassenach in Stilettos
Critic with a Claymore
The Stuntman and the Swordmaster
The Duke the Witch and the Party Planner

Stay tuned for the next Rosemount Manor series *The Price of Love*

To keep up on all the Rosemount Manor romances and all our other great books join our Newsletter